THE HAWAIIAN QUILT

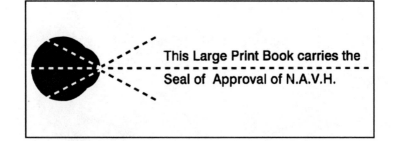

This Large Print Book carries the
Seal of Approval of N.A.V.H.

THE HAWAIIAN QUILT

WANDA E. BRUNSTETTER AND JEAN BRUNSTETTER

THORNDIKE PRESS
A part of Gale, Cengage Learning

Farmington Hills, Mich • San Francisco • New York • Waterville, Maine
Meriden, Conn • Mason, Ohio • Chicago

LIBRARY OF CONGRESS CATALOGING-IN-PUBLICATION DATA

Names: Brunstetter, Wanda E., author. | Brunstetter, Jean, author.
Title: The Hawaiian quilt / by Wanda E. Brunstetter & Jean Brunstetter.
Description: Large print edition. | Waterville, Maine : Thorndike Press, a part of Gale, Cengage Learning 2016. | Series: Thorndike Press large print Christian fiction
Identifiers: LCCN 2016041158| ISBN 9781410495624 (hardcover) | ISBN 1410495620 (hardcover)
Subjects: LCSH: Amish—Fiction. | Large type books. | BISAC: FICTION / Christian / General. | GSAFD: Christian fiction. | Love stories.
Classification: LCC PS3602.R864 H39 2016 | DDC 813/.6—dc23
LC record available at https://lccn.loc.gov/2016041158

Published in 2017 by arrangement with Barbour Publishing, Inc.

To LeAnna Lehman,
a special Amish friend who has
visited the Hawaiian Islands.
And to our friends,
Bob and Sue Miller, who have a
heart for the Amish people.

Be not forgetful to entertain strangers:
for thereby some have entertained
angels unawares.

Hebrews 13:2

PROLOGUE

Middlebury, Indiana

Mandy Frey gazed at the travel brochures lying on the kitchen table. The pictures were so vibrant and enticing she could almost smell the soothing scents of the tropical flowers and hear the gentle lapping of ocean waves. Ever since her Mennonite cousin Ruth went to the Hawaiian islands for missionary training two years ago, Mandy had yearned to visit. For a little over a year, she had saved toward the trip. She'd invited three of her closest friends — Barbara Hilty, Ellen Lambright, and Sadie Kuhns — to go on the cruise with her. They'd kept their plans secret until they had enough money and had made arrangements for time off from their jobs. They would leave in one month, traveling by train to Los Angeles. From there, they'd be on a cruise ship for four-and-a-half days until they reached their first Hawaiian island.

Paging through another brochure, dazzling pictures of cascading waterfalls and scenic mountains heavy with vegetation gave her goose-bumps. Everything seemed so colorful in Hawaii — even the exotic birds. She wished she was there right now.

Excitement bubbled in Mandy's soul as she envisioned herself sitting on the beach with her toes in the warm grains of sand, inhaling the salty air. "This is a trip of a lifetime," she murmured. It was one she would probably never make again, so Mandy wasn't about to let anything or anyone dampen her spirits.

But the hope of nothing spoiling her enthusiasm didn't last long. When she'd told her parents this morning about her plans, Mom wasn't happy and tried to talk her out of going, saying Hawaii was too far away. She'd also mentioned if Mandy had a problem while she was there, her family wouldn't be readily available to help.

Dad hadn't said much, other than telling Mom their only daughter was a grown woman and had the right to make her own decisions. Mandy could have hugged him right then and there, but held back, not wanting Mom to feel hurt or left out. Mandy's younger brother, Milo, had sided with Mom, but Mandy ignored his concerns. She and her friends had booked their trip to Hawaii through a local travel agency, and she would not change her plans. The only person left to tell was her boyfriend, Gideon. She hoped he would take the news well.

CHAPTER 1

Los Angeles, California
November 1
As Mandy sat with her friends, waiting to board the cruise ship that would take them to Hawaii, her thoughts went to Gideon. It had been difficult saying goodbye to him before their driver took them to the train station in Elkhart. She felt bad about his negative reaction when she'd told him she planned to make this trip with her friends. She should have said something sooner, so he would have been more prepared for her departure.

Diverting her thoughts, Mandy watched the young boy sitting across from her, bouncing in his chair while drinking a can of orange soda. He spilled it down the front of his shirt and started howling and kicking his feet.

Patiently, the child's mother got up and took him by the hand to the restroom.

Mandy leaned close to Barbara and whispered, "That little guy is sure a handful."

"*Jah.* I don't envy his mother. He'll probably keep her plenty busy on this trip."

Mandy listened to the steady hum of voices around her. The terminal was filled with an air of excitement, but her thoughts returned to Gideon, remembering his hurt expression as he held her hand. "I don't want you to go, Mandy, but if this is what you want, then you have my blessing and ought to follow your heart. I'll be here when you get back, and then we can talk about our future."

Mandy didn't know if her future was with Gideon. They'd been courting over a year, and she'd suspected for some time he wanted to propose marriage. He'd no doubt held back because she hadn't committed to joining the church. Since every couple planning to get married in an Amish community must first join the church, there was no point in him proposing until they both had been baptized and become church members.

I may feel ready when we return from this trip, she mused. *If I do, then I'll take classes to prepare for church membership.*

Ellen snapped her fingers, causing Mandy to jump. "Our number's been called. It's time to board the ship."

On the Cruise Ship
"*Ach,* this room is much smaller than I thought it would be, even if it is nicely decorated. It's not much bigger than the two tiny rooms we had on the train that brought us to California." Barbara's eyebrows rose as she made a sweeping gesture of the room they'd been assigned. "And how are the four of us supposed to sleep when there are only two beds?"

Mandy shrugged. "Maybe someone made a mistake and gave us the wrong room." She couldn't imagine how these arrangements would work. Their travel agent had told them the room they'd booked would sleep four, and it included two bunk beds. They'd either been misinformed or someone made an error. Perhaps two other people on the ship had been shown a room with four beds. They needed to get to the bottom of this before they unpacked their suitcases.

"Look, there's one of the Pullman beds! The other one is up there, too." Sadie pointed to the ceiling above one of the small beds on the floor, and then to the other. "Remember, our agent said it would be similar to a top bunk bed, except instead of being held up by posts extending from a

13

bottom bunk, it's supported by brackets attached to a wall. It can be folded up into the ceiling when not in use to create more space in the room."

"It's certainly folded up right now." Ellen raised her head, squinting her blue eyes. "How are we supposed to get the beds down from the ceiling?"

"We won't have to worry about putting them up or down, because one of the ship's attendants will pull the beds down for us at night and raise them again each morning when our room is serviced." Sadie's tone was typical — so matter of fact.

Mandy couldn't help grinning. *Leave it to Sadie to know all the details.* Even at home, whenever the four young women planned to do something together, Sadie made sure of the details. She was usually responsible for making all the arrangements, too. Last month when the girls got together to do some sewing at Sadie's house, she'd made certain everything was laid out before they arrived. She had even provided them with needles, thread, and scissors. All Mandy, Ellen, and Barbara had to bring was the material they planned to cut and sew. Sadie prepared a casserole for their lunch that day. The smell of it warming in the oven had

14

greeted them as soon as they'd entered the house.

Barbara cleared her throat, bringing Mandy's thoughts to a halt. "I hope I don't have to sleep in one of those upper bunks. I'd feel claustrophobic being so close to the ceiling."

"Me, too," Ellen agreed. "And I'd be worried about falling out."

Mandy folded her arms. She didn't want to sleep on a top bunk, either, but this problem would be resolved sooner if she volunteered. "I'll give it a try. How about you, Sadie?"

Heaving a sigh, Sadie gave a nod. "Since we've settled the sleeping arrangements now, why don't we unpack?"

"It can wait awhile. Right now, I want to take a tour of the ship." Smiling, Barbara pointed to the door.

"I'm all for that!" Ellen pushed a strand of golden-blond hair back under her white head covering and moved toward the door, no doubt as eager as Barbara to check things out.

"Let's go for a walk and look at what's available for us on a few of the outside decks. I'd like to see if there are any good books in the library, too," Sadie suggested. "Afterward, we can head up to the room

15

where lunch will be served buffet style."

Feeling a gurgle in her midsection, Mandy placed both hands on her stomach. "Thinking about all the food that'll be available to us on this cruise makes me *hungerich.*"

"I hope we don't run into bad weather or rough waters during our trip." Barbara placed both hands on her stomach. "It wouldn't be fun if any of us got seasick."

Mandy wrinkled her nose. "I don't even want to think about getting *grank.*"

"How about this." Sadie lifted her hands above her head, yawning nosily. "The first person who gets sick has to buy the rest of us lunch when we get to Maui."

All heads turned to look at her with furrowed brows.

"Okay, guess it's a bad idea. Let's just relax and have fun."

It took awhile to find their way up to the room where they would be served dinner each evening, but with the help of one of the ship's attendants, they finally made it. Mandy was glad when she and her friends were seated at their table a few minutes before 6:00 p.m., which was when the meal was supposed to be served. They would sit at this same table for all their evening meals during the cruise. They'd also have the same waiters.

"I don't know about anyone else, but I'm not used to having a four-course meal for supper." Ellen placed a linen napkin across her lap.

"Me neither." Mandy glanced at the fancy dishes, noticing the blue vine pattern on the rim, and several pieces of silverware beside each plate. She hoped she wouldn't mess up and eat with the wrong utensil or accidentally drink from her neighbor's glass. That would be so embarrassing.

"I'm still full from all the food we had for lunch." Barbara groaned. "Not sure I'll be able to eat all my dinner."

Sadie tapped Barbara's arm in a motherly fashion. "Eat what you can."

"I don't like to waste food. *Sis en sin un e schand.*"

Ellen rolled her eyes. "Wasting food is a shame, but I don't think it's a sin."

"Probably not." Barbara raised her slim shoulders in a brief shrug. "I can only imagine what my *mamm* might say if she were here right now and I didn't eat everything on my plate."

"Well, none of our mothers are here, so we should relax and enjoy ourselves." Sadie reached for the salt and pepper and sprin-

17

kled some on her salad.

After they prayed silently and began to eat, introductions were made among those sitting closest to them. Since the same people would be seated at their table every evening, Mandy thought it was a good idea to get acquainted.

"Are the four of you nuns?" the young Asian woman sitting on one side of Mandy asked.

"No, we are not." Sadie spoke up. "We're Amish."

Blinking rapidly, the woman tilted her head to one side. "Amish? But I thought by the way you prayed and the plain clothes you wear . . ."

Mandy stifled a giggle as Sadie shared a brief history of the Amish and their way of dress. "Nuns dress different than we do," she added.

As the meal progressed, Mandy and her friends discussed what an adventure it was being on the ship and how eager they were to get to Hawaii. From what Mandy's cousin told her about the Big Island, which would be the last island they visited, each day would be filled with many things to see and do. Of course, with only one day spent on each of the islands, they'd have to pick and choose what sights to see. They could either sign up to go with one of the tour groups or strike out on their own. It was logical to go with a group. But since they had to be back at the ship by a certain time each day, they'd have to make every minute count and see as much as possible.

If we ventured out on our own and didn't make it back in time, we could become stranded, Mandy thought, while cracking the crab shell on her plate. *We'll need to make sure it never happens.*

The first three courses of their meal were delicious, but filling. When it came time for the last course — a scrumptious-looking strawberry cheesecake — Mandy was too full to eat it. Their waiter came by the table and offered to box it up so she could take it back to her room. Mandy declined, saying she wouldn't be able to eat anything more tonight. Between breakfast in the morning, a buffet lunch around noon, plus tomorrow's evening meal, she didn't think she'd have room to eat much else. *Maybe I won't have a big lunch every day,* she thought. *Tomorrow, I may try some pizza or a hot dog at one of the snack areas I saw earlier today.*

"For a while I thought we weren't going to find our room," Ellen said as the four of them prepared for bed. "This ship is so big, and with several dining rooms on board, it's easy to get lost."

"I know." Mandy sighed contently as she brushed her long hair. "But it's worth getting lost to be able to say we were on this enormous boat."

"The dining room looked so nice. It's amazing how many details were put into the design of the ship's interior." Barbara sat on one of the twin beds, removed her hairpins, and placed her head covering on the nightstand next to her bed.

"Shall we play a game or sit and talk awhile?" Ellen asked.

Sadie yawned. "I don't know about the rest of you, but I'm *mied* and more than ready for bed." She glanced at one of the bunks overhead, which had been dropped down from the ceiling while they were out of their room. Two ladders had also been set in place, making it possible to climb up to the beds.

Mandy wasn't eager to sleep in either bunk. She'd had a terrible experience sleeping on one when she was younger and had ended up on the floor with a bruised tailbone. But at least the attached side rails on these bunks should keep her from falling out. "Which bed do you want, Sadie?" she asked.

"It doesn't matter to me. Why don't you choose?"

Mandy picked the bunk above Ellen's bed, and after telling her friends good night, she climbed the ladder and settled in. She didn't get up in the middle of the night most of the time anyway, so other than feeling cramped, she would manage. The mattress wasn't too bad — a littler firmer than she'd like, but it would have to do. As tired as she was, she didn't even care.

Curling up against her pillow, she closed her eyes and prayed for her family back home. She also prayed for Gideon and asked God to give her a sense of direction about whether she should join the Amish church or not. Before drifting off to sleep, Mandy prayed, *Heavenly Father, please keep us safe on this journey, and may we return home with many wonderful memories to cherish for the rest of our lives.*

CHAPTER 2

When Mandy awoke the following morning, she felt strange — almost as though someone had rolled her around while she was sleeping. She could sense the ship swaying and knew the sea must be rough. *What a contrast from the calm of last night.* She pushed her sheets aside and climbed carefully down from her bunk. Once her feet hit the floor, she rubbed her eyes, trying to clear her vision.

"*Sis mer iwwel.*" Ellen groaned from her lower bunk.

"If you're sick to your stomach, it's probably from the rocking of the ship." Mandy looked at Sadie and Barbara who were already up, but not dressed. "Do either of you feel seasick?"

"So far, I'm okay, but we should probably put some of those motion-sickness drops behind our ears, in case the rest of us do start to feel grank. It's a good thing I brought this along." Sadie took the bottle out of her traveling case and dabbed some behind both ears, then passed it to Ellen, who did the same. When Ellen was done, she gave the bottle to Mandy. After she'd put drops behind her ears, she handed it to Barbara.

"If I'd have known last night this would happen to me, I would have put some of the drops on before going to bed." Ellen sat up, clutching her stomach. "I won't be able to eat anything, feeling like this, but you three should get dressed and enjoy the breakfast buffet." Moaning, she continued holding her stomach.

"I wouldn't feel right about leaving you here alone." Barbara looked out the window and grimaced. "The rain is coming down hard. What a way to begin our day."

"I wouldn't feel right about leaving Ellen, either." Mandy opened the satchel containing her personal items and removed a homeopathic medicine she'd brought along. "This is for nausea and dizziness." She handed it to Ellen with a fresh bottle of water. "If it doesn't help, let me know, and I'll see what's available from the ship's infirmary."

Ellen took the remedy and reclined on her bed. "I'll be fine by myself while you're eating breakfast." She reached for the sheet and blanket, pulling them up to her shoulders. "I need to lie here awhile. I only wish the ship would stop moving so much."

Mandy looked at Sadie and Barbara, and when they both nodded, she hurried to get dressed. By the time they were ready to leave the room, Ellen was sleeping.

"Hopefully, she'll be okay," Sadie whispered. "One of us can check on her as soon as we're done eating."

As they headed out the door, Mandy turned to look at Ellen again. She wanted to stay with her childhood friend, but since Ellen had insisted everyone go to breakfast and couldn't be helped while she was sleeping, Mandy quietly stepped into the corridor and shut the door. She'd make sure to eat quickly and not be gone too long.

Ellen woke up with her stomach churning. She sat up for a moment, but the feeling didn't go away. All at once, her throat constricted, and she covered her mouth. Jumping out of bed, she dashed to the bathroom, barely making it in time. When the vomiting subsided, her ribs felt sore, and she was exhausted. With her stomach empty, and a feeling of shakiness, all she wanted to do was climb back in bed. *Will this ever go away? How long am I going to be seasick? Sure hope I don't feel like this the whole cruise.*

Tears welled in Ellen's eyes as she lay staring at the ceiling, still fighting waves of nausea. *So much for those anti-nausea drops and homeopathic medicine. Maybe they would have helped if I'd taken them sooner.*

Hearing a knock on the door, Ellen pulled herself off the bed. Since she was still in her nightgown and knew she looked a mess, she hoped it wasn't one of the ship's attendants. When she opened the door a crack, she was surprised to see Mandy.

"Sorry if I woke you. I forgot my room key," Mandy apologized.

"It's okay. I was awake."

"I ate a quick breakfast and brought these back for you." When Mandy stepped into the room and closed the door, she placed several packets of saltine crackers and a can of ginger ale on the small table between the beds. "How are you feeling? Did the homeopathic remedy help at all?"

"Not really. I threw up while you were gone, and I still feel a bit woozy and nauseous." Ellen sighed deeply. "Sure hope I don't feel like this the rest of the way. We still have three more days before we get to our first stop on Maui."

25

Mandy took a seat. "I hope this storm passes soon and the ship moves into calmer waters. Even though I'm not sick to my stomach, the rocking affects my equilibrium. Maybe it would help if we went out on our balcony for a while and breathed in some fresh air. For now, at least, the rain has stopped."

"I doubt it'll help me, but I guess I could try." Ellen slipped into her robe, and they stepped onto the small veranda. The blowing wind and choppy waters were reason enough for her stomach to be upset all morning. Grasping the railing, she drew in several deep breaths, which helped a little, but those lingering gray clouds above didn't remove her dismal outlook.

Mandy placed her hand gently on Ellen's shoulder. "I'm sorry you're not feeling well. This is supposed to be a fun trip for all of us."

"It will be once we're on dry land." Ellen groaned. "I must be a land lover."

"Same here. Since I can't swim, it makes me *naerfich* looking out at nothing but water and seeing no escape except the ship we're on."

"Then why'd you want to take this trip so badly?"

"Because I wanted to see Hawaii. And

26

even though I haven't joined the church, I knew my folks would disapprove of me flying."

"Same here."

"We'll keep praying this will go away for you, and you'll soon be back on your feet." Mandy stared out at the rough waters. "I'm excited to see Maui, but I wish we could spend more time there. There's only so much we can see in a day."

"Guess we should be happy for what we get. At least we'll have a taste of Hawaii and should have a lot to tell our families when we go home."

"I'm glad I purchased a digital camera before we left. I plan to keep a journal and put together a scrapbook with pictures from our trip. Then whenever I miss Hawaii, I'll take it out and relive all our precious memories."

Ellen snickered, despite her fluttering tummy. "How do you know you're going to miss Hawaii? You haven't been there yet. Maybe it's not as special as you think."

"Of course it's special." Mandy gave a playful grin. "I've seen the pictures my cousin took from her time on the Big Island. Looking at them made me want to see all the beautiful flowers, palm trees, and colorful birds for myself." Mandy tried tucking the blowing stray hairs back under her head covering, but it was no use. The wind had a mind of its own.

"Don't forget about the coconuts, pineapple, and papaya we'll get to taste. Didn't you say Ruth brought back a pineapple for you to sample?"

"She did, and I loved it." Mandy smacked her lips. "I ate some at breakfast this morning, as well as slices of mango. They were *appeditlich.*"

"Nothing sounds delicious to me right now." Ellen shivered, rubbing her arms. "It's chilly out here. Think I'd better go back inside."

When they stepped into the room, Barbara was lying on her twin bed, reading a Hawaiian magazine. Sadie sat on a chair nearby, mending one of her dresses that had somehow gotten torn.

"I didn't realize you were back," Mandy said.

"We've been here about five minutes." Sadie held up her turquoise dress. "I brought this one along because it's kind of a tropical color."

Mandy smiled, then pointed to the crackers and ginger ale. "Why don't you try those now, Ellen? A little something in your *bauch* might help, and you do need to keep hy-

28

drated."

"I like saltines anytime," Barbara commented, before sticking her nose back in the magazine.

"Guess I will try a little." Ellen opened one pack of crackers and took a seat on her bed. Nothing appealed, but maybe the saltines would help settle her stomach. Her mother always gave them to Ellen and her siblings whenever they got stomach flu and couldn't keep anything else down. Maybe tomorrow she would feel better and could explore more of the ship.

Middlebury

Gideon stood at the entrance of the barn, sipping hot chocolate and admiring the snowflakes glistening in the sunlight like crystals. As a young boy, he had loved to take his sled up the small hill behind their place and slide down at unimaginable speeds. Back then, he'd thought it was pretty exciting. When Gideon and his siblings came inside afterward, Mom always had a cup of hot chocolate waiting for them. Now he was in his early twenties, and this kind of weather seemed like an inconvenience, not to mention downright cold. Gideon still thought the snow was pretty, but it gave him more things to worry about.

"It's too early for *schnee,*" he muttered. "Sure hope the roads don't get bad." Most horse and buggies did well in the snow, but the cars on the roads were what he worried about. Some drivers went too fast, while others crept along at a snail's pace.

As Gideon turned toward the stalls needing to be cleaned, his thoughts went to Mandy. No doubt she and her friends were on the boat by now, enjoying better weather than this. He disliked having her so far away. Gideon still didn't understand why she wanted to go to Hawaii so bad. He was eager for Mandy to come home and make a decision about whether she would join the church or not.

He paused and closed his eyes, as an image of Mandy's pretty face came to mind. Her eyes, matching the color of her silky brown hair, seemed so expressive when she talked. Gideon had never seen eyes as beautiful as hers. They were a rich coffee color, but what made them so unique was how they almost turned green, depending on the color of dress she wore. Mandy smiled a lot, too, and got along well with others. *It's no wonder she enjoys being a waitress,* Gideon thought.

He wondered what she was seeing and doing on the cruise ship. Gideon supposed it was a fun adventure, but being here was all he needed to be content. *I wonder if she's nervous about traveling so far from home, especially on a ship floating in a big body of water like the Pacific. Since Mandy's never learned to swim, I would think she'd be scared being surrounded by all that water. Sure hope she gets this trip out of her system and will be content when she comes home.*

He gave himself a mental shake. *I probably shouldn't be worried. Mandy will be back in a few weeks, and everything will be fine. If we are truly meant to be together, she'll be ready to take classes preparing her to join the church soon after she arrives.*

CHAPTER 3

On the Cruise Ship
Ready to leave their cabin, Mandy took a moment to write in her journal:

Today is Sunday, our third day at sea. Before we went for breakfast this morning, we sat in our cabin and had our devotions. It was nice to set a time aside to read God's Word and reflect on His promises.

The weather's improved, and Ellen's feeling better. I'm glad things are looking up for her now that the ship isn't swaying like it was before. The storm was a bit un-nerving to our group, and probably for a lot of other people on board as well.

It was nice all four of us could sit together and share the morning meal. A few min-utes ago, we got back from breakfast. I ate too much again. It's hard to pass up all the delicious food; especially the fruit and seafood. It would be easy for a person to put on extra pounds, taking in all the tantalizing food and lounging on the deck or in our room. Maybe I'll visit the exercise room later today and use the treadmill. I need to burn off the extra calories.

No matter how many times I look out the door of our balcony, it seems strange to see nothing but water, with no land at all in sight. It's kind of eerie and makes me feel somewhat isolated, even though we're on a ship with over two thousand passengers. I'd love to see some dolphins, like some of the folks at our dinner table said they had earlier today. Maybe we'll still get the chance.

"Are you ready to do some exploring?" Ellen placed her hands on the desk where Mandy sat.

"Give me a moment." Mandy set her pen and journal aside. "I want to put on some sunscreen, since it's so bright out today."

"Good idea." Ellen picked up her tube of sunscreen and put it in her tote bag, along with a pair of sunglasses. "Since Barbara and Sadie have already gone out to sit by the pool and read, I'd better take this along. I don't think they took theirs."

"They did seem in a hurry to get going."

"No more than I am. After feeling so sick

and staying in the room yesterday, I'm anxious to get out for some fresh air and sunshine."

Mandy slathered some sunscreen on her face and arms, then put the camera in her tote. "Let's go!"

After sitting in one of the lounge chairs by the pool awhile, Mandy saw an elderly couple walk by and pick out two empty chairs. Based on their conversation, they seemed eager to get some fresh air by the pool. The woman took her seat carefully and waited for her husband to do the same. He, though, sat rather abruptly, sending the lounge chair crashing as it flattened like a pancake.

"Oh, dear! Robert, are you all right?" With a worried expression, his wife turned toward him.

"Only my pride is hurt," he panted, struggling to get up.

Before Mandy could react, Sadie jumped up and went to help him. Once he was on his feet, she stood his chair up and made sure it was locked in place.

"Thanks for coming to my rescue." His face was bright red. "Bet I looked pretty foolish."

"I'm glad you weren't hurt." Sadie smiled

and returned to her seat beside Ellen. "I can't believe how many people sat there watching and didn't even try to help."

Ellen nodded. "A lot of them had their phones out. Sure hope they weren't taking pictures of the poor fellow."

Some people don't seem to care about others, Mandy thought. *I'm glad Sadie helped the elderly man. He could have been seriously hurt.*

After lounging awhile, Sadie said she was craving some ice cream. "Why don't we all head for the sundae shop?" she suggested.

Mandy glanced at her cell phone, noting the time. "It won't be long till it's time to eat lunch. If we have ice cream now, it'll ruin our appetites."

"Not mine." Sadie shook her head. "If anything, an ice-cream cone will whet my appetite."

Mandy fought the urge to roll her eyes. One thing she and Sadie disagreed on was the kind of food they ate. Mandy treated herself to ice cream once in a while, but she didn't go overboard on sweets — especially not before eating a big meal. "You can go to the sundae shop if you want to." She licked her lips, trying not to think how good an ice-cream sundae would taste. "I'm gonna stay here and enjoy the sunshine. When I talked to Mom last night, she mentioned they were getting snow in Middlebury."

Barbara clicked her tongue. "I can't believe they're getting schnee so early in November. I hope it's all gone by the time we go home."

"They could have more by then, which is why we'd better enjoy the sun while we can." Sadie stood. "Who's going with me to get ice cream?"

"Guess I'll come along." Barbara gathered up her things and left her chair.

"I'm going to stay here with Mandy. It's fun to watch the children play in the pool." Ellen lifted her arm up and grinned. "Think I'm getting a little color, too."

"Okay, then, we'll see you two at the lunch buffet." Sadie waved and headed off, with Barbara at her side.

Mandy glanced over at Ellen and grimaced. "I bet those two won't be able to eat much lunch."

Ellen gave her stomach a few thumps. "I will. After only crackers and ginger ale for the past twenty-four hours, I'm more than *eiferich* to eat."

"I'm eager, too, but I won't overdo. I want to save room for our supper this evening." Mandy glanced at the cute little blond-haired girl sitting on the side of the pool.

36

Despite her mother's coaxing, the child refused to get in the water.

She might be afraid because she can't swim. Mandy brushed a strand of hair away from her face. Since she had never learned to swim, she could relate to the young girl. Mandy feared going into the pond on her parents' property, which her four brothers enjoyed. Mandy's dread of water kept her from learning to swim or even float. She remembered how, on hot summer days, she would hold her long dress up so it wouldn't get wet and wade into the shallow part of the pond near the shoreline. The cool water felt good on her bare legs and feet, and she'd been satisfied with that. When Mandy was eight years old, her brother Michael, who was ten at the time, pulled her into the water where it was over her head. Certain she would drown, Mandy flailed her arms and screamed so loud their father came running. Within seconds, he dove into the water and rescued her. Sobbing and clinging to Dad's neck, she vowed never to go in the pond again. Of course, she had, but only knee deep. On several occasions, Dad had offered to teach her to swim, but Mandy flatly refused. Even with her fear of the water, she found it fascinating and looked forward to watching the waves hit the shore when they were on dry land.

Mandy's brother Mark had kidded her about making a trip to Hawaii by boat, since the ship would be surrounded by water. Mandy's response was, "I'm not worried about it, because I won't go anywhere on the ship where I could fall overboard."

Then her youngest brother, Melvin, piped up. "What if the ship sinks, like the *Titanic?*"

Mandy squeezed the arms on her deck chair. *Leave it up to my* bruder *to give me a hard time.* She could only imagine how horrible it must have been on the *Titanic,* with nowhere to go but the cold ocean water. Even so, she couldn't let these feelings get the best of her. Thinking happier thoughts, she reflected on how her parents had given each of their five children a name beginning with the letter *M.* Michael, almost twenty-three, had recently married Sarah Yoder. Milo was eighteen; Mark, fifteen; and Melvin, twelve. Mandy would celebrate her twenty-first birthday on January 28. She would be home from her trip way before then and figured her parents would do something special for her. Maybe Mom would cook a big meal and invite Mandy's closest friends to join them. Or perhaps they'd all go out to one of her favorite restaurants in the area.

Growing up with teasing brothers hadn't been easy, but she'd survived her childhood — although she had always longed for a sister.

Of course, she reasoned, *I have my three best friends, and they're almost like sisters.*

"Are you daydreaming?" Ellen nudged Mandy's arm. "I've been talking to you, but I don't think you heard a word I said."

"Oh, sorry. I was deep in thought." Mandy turned to face her friend. "What did you say?"

"It's getting windy, and I've had enough sun." Ellen unrolled her sleeves.

"You're right, the wind has picked up. Why don't we go check out one of the gift shops? Or would you rather go back to the room and rest awhile before lunch?"

"I've been in our room too much already. Let's go shopping." Ellen stood and smoothed the wrinkles in her dress. "Maybe I can pick up a few trinkets to give to family members back home."

The two friends gathered up their things, but before they left the pool area, Mandy paused and took a picture of the little girl she'd been watching earlier. *I hope someday I'll have a daughter as cute as her.*

■ ■ ■ ■

Middlebury

"Miriam, it's good to see you." Peggy Eash smiled when Mandy's mother entered her quilt-and-fabric store on Monday morning. "Is there anything I can help you with?"

"I need some thread."

"Well, you know where the notions are kept." Peggy pointed to the notions aisle.

Miriam nodded, picked up a shopping basket, and headed down the aisle. She had almost reached the thread display when she noticed Peggy's son Gideon. "I'm surprised to see you here this afternoon. Aren't you still working at the upholstery shop?"

"Things are a little slow there right now, so I have the day off. I'm helping unload a shipment of fabric and some other things that came in this morning." He brushed his dark hair off his forehead.

"I'm sure she appreciates your help, especially with Barbara gone." Miriam picked out two spools of thread then stepped aside so Gideon could set down the box he held.

"Have you heard anything from Mandy?" he asked, kneeling beside the box.

"We talked for a while last night." She

dropped the thread into her basket.

"Are she and her friends still on the boat?"

"Jah. They should be almost to Hawaii by now. They're scheduled to reach land tomorrow."

"How's Mandy doing?" He looked up at her with a curious expression.

"She's fine, but Ellen got seasick on Saturday."

Gideon's forehead wrinkled. "You'd never get me on a boat for all those days. I'd probably be grank as soon as I got on board."

"From what Mandy said, the ship is quite large, so unless the waters get really rough, I wouldn't think the boat would sway too much." Miriam picked out a few more spools of thread. "I hope she's enjoying herself and will return with lots of good memories."

"Aren't you worried about your *dochder* being so far from home?"

"I'm not fond of the idea, but as you know, Mandy is twenty years old. I certainly couldn't forbid her to go. She's old enough to make her own decisions." Miriam pursed her lips. *Although if I had my way, Mandy would be here right now — not off on a cruise to see what Hawaii is all about.*

"I didn't want her to go," Gideon admitted, "but I gave her my blessing."

41

"If you'd asked her not to go, maybe she would have stayed. As long as you two have been courting, I would think she'd want to please you and not go gallivanting off to see what a tropical island looks like."

"If I'd asked Mandy to stay, she might have resented me, and it could have affected our relationship." Gideon began pulling new skeins of yarn from the box.

"You may be right." Miriam hoped Mandy appreciated her boyfriend and would make a commitment to join the church soon. Maybe after this trip, she would settle down and take life more seriously.

CHAPTER 4

The Island of Maui

Since Mandy and her friends had stayed up late Monday night, visiting and looking at the stars and the full moon, it was hard to get up the next morning. However, the excitement of arriving at the port in Maui and the sounds of people in the hallway talking got them all out of bed.

Mandy and Barbara had signed up to go with a tour group to the visitors' center at the Haleakalā volcanic crater, as well as the Ali'i Kula Lavender Farm. Sadie and Ellen would tour the huge aquarium at Maui Ocean Center and explore the town of Lahaina, where many shops and restaurants were located.

Watching from one of the decks as the ship entered the harbor with a smaller boat guiding it into place, Mandy's enthusiasm mounted. After seeing nothing but water for the last four days, it was a thrill to finally spot some green. She could hardly wait to step on dry land and view the beautiful sights awaiting them.

Lahaina

"Wish we could have gone on a tour watching for humpback whales," Sadie commented as she and Ellen, along with the others in their tour group, started their walk through what appeared to be quite an old town. "Unfortunately from what I read in the brochure, the whales won't migrate here from Alaska until December."

"I agree it's a disappointment, but it'll be fun to do some shopping." Ellen gestured to an enormous tree with a twisted trunk, growing across the street. "That tree is certainly unusual. I wonder what it's called."

"It's a banyan," their tour guide explained. "A lot of them grow here on Maui." Everyone stopped walking as she told about this particular tree, and how it covered over two-thirds of an acre, with a dozen main trunks. "The Banyan tree was originally brought to Maui from India and planted over 140 years ago. Back then it was only eight feet tall, but now it's grown to a height of sixty feet."

Sadie tipped her head back, shielding her eyes from the bright glare of the sun as she studied the monstrous tree. It was nothing

44

like any of the trees they had back home.

With her camera ready, Sadie suggested she and Ellen take their picture by the Banyan tree. Since neither of them had joined the church yet and they wouldn't put their photos on display, it should be okay. Handing her camera to an older woman who was on the tour, they posed for a picture.

After the photo was taken, they continued the tour, pausing along the waterfront to watch some of the boats going in and out of the harbor. It was a clear, sunny day, and Sadie was glad she'd remembered her sunglasses.

Everyone went their own way for a while, visiting shops. They would regroup at a set time to board the bus that would take them to the Maui Ocean Center. Sadie looked forward to going because she'd read a beautiful pamphlet describing the center's unique attractions.

"Let's get one of those." Ellen pointed to a Hawaiian Shave Ice stand. "It looks similar to an ice-cream cone, only I've heard it's more refreshing."

"Jah, let's do." As Sadie and Ellen started walking, Sadie bumped her toe against the sidewalk and lost her footing. She regained her balance in time to right herself, and kept going.

"Are you okay?" Ellen clasped Sadie's arm.

"I'm fine. Jarred my back a bit, but at least I didn't fall. It was embarrassing, but it could have been worse." Taking a deep breath and exhaling, Sadie moved on.

When they stepped up to the stand, Sadie studied all the different flavors they offered. "Now I don't know which one to choose."

"Think I'll try a coconut-flavored shave ice." Ellen reached into her purse for the money. "As soon as you decide, we can order, and it'll be my treat."

"*Danki.*" Sadie continued to study the list of flavors and finally decided on a *li hing mui,* which meant "salted plum." In case she didn't care for the taste, she added a bit of cherry flavor to it, as well.

They sat on a bench to eat the delightful, cooling treats and watched the people from all walks of life passing by. Sadie had thought people might stare, wondering about their plain clothes, but with so many others representing different parts of the world, their way of dressing seemed to go unnoticed.

When they were almost finished with their shave ice, Sadie noticed some syrup from the bottom of the paper cone had dripped out. "Oh, no!" She pointed to the front of her blue dress. "I hope it won't leave a stain." She threw the remainder of the treat in a nearby garbage can.

"I packed some stain applicator for the trip," Ellen said. "When we get back to the ship you can put some on your dress. Good thing we brought extra clothes with us."

"It's also good we had our picture taken before this happened."

"Let's look for a restroom so you can try to get some of the mess out now," Ellen suggested.

Sadie picked up her tote bag and held it in front of her dress. "If I can't get the syrup out with soap and water, I'll carry my bag in front of me the rest of the day."

Ellen snickered.

After they located the public restrooms, Sadie took care of the stain as best as she could. Following that, they went into a few of the shops. In one, she spotted some petrified shark's teeth.

"Were those found here on Maui?" Ellen asked the woman behind the counter.

"No, they were actually discovered off the shores of Florida, along the Gulf of Mexico."

Sadie thought it would be strange to buy

something found in Florida when they were here on Maui, but then she'd also seen souvenirs and clothing in some of the shops that had been made in other countries.

"I'm looking for something inexpensive to take home to my family," Ellen said after they left the store selling shark teeth. "And I'd like it to be useful."

"I saw some Hawaiian-made purses at one of the shops. Those might be nice for the women in your family. There are some wooden items in this shop right here that might be useful." Sadie stepped up to the window for a closer look. "What do you think? Should we go inside and look around?"

Ellen drew in her lower lip and squinted. "Maybe I'll wait till we visit some of the other islands before I buy any gifts. I'm sure we'll have plenty of opportunities to shop."

Sadie shrugged. "Okay, but if we see something along the way that catches our eye, we ought to get it because you never know if you'll see anything like it again."

Haleakalā Crater
"Did you ever see anything so strange?" Barbara asked as she and Mandy stood with several others at one of the observation areas, looking at the lava formations.

"Seems like we've landed on the moon." Mandy giggled. "Course, I've never been to the moon, so I really can't say."

Barbara tipped her head back and looked up. "Did you hear that *gedumor*?"

"What noise?"

"It sounded like geese honking."

"Oh, those are the nēnē geese," their guide explained. "They're an endangered species and live on the wooded slopes of Haleakalā."

Mandy took out her camera and snapped several photos of the surrounding area. She could see for miles, clear out into the ocean. There was no way she could ever describe this unusual place without showing her family and friends a few pictures. She felt thankful she'd come to Hawaii, and what they were seeing today was only the beginning.

On the Cruise Ship
After Sadie and Ellen boarded the ship again, they headed for their room to get ready for the evening meal. They found Barbara and Mandy there.

"We had a good time today." Ellen yawned. "I'm tired, but no worse for wear."

"I don't know about the rest of you, but I can't wait to eat." Mandy gave a sheepish smile when her stomach growled. "I've snacked on a few roasted macadamia nuts. It's hard not to get carried away because they're so good."

"I tried a couple of them, but they're not as appealing to me, so I've been snacking on chips." Barbara sat in a chair with a bag of Hawaiian-style chips in her lap. "You're all welcome to try some if you want."

"Those sound tempting." Ellen walked over and reached into the bag. "They even smell good."

"What's on the front of your dress?" Mandy pointed.

"Ellen and I had some shave ice today. Mine ended up leaking on me." Sadie helped herself to a few macadamia nuts. "These are so good." She glanced at the clock. "There's still a little time before we head up for dinner, so I'm going to change out of this dress, put some stain remover on the spot, and soak it in the sink."

"Hopefully it'll come clean." Mandy moved to the window with her camera to take a few pictures of the beautiful sunset. "Would you look at that? We're seeing the hand of God again, jah?"

During dinner, the girls talked about the things they'd seen that day.

"The best part for me," Barbara said, "was

50

visiting the Ali'i Kula Lavender Farm. It was beautiful, and I bought a few lavender gifts at the Gallery Gift Shop to take home for family."

"It was a nice place to visit," Mandy agreed, while reaching for her glass of water.

"What was it like?" Ellen asked.

Eyes sparkling like fireflies on a hot summer night, Barbara told about the breathtaking views and walking paths. "It was interesting to hear the history of how the farm came to be, and we got to see and smell the pretty lavender plants."

"We were thankful for our tour guide, who explained everything," Mandy interjected. "It was so peaceful. We wished we could have stayed longer."

"That's how I felt when the group Sadie and I were with visited the Maui Ocean Center." Ellen blotted her lips with a cloth napkin. "My favorite part was the outdoor turtle lagoon. It was fun to see the turtles playing in the water and basking in the sandy area provided for them."

Sadie took a bite of roast beef, then set her fork down. "Watching the turtles was enjoyable, but the best part for me at the ocean center was the indoor part of the aquarium, where we saw many species of native Hawaiian fish."

Ellen smiled. "After our tour we ate lunch at the Aquarium Reef Café and browsed the gift shop, where they had all kinds of treasures."

"Did you buy anything?" Mandy asked.

"No, I'm waiting until we get to the next island in the morning."

"Speaking of which . . ." Mandy tilted her head. "I hear the ship's motor running below, which means we're getting ready to leave port." *I can hardly wait to see what adventures await on Oahu tomorrow.*

CHAPTER 5

The Island of Oahu

Mandy shivered in anticipation as she waited to leave the ship. She and Sadie would tour Pearl Harbor while Barbara and Ellen explored the Polynesian Cultural Center. There wasn't time to go on both tours, so the four friends had decided to split up and then share their experiences during dinner. Later on, they'd also exchange pictures.

Mandy chose Pearl Harbor because she'd studied the World War II attack and was saddened to think how many people lost their lives because of it. Sadie was also interested in history, and especially wanted to visit the USS *Arizona* Memorial, which she'd heard was one of the most popular visitor attractions in Hawaii.

"I'm eager to see the cultural center. The brochure I have mentions it's a forty-two-acre lagoon park." Ellen placed the brochures in her tote bag. "We'll be able to see Polynesian dance, costumes, and songs, and learn how they used to live. From the pictures I've seen, it appears to be a special place with natural beauty, showcasing the culture of the Pacific. There will be so much to see and do, all in a single day."

"I'm excited, too," Barbara agreed. "It will be interesting to learn about the various aspects of Polynesian culture."

"Oh, look, there's a beautiful *reggeboge*! It must be raining somewhere on the island."

Mandy looked in the direction Sadie pointed. Sure enough. A gorgeous rainbow spanned the sky. Its bright colors pierced the clouds, captivating her as she admired the rainbow's beauty. Looking closer, she noticed a double rainbow, but the colors were in reverse of the brighter one.

Mandy thought about the Bible passage where God placed a rainbow in the sky after the flood as a promise to never again destroy the earth by water. Whenever she saw a rainbow, she remembered God's promise, and it made her feel closer to Him. *Our heavenly Father created many wonderful things for our enjoyment,* she thought. *Too bad some people take them for granted or don't notice at all.*

■ ■ ■ ■

Polynesian Cultural Center

"This is fun!" Ellen could hardly contain herself as she and Barbara sat in a canoe.

Their paddling guide led them through a lovely lagoon, slowly maneuvering from one end of the cultural center to the other. After spending most of the morning on their feet, looking at many of the exhibits, it felt good to sit and enjoy a more leisurely pace. She'd picked up a disposable camera at the first gift shop they'd visited and had already taken several pictures. Her camera wasn't fancy like the digital one Mandy purchased before leaving on their trip, but it would capture some of the special places Ellen was seeing today. Tomorrow, she'd also have more picture-taking opportunities when they visited the island of Kauai.

She leaned back, closing her eyes for a brief time, enjoying the perfumed fragrances in the air. "Can you smell the flowers?" Ellen tilted her head farther and sniffed deeply, to catch more of the pleasant aroma.

Turning to face her, their handsome young guide spoke up. "The fragrance you're enjoying is from the gardenia flower growing over there." He pointed toward the bank of the man-made freshwater lagoon. "They do smell wonderful."

Barbara smiled. "I agree. The scent of those flowers is so different than any we have back home."

"Where are you two from?" he asked.

"Middlebury, Indiana," Ellen replied.

"You're a long way from home. How do you like Hawaii so far?"

Ellen's cheeks felt hot as she murmured, "It's amazing."

"I couldn't agree more." Barbara dipped her hand into the water as they glided quietly along.

"Maybe you'll come back someday. We see a lot of returning guests here at our center." He winked at her.

Stifling a snicker, Ellen exchanged looks with her friend. Then to ease her embarrassment, Barbara leaned closer to Ellen and whispered, "What should we do after this?"

"I'm hungerich, so maybe we should eat lunch."

"Sounds good to me. There's a snack stand at the Marquesas Village inside the center."

"They have good food, and the prices aren't bad." Their guide smiled and winked at Barbara again.

Ellen wondered if he was flirting with her friend. If so, she was glad Barbara wasn't flirting back.

"Thank you for the information." Barbara turned to look at Ellen. "After we eat, maybe we should stop by the Polynesian Marketplace, which has many handcrafted items. I bet we can find some nice things to buy."

"They do have some interesting items," their guide interjected.

"I need to be careful not to spend all my money in one place," Ellen said. "We still have two islands to see, not to mention our stop in Ensenada, Mexico, before returning to Los Angeles."

"So you came by cruise ship?" the young man asked.

Before either Barbara or Ellen could respond, he added, "I've never been on a big boat like that." He paused, lifting his oar out of the water. "So, what's it like?"

"It's an interesting way of traveling," Barbara replied. "There are a variety of shows to see on board and incredible amounts of elaborate food to eat. It's like a small floating town, with shops, swimming pools, and many other things to see and do. So far, it's been quite enjoyable."

"Except for me getting seasick one day."

Ellen leaned closer to Barbara. "I wonder how things are going with Mandy and Sadie."

Pearl Harbor

A lump lodged in Mandy's throat as she stood on the USS *Arizona* Memorial platform, looking into the water. She could see an outline of the submerged ship. A taped narration played close by, telling about the attack. This was the final resting place for the 1,177 crew members who lost their lives when the ship was sunk by the Japanese on December 7, 1941.

"This is so sad," she whispered.

Sadie nodded slowly, clutching her handkerchief.

Mandy could hardly fathom the horrible chaos that went on during the bombings. This wasn't the only ship that had been attacked in the harbor. The *Nevada, Tennessee, West Virginia, Maryland, Oklahoma,* and *California* were also hit. The battleship *Pennsylvania* was in dry dock that day for repairs.

Since the Japanese attack had been a surprise, many of the bombs and torpedoes hit their targets. The damage to the ships was severe, causing great loss of life and many ships to sink.

When Mandy closed her eyes, she could

almost smell the pillars of smoke and hear the loud booms as the enemy aircraft swept in. She shuddered thinking about the shouts of anguish from those who'd been injured and the sorrow of family members who lost a loved one that fateful day. War was a terrible thing. She wished there could only be peace.

"It's time to go, Mandy." Sadie touched her arm. "They've announced the boat that brought us here is ready to transport us back to the visitor's center."

Glancing once more at the remains of the ship beneath them, Mandy turned away.

"What shall we see next?" she asked Sadie when they reached the visitor's center a short time later.

"I'd like to walk through the USS *Bowfin*. The submarine is docked outside the Bowfin Museum. The cost for museum admission and a tour of the sub is twelve dollars, which includes getting a digital audio player to narrate the tour."

"It does sound interesting. It's a good thing neither of us is claustrophobic, because from what I've read, submarine quarters are tight."

"When we're done touring the *Bowfin,* if there's still time, we could visit the USS *Missouri,*" Sadie rushed on. "It's famous for being the site where Japan signed the formal surrender, ending World War II in 1945."

"You certainly know your history." Mandy moved in the direction of the submarine.

"I've often wished I could have lived in the past. Course, not through something as serious as a world war," Sadie quickly added.

On the Cruise Ship

When the girls sat down to dinner that evening, they shared their adventures of the day.

"The best part of visiting the Polynesian Culture Center was learning how to make a fire by rubbing two sticks together." Barbara's eyes gleamed. "It was hard work, but the Samoan villagers made starting a fire look effortless."

"I'll bet it was fascinating." Mandy cut into a piece of baked chicken. "Pearl Harbor was not only interesting, but quite emotional. Too bad we didn't have time to see the cultural center, too."

"What was your favorite part of the day?" Sadie focused her gaze on Ellen.

"I enjoyed the canoe ride, but even though it was relaxing, our tour guide made me kind of naerfich. He seemed overly talkative and flirted with Barbara." Ellen's brows pinched together. "But watching several skilled artisans carve some beautiful pieces from various types of wood was also interesting."

"Oh, and don't forget the food," Barbara interjected. "We had a tasty lunch at one of the snack stands inside the center." She looked at Mandy. "Where did you and Sadie eat?"

"Between the USS *Arizona* Museum and the USS *Bowfin* Museum there's an open-air café." Mandy paused for a sip of iced tea. "Of course, the food wasn't nearly as good as what we're being treated to tonight."

"We have had some delicious meals on this trip." Sadie lifted her fork and took a bite. "I wouldn't be surprised if I've gained a few pounds. When we get home, I'll most likely have to diet and exercise."

"Speaking of home, have any of you heard from your family lately?" Ellen asked.

"I got a call from my mamm this afternoon," Mandy replied. "She mentioned the weather there has warmed a bit. Instead of snow, they're now getting rain."

"We had some rain today, too," Sadie reminded. "Although it was a warm rain, so I didn't really mind it."

Barbara's forehead wrinkled. "I almost

61

feel guilty being here where the days and nights are so balmy, while our family and friends are dealing with pre-winter weather."

"We should enjoy it while we can." Mandy's enthusiasm slowly diminished as reality sank in. "Because all too soon our *wunderbaar* vacation will be over." She didn't tell the others, but part of her wished she never had to go home. Mandy didn't dislike her home in Middlebury — it was where she'd grown up and met her friends. But the sensation of being somewhere new made her feel like all her burdens had been removed. *Of course,* she reminded herself, *if I lived anywhere else, I'd miss my family and friends.*

CHAPTER 6

The Island of Kauai

"Don't forget your cell phone, Barbara. I may want to borrow it to call my folks today," Sadie said as they prepared to leave the boat Thursday morning.

"No problem." Barbara held up her phone. "It's charged up and ready to go in my travel tote."

"Are you two sure you don't want to go with us to see the Waimea Canyon?" Sadie turned to face Mandy and Ellen.

Mandy shook her head. "I'm sure the canyon is beautiful, but I'd rather see a few things on my own this time, instead of going with a tour group." She looked at Ellen. "Do you still want to explore with me, or would you rather go with Sadie and Barbara?"

"I'd like to go with you and see Spouting Horn, or whatever else we have time for before the ship moves on this evening." Ellen smiled. "It'll be fun to be on our own."

"We'll be going to see the canyon on a bus with our tour group," Barbara stated. "But how will you two get to the places you want to see?"

"Guess we'll have to call a taxi, because only the town of Lihue is within walking distance of the port," Mandy replied.

Sadie squeezed Mandy's shoulder. "Be careful out there, and make sure you're back on time. The boat will probably head for the Big Island sometime during our evening meal."

"Don't worry. We'll be here in plenty of time." Mandy pulled her cell phone from her purse and held it up. "The clock on this device keeps me right on track."

Koloa Estate

When Ellen and Mandy stepped out of their taxi cab, Ellen paused and sniffed the air. "Can you smell it, Mandy?" Her excitement mounted. "The wunderbaar aroma of *kaffi* is all around us."

Mandy chuckled. "Of course it is — we're at a coffee farm."

"Jah, but I never thought it would smell like this." Eager to go inside the visitor's center, Ellen grabbed Mandy's hand. "Let's ask about taking the walking tour."

"Don't you want to try some kaffi first? The brochure I picked up says there are several kinds to sample inside the visitor's center."

"Good idea." Ellen started walking in that direction, and Mandy followed.

The aroma of coffee greeted them inside the building, even stronger than it had been outside. It didn't take Ellen long to find the room where the free samples were located. She and Mandy tasted all of them — chocolate, dark-roasted peaberry; coconut caramel; vanilla; chocolate macadamia nut; hazelnut; and Hawaiian-style Irish crème.

Ellen turned to Mandy and grinned. "After all those samples, we should have enough energy to keep going for the rest of the day."

Mandy nodded. "Maybe a little too much energy. I'm not used to drinking so much kaffi at one time."

"Let's go on the walking tour, and then we can check out the gift shop before our taxi picks us up." Ellen reached into her tote bag to get her camera. "Oh, oh."

"What's wrong?"

"I can't find my camera. I must have left it in our room on the ship."

"No problem. I have mine, and I'll share

it with you. We can take all the pictures we want."

Since they had the option of meandering through the shade of the coffee trees on their own or waiting for a time when a tour would take them, Mandy suggested they start walking by themselves. "There are signs along the way identifying the different coffee varieties, as well as telling about the coffee process. We can learn what we want to know without a tour guide." She quirked an eyebrow. "After all, this day is supposed to be about branching out on our own."

Ellen stopped, pointing to a sign. *"Aloha e komo mai."*

"I wonder what it means."

Ellen smiled. "It means 'Welcome.' " Before Mandy had a chance to ask, Ellen explained that she found the words in a little Hawaiian booklet she'd bought at the Polynesian Cultural Center the previous day. "I left it in our room on the ship, but wish now I had it with me."

"Guess we should both study your book so we can say a few Hawaiian words while we're here."

"Good idea. I'll take it out of my suitcase when we get back to the ship, because it won't do us any good unless we have it with us when we're touring the islands." Ellen's forehead wrinkled. "I'm surprised I even remembered what I'd read about how to say 'welcome.' "

As they moved on, they came to other signs identifying the different coffee varieties. Up ahead, they found even more informational markers explaining the process from initial blooming, through harvesting and processing, to the final roasting.

They ended the tour by sitting on the veranda to enjoy sweeping views of the plantation and coffee trees, leading down to the ocean. The palms moved in the gentle breeze as Ellen and Mandy sat together eating the ice-cream cones they'd purchased at the snack bar.

"I'm glad we came here." When Mandy finished her cone, she stood and tossed her napkin into the trash can. "It's time to check out the gift shop and call our taxi so we can move on. Also, maybe we should get a high-protein snack to take with us."

"You're right," Ellen agreed. "With nothing in my stomach but ice cream and coffee, I feel a bit shaky."

Mandy glanced at her cell phone. "The time is going quickly, and I do want to see Spouting Horn yet, don't you?"

"Of course. According to the brochures I have, it's a sight to behold." Ellen finished the rest of her cone and rose from her seat.

Waimea Canyon

"I wonder how things are going with Ellen and Mandy," Sadie said as she sat beside Barbara on the tour bus taking them up the long, curvy road to the viewpoint.

Barbara's brows lifted. "I still can't believe they went off by themselves. They're gonna miss seeing what some call the 'Grand Canyon of the Pacific.' "

"It was their choice, and I'm sure they'll get to see some things as awesome as what we'll be witnessing today. Besides, we'll take plenty of pictures."

"I suppose." Barbara looked away, staring out at the scenery as the bus traveled along.

"This has sure been a wonderful trip, getting to see so many unusual and beautiful things." Sadie sighed. "It's almost like stepping inside the pages of a book."

"It has been pretty amazing," Barbara agreed. "Too bad we can't spend more time on each of the islands. But then again, we should be glad for what we have been able to see. Our trip might be more expensive if the ship remained docked for more than a day on each island. We'd probably still be at home, working to save more money, instead of being here, enjoying ourselves." She pulled a package of mints from her purse and offered one to Sadie.

"Danki." Sadie smiled and put one in her mouth.

When the bus came to the viewpoint, it stopped and everyone got out. Sadie stood staring at the panoramic view of the colorful canyon, with its rugged, craggy surface and deep valley gorges. The rock formations of beige, red, and green seemed almost surreal. "How could anyone believe there is no God?" she whispered in awe.

"I understand what you're saying. Oh my, I wonder how it all came about." Slowly, Barbara shook her head.

"It was formed from the steady process of erosion, due to a catastrophic collapse of the volcano that created Kauai millions of years ago. At least, that's what it says here." Sadie lifted the brochure she held. "When Kauai was still continually erupting, a portion of the island collapsed. It then formed a deep depression, which became filled with lava flows."

Barbara sucked in her breath. "All I know is, what we are looking at is gorgeous. I see it as the handiwork of God."

Sadie nodded. "Well said."

■ ■ ■ ■

Spouting Horn

"Watch now! Watch real close, 'cause it's gonna blow." Mandy lifted her camera in readiness to see water shoot upward through an opening of lava rock, as she'd read about.

Ellen stood beside her, holding tightly to the rail. "I don't see anything, Mandy. When is it supposed to happen?"

"I don't know the exact moment; that's why we need to watch."

A minute later, it happened. As a huge spray of water shot upward through an opening, it created a great moaning sound. "I got it!" Mandy shouted as she snapped a picture. "That was absolutely incredible!"

"And it never ceases to amaze me."

Mandy's head jerked at the sound of a deep voice close to her ear. Startled, she turned to see a young man with tousled sandy-blond hair hanging almost to his shoulders. He stood right beside her and wore a pair of dark blue cutoffs and a white T-shirt.

"You've seen it before?" she questioned.

"Oh yeah, many times." His cobalt-blue eyes twinkled as he gave her a dimpled smile. "I live on the island, so I can come here whenever I have time. The spray from Spouting Horn can shoot as high as fifty feet in the air. Oh, and you might also like to know that the original name for this natural wonder is *'puhi,'* which means, 'blowhole.' "

"It sounds like you know a lot about it." She tossed the ties on her head covering over her shoulder to keep them from blowing in her face.

"Sure do. According to Hawaiian folklore, a giant lizard protected this area, until a young man named Liko challenged it. Of course, this threatened the people who came here to fish or swim." He paused, his thick lashes brushing his cheeks as he blinked. "During the battle, Liko plunged a sharp stick into the lizard's mouth."

"What happened next?" Mandy felt drawn into his story.

"Well, Liko leaped into the water, luring the lizard in, too. Then he swam into a small lava tube in the rocks, leading to the surface. The lizard followed and got stuck in the tube. So today, what you witnessed when the water shot up was the lizard's roar. And he does it every time Spouting Horn blasts into the air."

Mandy giggled. "What a great story. Thanks for sharing it with us."

"Us?" He tipped his head, looking at her curiously.

She glanced to her left, thinking Ellen was still there, but her friend had wandered off and was kneeling beside a mother hen and her baby chicks in the grassy area. Mandy had read about all the chickens roaming free on Kauai, but these were the first she had seen. "My friend is over there." She pointed over her shoulder with her thumb. "This is our first time to Kauai, and I'm impressed with what we've seen so far. There's so much colorful foliage and beautiful flowers — even more so than the other two islands we've already seen."

"It is beautiful here." His hands made a sweeping gesture of the landscape. "That's why it's known as 'The Garden Island.' "

"I'd heard that, and it makes sense to me now." Mandy took a picture of Ellen and the chickens. She would surprise her with it when they got home.

"Where are you from?" he asked.

"We live in northeastern Indiana."

"Amish country?" He slipped his sunglasses on.

She nodded.

"I figured you were Amish by the way you're dressed." He kept his focus mainly on Mandy, glancing briefly at Ellen as she watched the mama hen and her chicks.

"Have you ever been to Indiana or met any Amish people?" Mandy asked.

"Nope. I grew up in Portland, Oregon, but I've read about the Amish and seen some shows on TV about them."

Mandy frowned. "Don't believe everything you read and especially what you see on television. Not everything people say or think about us is true."

He rubbed the bridge of his nose. "Figured as much. Not everything people say about those who live on the Hawaiian Islands is true, either."

Ellen returned to Mandy's side and tugged her sleeve. "Should we go look at some of the souvenir booths now? I'd like to see if there's anything I might wanna buy to take home."

"You'll find some nice locally-made items," the young man said.

Mandy smiled. "It's been nice talking to you. Thanks again for the information about the blowhole — even the story you made up."

"Oh, I didn't make it up. The legend's been around a long time." He lifted his hand to wave. "Enjoy your time here on the island."

As the girls made their way toward the

booths, Ellen leaned close to Mandy. "Do you always talk to strangers?"

"I do when I want to learn something." Mandy giggled. "I thought what he told us about the blowhole was interesting."

"Told *you,* don't you mean? I was looking at the chickens."

"You should have been looking at the water shooting up. It was much more interesting."

"I did see it blow, but when the stranger engaged you in conversation, I let someone else take my place at the railing."

"If you'd stayed, you would have heard an interesting folk story about a lizard and a man doing battle in the ocean."

Ellen rolled her eyes dramatically. "Really, Mandy, I'd never have believed something so *narrisch.*"

"It wasn't foolish. It was fun." Mandy gave Ellen's arm a gentle tap. "You need to relax and be more outgoing. A person can learn a lot from talking to strangers."

Lihue

After stopping for a late lunch and doing a bit of shopping, Ellen suggested they start back to their ship.

"I'm sure we have plenty of time." Mandy reached into her purse to retrieve her cell phone and was surprised it wasn't there. "That's *fremm*."

"What's strange?"

"I thought I put my cell phone in my purse after we were done eating, but it's not there."

"Maybe you laid it down somewhere. Could you have left it in your seat or on the table at the restaurant?"

"I'm not sure. I suppose it's possible." Mandy started moving in that direction. "We need to go back and see."

When they entered the restaurant, Mandy told the hostess she'd lost her cell phone and thought it might be there, but she was told no cell phone had been found when their table was cleared.

"Okay, thank you." Mandy felt her heart beat faster. She needed her phone to keep in touch with her family, not to mention keep track of the time.

"Where else could you have left it?" Ellen's gaze flitted around the area.

"I have no idea." Mandy took several deep breaths to calm herself. "I need to find it, Ellen. Help me think where it could be."

"Let's retrace our steps."

"Okay." Fear clutched Mandy's heart. Losing her phone was much worse than if she'd lost her camera.

After looking in several places with no luck, Mandy finally gave up. "Guess we'll have to discontinue our search. We need to get back to the ship."

"You're right." Ellen rested her hand on Mandy's arm. "I'm sorry I wasn't paying closer attention. If I had, I may have seen where you laid the phone down."

"It's not your fault. I was careless." She turned away from Ellen and bit her lip.

They were several blocks from their cruise ship, so they had plenty of walking to do. The sun was beginning to set over the horizon, reflecting off the water's surface. Hot and cool colors swirled in the sky and waves. It looked like something one would see in a painting, but this was even better because it was real.

Mandy and Ellen walked at a fast pace, yet Mandy's heartbeat slowed while she gazed at the sunset. *I wonder if there are any legends about the sun in Hawaii,* she mused. *If there are, I'd love to listen.*

As they approached the dock, Mandy's eyes widened, and her stomach churned. She turned to Ellen. "Where's our cruise ship?"

With a trembling hand, Ellen pointed.

Mandy saw it then, some distance away.

The boat had already headed out to sea. She gasped. "Oh, no! We missed it!"

CHAPTER 7

On the Cruise Ship

Sadie squeezed her purse handles so tight, the veins stood out on her hand. "Oh, dear. I'm getting nervous, Barbara. The ship's on its way to the Big Island, and we haven't seen any sign of Mandy or Ellen."

"I'm sure they're somewhere on the ship," Barbara said. "We must have missed them on our way to dinner. This boat is enormous, and a lot of passengers are milling around, so at this point, let's not worry."

"I realize that, but it's time for supper. Mandy and Ellen should be sitting here beside us at the table." Sadie looked around, hoping their friends were on their way and would join them any minute.

Barbara shrugged. "Maybe they couldn't find the dining room."

"It doesn't make sense. As many evenings as we've all come up to this deck, they surely would be able to find their way here

78

by now."

Barbara drank some water. "Perhaps they ate too much for lunch and decided to skip the evening meal. I remember the time Mandy mentioned she'd like to visit the exercise room on the ship. Maybe she and Ellen are there, working out on one of the machines."

Sadie's brows lifted. "And miss dinner? I don't believe it."

"If they're too full to eat anything right now, I can understand them not wanting dinner." Barbara leaned forward. "Or maybe they went to the ship's library and became lost in a novel."

"They should have been in our room when we went there to change before coming up to dinner." Sadie pursed her lips. "I hope you're right about why they're not here, but I have a horrible feeling they didn't make it back to the ship before it pulled away from the dock."

Barbara coughed, nearly choking on her water. "Ach, that would be *baremlich*! If Mandy and Ellen didn't get to the ship on time, they're stranded on Kauai!"

Lihue

Ellen clutched Mandy's arm. "What are we going to do? The boat left without us, and

79

now we're stuck here for who knows how long and without our luggage." For the first time since they'd begun their journey, she sounded desperate to go home.

"Calm down." Mandy spoke softly, hoping to ease her own fears. She had to admit, even with her friend standing right beside her, it was a lonely feeling being so far from home in an unfamiliar place. "It won't do us any good to get *umgerrent.*"

"How can we not be upset?" Ellen's voice rose while she twisted her head covering ribbons around her fingers. "We're stuck here, with no place to even stay the night. And remember, you don't have your cell phone anymore. If you still had it, you could at least call Sadie and Barbara and tell them what's happened. Imagine how worried they are by now. I sure would be if our roles were reversed."

While Mandy and Ellen talked more about their situation, an elderly man and woman walked up to them.

"I don't mean to interrupt," the lady said, "but my husband and I couldn't help overhearing what you two were saying about missing your ship."

Mandy barely managed a nod.

"I'm sorry to hear it. If you're looking for overnight lodging, perhaps you'd be interested in staying at the lovely bed-and-breakfast where my husband and I have been staying in Kapaa for the past two nights. I heard the owner mention they have a vacancy, so I don't think getting a room would be a problem." She brushed her thin, gray bangs to the side of her forehead before looking at her husband who nodded.

Mandy's ears perked up when the elderly man mentioned the people who ran the B&B were Christians. "That's why my wife and I have come back to stay there again. The Palos are so kind and down to earth. Real nice, genuine folks. We'd be happy to give you girls a ride to their place." He held out his hand. "My name is Frank Anderson, and this is my wife, Dottie. We live in California, and this is our third time on Kauai."

Ellen and Mandy introduced themselves, then Ellen turned to Mandy. "What do you think we should do?"

"I don't believe we have much choice. We need a place to stay this evening."

As Mandy sat in the backseat of Mr. and Mrs. Anderson's rental car, her throat constricted. *This whole mess is my fault. If only I hadn't lost my phone. What's going to happen to us now? Surely the ship won't*

81

come back to get us. I remember what we were told when instructions were given to all passengers about not being late. Now we we'll need to find another way home.

She glanced at Ellen, sitting behind the driver's seat, while fingering her head covering ties again. *What is she thinking?* Mandy rubbed her hand on her chest. *Is Ellen as upset with me as I am with myself?* She had told her friend to calm down a while ago, but now Mandy was upset. She needed to pray and ask God to help them.

Closing her eyes, she sent up a silent prayer. *Dear Lord, please help us find a way to get in touch with Sadie and Barbara. And show us what we need to do in order to get home.*

Kapaa

Sometime later, they pulled up in front of a large, two-story house. The sun was about to disappear below the horizon. Mandy didn't know if it was because they were in Hawaii, but the sky was breathtaking as it turned from a brilliant orange to a deep scarlet red. The porch light was on, and Mandy could read the sign by the front door: The Palms Bed-and-Breakfast. The name seemed appropriate, since two large palm trees, silhouetted by the sunset, stood in the yard.

Frank turned off the engine, and when he and Dottie got out, Mandy and Ellen did the same. Going up to the door without any luggage seemed strange. Since she and Ellen had not made reservations, she wondered if they would be allowed to stay.

Both of them held back until the Andersons entered the house. A pleasant-looking Hawaiian couple, who appeared to be in their late forties, greeted them.

"Luana and Makaio, these two young women missed their cruise ship and need a place to stay tonight," Dottie explained. "They're Amish, and their names are Mandy Frey and Ellen Lambright. Would you have a room for them?"

"I'm sorry to hear of your predicament." A look of concern was quickly replaced by Luana's pretty smile, revealing perfectly white teeth. "We have two rooms left, but one is reserved for some people who are expected to arrive later tonight. Would one room with twin beds work for you?" She directed her question to Mandy. "It's the Primrose Room."

"That would be fine." Mandy hesitated, biting her lip. "How much does the room cost?"

"For a single room with a shared bathroom, the cost is ninety-five dollars per night," Makaio spoke up.

"We'll take it." Ellen's cheeks turned pink when she looked at Mandy. "Is that okay with you?"

Mandy nodded. It wasn't like Ellen to speak up so boldly, but in this case, she was glad she had. Mandy was relieved they had enough money between them, even though it wouldn't last forever. They wouldn't be able to stay here too many nights, but for now, what other choice did they have? Mandy was dog-tired and stressed out from all the drama they'd gone through today. Ellen had to be feeling it, too. *I wonder if Barbara and Sadie are exhausted from worrying about us.*

Mandy couldn't wait for her head to hit the pillow; although she wished she and Ellen were on board the cruise ship. *On a positive note,* she thought, *I'll have a nice bed to sleep in tonight rather than a tight upper bunk in our ship's cabin.*

She suddenly realized that they needed to get in touch with their folks as soon as possible to let them know what had happened. Hopefully, they could send them enough money for tickets on another cruise ship that would take them back to the mainland.

"Could we borrow your phone?" Mandy

asked Luana after the Andersons headed down the hall to their room. "I'll pay you whatever it costs for the long-distance call."

"Certainly, but don't worry about paying us back. We have unlimited long-distance." Luana spoke in a bubbly tone as she pointed to the phone sitting on a desk where the guest book lay. "Please, help yourself, and don't forget to sign our guest book."

"Thank you so much." Mandy looked at Ellen. "I'll call my folks first, and then you can call yours."

"What about Sadie and Barbara? How are we supposed to let them know where we are?"

"That's a problem. I can't call Barbara's cell phone, because her number was programmed into my phone and I didn't write it down." Mandy released a frustrated groan.

"Maybe when you call your parents and explain what happened, you could ask them to get ahold of Barbara's parents, because they surely have her cell number," Ellen suggested.

"Good idea." Mandy picked up the receiver and punched in the number for home. After getting her parents' voice mail, she left a message explaining what happened. She also gave them the phone number for the B&B, reminding them of the five-hour difference in time between Indiana and Hawaii. Then she handed Ellen the phone. "Your turn."

"I'm bummed. The last thing I want to do is make this call to my folks. They'll be so worried when they get my message." The sound of dread in Ellen's voice was evident.

Hopefully by tomorrow, one of them would hear something from someone back home. Mandy prayed everything would work out.

On the Cruise Ship

"Did you get ahold of Mandy?" Sadie asked when she stepped out of the bathroom and saw Barbara with her cell phone.

Barbara lay back on her bed. "Unfortunately, no. I did leave a message, though."

"How many messages does that make now?" Sadie sipped a cup of tea she'd made for herself.

"Three." Barbara sighed. "If they did miss the boat, which I'm almost sure is what occurred, what's gonna happen to them?"

Sadie sat down on Ellen's bed. "I don't know, but they're both *schmaert*. I'm sure they'll figure something out. We'll pray they get help this evening and things will work out as smoothly as possible under the circumstances they're facing."

"It's hard to have faith sometimes — especially when something like this happens." Barbara's voice cracked. "This is horrible. It's sure put a damper on our vacation."

"I agree. It'll be hard to get off the ship in Hilo tomorrow morning and go with the others who signed up to see the volcano." Sadie looked down at the bed and brushed her hand over the blanket. "It's probably not the right time to say this, but . . ."

"What were you going to say?"

"I'm taking Ellen's bed and leaving the cramped upper bunk behind."

"I don't blame you for choosing to sleep there, and Ellen can't say anything if she's not here to talk you out of it." Barbara's eyes teared up. "Maybe we shouldn't go sightseeing tomorrow. We should probably stay here and keep trying to get in touch with Mandy and Ellen."

"What would that solve? You can keep calling her when we're on the Big Island."

"True." Barbara picked up her cell phone again. "Think I'd better give my folks a call and tell them what happened. I'll ask Mom to let Ellen and Mandy's parents know about them missing the boat. After that, you can call your parents." She grimaced.

"Everyone — especially Mandy and Ellen's family — will be *umgerrent* when they hear the news."

Chapter 8

The Big Island

Sadie stretched her arms over her head and released a noisy yawn. She hadn't slept well last night, despite being in her friend's bed. Thoughts of Ellen and Mandy kept her awake. Now she and Barbara were scheduled to take a tour to see the volcano, but neither of them felt like going anywhere. How could they have fun while their friends were stranded on Kauai?

"Even if we're not in the mood for sightseeing, we need to leave the ship and join the tour." Barbara gathered her sunglasses, along with her phone, and put them in her purse.

"You're right. We may never visit Hawaii again, so we should try to make the best of this beautiful sunny morning. I hope we hear something from Mandy today."

"Jah." Barbara reached for her sweater and held it up. "You may want to bring yours, too. I heard it can be a bit chilly near the volcano."

"I'll get mine." Sadie gathered up the rest of her things and put them in a tote. "Let's be off."

Kapaa

"This is a lovely room," Mandy commented as she and Ellen put their only dresses on Friday morning before joining the other guests for breakfast. "The Primrose Room — what an appropriate name. The entire space looks like a beautiful flower."

"And don't forget these." Ellen gestured to the twin beds, each covered with a lovely quilt. "Wouldn't it be nice to buy a Hawaiian quilt to take home when we go?" Ellen walked to the bed and ran her fingers over the material.

Mandy brought her hands to her chest. "I would love to own one, but I hear they're expensive." She moved over to the mirror and put her head covering on. "If we end up staying here awhile, maybe we could make one. I don't think they're much different than our Amish quilts."

"That may be, but we won't be here long enough to make a quilt." Ellen moved toward the door. "We'd better go downstairs. From the delicious aromas coming up the steps, breakfast must be ready."

Mandy was almost to the door when she dropped her handkerchief. She bent to pick it up and noticed a little wooden statue on the floor under the dresser. "I wonder what this is."

Ellen turned around. "What?"

Mandy reached for the small object and held it up. "Have you ever seen one of these before?"

"No, I have not." Ellen ran her finger over the dark-colored sculpture. "It's smiling face carved into the wood looks so peculiar. Let's ask Luana or Makaio about it."

When Mandy and Ellen entered the dining room a short time later, they were greeted by Mr. and Mrs. Anderson, already seated at the table.

"Did you two sleep well?" Dottie asked.

"I did." Mandy grinned and pulled out a chair at the table. "The bed was a lot more comfortable than the upper bunk I slept on during our time on the ship."

Ellen pulled out a chair and sat beside Mandy. "I had a good night's sleep, too."

Two other couples entered the room and took seats at the table, and everyone introduced themselves. The middle-aged couple were from Washington State, and the newly-weds who'd arrived last evening lived in

Canada.

Smiling cheerfully, Luana stepped into the room carrying a plate of scrambled eggs. Makaio, wearing a pale green shirt with palm trees on it, was right behind her, bringing a platter of sausages and a bowl of white rice. Already on the table were two bowls of fruit — one with pineapple and strawberries, the other with papaya and blueberries.

Mandy's mouth nearly watered, thinking how good everything looked. No doubt it would taste equally yummy.

"If anyone would like Spam instead of sausage, I'd be happy to bring some out." Makaio's prominent cheekbones rose. "I kinda like the stuff."

Luana poked her husband's arm and chuckled. "Don't let him fool you. My man is addicted to Spam."

"I especially like it with scrambled eggs and rice," he added. "My dad likes it, too. He raised me on it."

"Thanks anyway, but I think I'll pass." Mandy averted her gaze. Although she wasn't a picky eater and was willing to try many things, she'd never gotten acquainted with Spam until she'd tried it on the cruise ship during breakfast their first morning. One glance and one sniff was all it took for her not to like it. She didn't understand how anyone could eat the stuff. *Then again,* she thought, *some people might question my taste for seafood.*

"Did you both sleep well?" Makaio asked.

"Oh yes," Ellen replied. "It was good to sleep in a bed that didn't feel like it was swaying back and forth."

"I have a question." Mandy held out the small statue she'd discovered. "I found this under the dresser in our room and wondered what it was."

"It's a tiki," Makaio explained. "One of our previous guests must have bought it from a gift shop and left it in the room. Guess we missed seeing it there when we cleaned."

"Do the little statues have a special purpose or meaning?" Ellen asked.

"Well, some who live on our island believe if a totem such as this has been carved with a scary expression, it will keep away evil spirits."

"Others with a friendlier appearance, like the one you're holding, are thought to bring good luck," Luana added. "Of course, as Christians we don't believe in such superstitions." She held out her hand. "Unless you want to keep the tiki, I'll dispose of it, because I don't feel comfortable keeping it around. I wouldn't want anyone to get the impression we worship idols or even believe in the fantasies surrounding the carvings."

Mandy was glad the Hawaiian couple didn't believe in such things, and she gladly handed the tiki to Luana.

"If everyone is ready, we can eat breakfast now." Makaio then asked if anyone objected to him saying a prayer before the meal.

The guests all shook their heads. Even though she was used to praying silently, Mandy had no objections to a prayer spoken aloud. She was glad the Hawaiian couple were Christians and remembered seeing a Bible lying on the coffee table while walking through the living room last night. It eased some of Mandy's inner tensions and gave her a sense of peace.

"Dear Lord," Makaio prayed. "We thank You for this food and the hands that prepared it. Bless the meal, and may it bring nourishment to our bodies. Thank You for the opportunity to make new friends and get reacquainted with those we have met before. In Jesus' name we pray, amen."

Mandy felt certain Makaio and Luana were devout Christians, not only because of the heartfelt prayer he'd given, but from the scripture verse on a plaque hanging above the buffet at the other end of the room. It quoted Hebrews 13:2: "Be not forgetful to entertain strangers: for thereby some have entertained angels unawares." She had a feeling every visitor who came to this bed-and-breakfast was treated special — as though they were an angel.

Middlebury

Stepping around mud puddles, Miriam headed down the driveway to the phone shack to check for messages. She'd meant to see if there were any this morning, but it had been raining so hard she'd waited. Even now, at one o'clock in the afternoon, the rain fell, although it had been reduced to a drizzle. She was glad there'd been no more snow, but they'd had rain for the last several days, leaving the yard a mess. She looked forward to spring when the weather warmed and she could be outside in her garden. Miriam longed to see budding trees and flowers opening their petals. She glanced at one of the maples in their yard and frowned. Like all the rest, it was barren of leaves. The birds sitting on its branches looked as miserable as she felt. None of them even chirped a tune.

Miriam moved on. When she approached the phone shack, she shook the rain from her umbrella and stepped inside. The blinking light on the answering machine signaled messages waiting. She took a seat in the folding chair and clicked the button. The first message was from Gideon's mother, asking if Miriam needed any more thread. They had an overstock of both black and white, which would be on sale for half price.

The next message was from Miriam's driver, saying she would be free to take her to the chiropractor's later in the week. *Good to hear. With the pain I've had in my neck the last few days, I need to go in as soon as possible.*

As Miriam listened to the beginning of the third message, she smiled. It was from Mandy.

"Hi, Mom and Dad. I wanted to let you know Ellen and I missed the ship last evening. We are staying at the Palms Bed-and-Breakfast, in the town of Kapaa, on the island of Kauai." Following a short pause, her message continued: "Barbara and Sadie are on the boat, heading for the Big Island, but I have no way of contacting them. Unfortunately, I lost my cell phone, which is why we were late and missed the ship's departure." Another pause. "Don't worry about me, okay? Ellen and I have a nice place to stay until we're able to book passage home. Ellen has called her parents, too.

96

If Barbara should call, please let her know we're okay. Oh, and if you could please call Barbara and Sadie's folks and tell them what's happened, I'd appreciate it. I'm going to give you the phone number for the B&B so you can contact me. When you call Barbara's mamm, would you please ask her for Barbara's cell number? It was programmed into my cell phone, but I didn't write it down. Oh, and don't forget about the time difference here when you call me back, because I'm five hours earlier than you are in Indiana. I need to let you go for now, so Ellen can call her folks. I hope to hear from you soon. I miss you all. Please give my love to everyone."

Miriam wrote down the phone number her daughter gave for the place they were staying, and then she listened to the message a second time to make sure she hadn't missed any information. Without listening to any of the other messages, she called and left messages for Barbara's and Sadie's parents. Immediately after, Miriam dialed the number for the B&B and brought her hand to her forehead. *It's no wonder I didn't want Mandy to go on that trip.*

Kapaa

"We've had many people at our B&B, but

no one quite like Mandy and Ellen," Luana said after she and Makaio returned to the kitchen. "I've heard about Amish people but never imagined we'd have the chance to meet any. They're nice young women, don't you think?"

"Yes, they seem to be. They sure dress different than other people here on the island, though." Makaio opened the refrigerator and removed a pitcher of guava juice. "I put some pineapple juice on the table earlier, but maybe our guests would like some of this."

Luana smiled. Her husband thought of everything this morning. "I can't help but wonder if the Lord may have brought Mandy and Ellen to us for a reason." She lowered her voice, to be discreet.

He tipped his head while squinting his dark eyes and leaning in closer to her. "What reason?"

"I'm not sure, but I feel like they are supposed to be here. It's as though God brought them to us for a purpose."

"Maybe so. You've had feelings about certain other guests in the past."

"I've also been thinking, since the girls have only the clothes on their backs, after breakfast, I'll see if they'd like to go shopping to look for a few modest dresses, some sleeping attire, undergarments, and sandals."

"Good idea. They sure can't wear the same dress every day they're here." Makaio started for the dining room but turned back around. "How long do you think they will stay?"

Luana was about to respond when the telephone rang. "I'll get it. You can go ahead and take the juice in to our guests." She reached for the phone and picked up the receiver. "The Palms Bed-and-Breakfast."

"Hello. This is Miriam Frey. Is my daughter, Mandy, there?"

"Yes, she is. I'll go get her." Luana set the receiver on the counter and hurried to the dining room. "Mandy, your mother's on the phone. If you like, you can take the call on the extension in the kitchen."

Mandy jumped up, dashed into the kitchen, and eagerly grabbed the phone. "Hi, Mom."

"Ach, Mandy, it's so good to hear your *mundschtick.*"

Tears welled in Mandy's eyes, blurring her vision. "It's good to hear your voice, too. I guess you got my message."

"Jah. I called as soon as I heard it." Mom sniffed. "Are you and Ellen all right?"

"We're both fine. Makaio and Luana Palu,

the owners of the B&B where we are staying, are nice Christian people. They welcomed us with open arms."

"I'm glad to hear it. Being stranded in a place where everyone is a stranger has to be frightening."

"We were scared at first, but not anymore." Mandy switched the receiver to her other ear.

"How's the weather there, Mom?"

"Cold and rainy."

"I don't miss the colder weather. It's eighty degrees here on Kauai."

Mom sighed. "Must be nice. I'm anxious for spring to come and bring warmer weather."

"Did you get ahold of Barbara's parents?" Mandy asked.

"I left a message for the Hiltys, as well as the Kuhns, but it could be awhile before I hear anything back. When I do and they give me Barbara's cell phone number, I'll be sure and call you again so you can get ahold of her."

"Good. She and Sadie are probably worried about us."

"I imagine they would be. It's hard to believe they'll be coming to Middlebury without you and Ellen." Mom paused. "What can your *daed* and I do on this end to get you home again?"

"Nothing yet. I'll need to find out when another cruise ship will be coming this way from Los Angeles and how much it will cost for Ellen and me to make the journey. It should be cheaper this time, Mom, because it will only be one way."

"It will be less, and if you need money for your ticket, we'll see what we can do."

"Danki, Mom. Tell Dad and the rest of the family I said hello. I'll call you again soon."

Mandy remained in the kitchen a few minutes after she hung up the phone, thinking things through. It took her a year to save enough money for this trip to Hawaii. Could her parents afford to pay for her ticket home?

CHAPTER 9

The Big Island

"I'm glad we brought our sweaters along, because the breeze blowing here isn't helping things." Sadie pulled hers closer and fiddled with one of the buttons. "It's much cooler up here by the Kīlauea Volcano than in Hilo, where our ship docked."

"The cooler temperature feels kind of good." Barbara pointed to the lava tube up ahead. "I'm glad we were able to come. I mean, how often does a person get to see an erupting volcano, much less be so close to one?" She spoke excitedly.

"You're right." Shuffling her feet, Sadie pressed her lips slightly together. "It's too bad Ellen and Mandy couldn't be with us today. They're missing out on this experience, not to mention the unusual scenery. There is no way we can adequately tell them about this, except for the pictures and postcards we'll bring home." She paused.

"Have you tried calling Mandy again?"

"I've called three times again this morning. All I ever get is her voice mail." Barbara frowned. "I can't figure out why she doesn't answer her cell phone. It's usually stuck to her like glue."

"Maybe the battery is dead. Or perhaps she has it muted or in vibration mode." Sadie stepped around a fallen branch on the path. "But with all the messages you've left, she really should have called you back by now."

"I agree, and my fear that something bad happened to them is increasing by the minute. I've been praying for their safety."

Sadie nodded. "I've been praying for them, too, so let's try not to worry. Since there's nothing we can do, we ought to make the most of our day."

As they walked up the trail, Barbara's cell phone rang. "Maybe it's Mandy." She reached into her tote bag and withdrew the phone. "Hello. Oh hi, Mom. How are things going? You did?" Barbara turned to face Sadie and gave her a thumbs-up.

"What's going on?" Sadie asked as she stepped aside from the path.

"I'll tell you as soon as I hang up."

While Barbara continued talking to her mother in Pennsylvania Dutch, Sadie studied one of the brochures their tour guide gave them during the bus ride. According to the brochure, two active volcanoes were on the Big Island — Kīlauea and Mauna Loa. Kīlauea was the more accessible of the two, which was why the tour guide had brought them here.

Since Sadie and Barbara had stopped walking while Barbara talked to her mother, the others in their tour had gone ahead and were probably making their way through the lava tube already. Sadie was eager to go, but equally anxious to hear what Mrs. Hilty had to say, so she waited patiently.

Barbara looked at her expectantly. "Sadie, would you write down this number for me?"

"Sure." Sadie took a notebook and pen from her purse and wrote down the number Barbara told her.

After a bit more conversation, Barbara finally clicked off the phone. "I'm so glad my mamm called. The good news is she heard from Mandy's mother. The bad news is Mandy called her to say she and Ellen missed the boat and are stranded on Kauai."

"Which is exactly what we suspected." Sadie clasped her tote tightly. "How in the world did they miss the boat? Why weren't they paying attention so they could get back to the ship on time?" She shifted her weight to the other foot.

"Apparently, Mandy lost her cell phone and, after spending too much time looking for it, when they arrived at the port where our ship had been docked, it had already left." Barbara rubbed the side of her face, where a mosquito had bitten her. "Now our two friends are staying at a bed-and-breakfast, and Mom got the phone number from Mandy's mamm."

Sadie was relieved Mandy and Ellen were okay, but she also felt a bit irritated. If they'd gone on the tour to see the beautiful canyon with them, this would never have happened. All four of them would be here right now, preparing to see the volcano's crater at the Kīlauea Visitor Center.

Kapaa

Luana smiled with anticipation as she entered one of the dress shops at the Coconut Marketplace with Mandy and Ellen. It felt nice to be able to help the girls out. The garments here were much brighter, with bold prints, than what the young Amish women normally wore. She hoped they wouldn't be offended by her suggestion to wear one of the dresses sold in this store.

"There's certainly a lot to choose from, isn't there?" Mandy reached up and touched a dark purple dress. "They're so beautiful."

Luana looked at Ellen, who stood off to one side, eyes wide. *She's probably never seen dresses like this before.*

"I'm going to try this one on." Mandy took down the purple dress. "Ellen, have you found one you like?"

Slowly, Ellen shook her head, looking back at her friend with a bewildered expression.

"How about this one?" Luana pointed to a pretty blue muumuu. Like the purple dress Mandy chose, this one was also long enough to cover most of her legs.

Ellen hesitated at first, but finally removed the dress from the rack. "I suppose I could try it on."

The store clerk showed the girls to the dressing rooms. While they tried on the dresses, Luana looked at her cell phone to check for any messages. Seeing none, she made a mental note of the other places she wanted to take Mandy and Ellen. Unfortunately, the marketplace didn't have shoe stores anymore, but Sole Mates on Kuhio Highway had plenty of sandals and flip-flops to choose from. Luana would stop there on the way back to the B&B. For underwear and sleeping attire, they would visit another clothing store near Kapaa.

When Mandy stepped out of the dressing

room, Luana's breath caught in her throat. The deep purple offset by Mandy's chestnut hair and brown eyes was stunning. Of course, the stiff white cone-shaped bonnet on the young woman's head looked out of place with a muumuu. *I wonder how Mandy would look with her hair down and a hibiscus or plumeria flower behind her right ear. When we get back to my house, I'll look and see if I have some nice scarfs the girls can wear over their hair instead of their white bonnets.*

A few minutes later, Ellen exited the dressing room. Her cheeks were flushed pink, and she kept her gaze to the floor. The blue dress she wore was lovely, but Luana sensed the poor girl felt uncomfortable wearing a garment such as this.

"You both look so nice." She smiled. "Are your dresses comfortable, and are those the ones you would like?"

Mandy nodded enthusiastically, but Ellen barely moved her head up and down.

"All right then, if you want to change back into your Amish clothes, I'll pay for your dresses and we can be off. There are some other stops we need to make."

"Oh, no." Mandy shook her head. "You don't have to pay for our dresses. We both have money."

Luana held up her hand. "Save it toward

your tickets home or anything else you may need. I want to buy the dresses — it'll be my treat."

Mandy took a seat at the desk in the room she and Ellen shared at the B&B and opened her journal. Before starting to write, she thought about their friends. *Sadie and Barbara are probably seeing something interesting today. I hope they take pictures. I can't wait to check out all the photos from our combined trip when we're all back home.*

Refocusing on her journal, she began to write:

It was fun shopping with Luana today, but the dress I bought feels a bit strange — almost like a nightgown. It's called a muumuu. Mine is a dark purple with pretty lavender flowers. Luana said they are called plumeria. The room Mr. and Mrs. Anderson are staying in here at the bed-and-breakfast is called the Plumeria Room. It has a king-sized bed and private bath. Ellen and I share our bathroom with guests in the Gardenia Room. After tomorrow, no one will be staying there for a while, so we will have the bathroom all to ourselves.

Mandy paused and lifted her pen. The dress she wore was actually quite comfortable, even if it felt odd to be wearing something with such a bold print. She and Ellen would probably need to wear clothes like this for as long they were visiting. Mandy felt like she was ready to step out of her comfort zone. Being here in Hawaii was a whole new experience for her and Ellen.

Looking in the mirror, she chuckled at the image staring back at her. *I do look funny, though.* She reached up and touched her white head covering. *It looks out of place with the Hawaiian dress. Think I'll wear the black scarf Luana gave us.*

Mandy removed her head covering, and was about to pin the black scarf in place, when Ellen entered the room. "What are you doing?" She stepped up to her.

"My traditional head covering doesn't go with my muumuu, and besides, I don't want it to get dirty. I've decided to wear the scarf instead." Smiling, Mandy picked up the scarf and pins. "We wear scarves when we're working in the yard or around the house at home, right?"

"Jah, but we're not working here." Ellen moved away from Mandy and flopped down on her bed. "I'm only going to wear the Hawaiian dress when my Amish dress is being washed, like it is now, and never out in public." She pointed to the bodice of her blue muumuu with white hibiscus flowers. "When I'm wearing this, I don't feel like myself. I feel as though I'm dressing up for one of those silly skits we sometimes put on during family get-togethers." Crossing her arms, she frowned. "It wouldn't feel right to wear this dress all the time. And if my parents were here, they'd agree with me."

Mandy moved over to the mirror to secure her scarf. "You can do whatever you want, but since neither of us has joined the Amish church yet, we're not breaking any rules by wearing these Hawaiian dresses."

"True."

"And they are quite cozy."

"I guess." Ellen slid off the bed and moved over to stand by the window, "Oh look, there's a nice *gaarde* at the back of the house. It looks like a vegetable garden."

Mandy joined her, leaning her elbows on the windowsill. "I'll bet Luana and Makaio raise all, or most, of their own produce. Should we take a walk outside and see what's growing?"

Ellen nodded but remained motionless. Then she lifted her hands and removed her own covering. "Maybe I will replace this with a scarf for now. I wouldn't want my white head covering to become soiled."

Mandy smiled. "I hope you're not doing this because of me."

"Well . . ." Ellen dropped her chin. "You do have a point. They don't go with what we're wearing."

After they both had secured their scarves, Mandy hurried to the door and opened it. She would finish writing in her journal later.

CHAPTER 10

Middlebury

Gideon didn't feel like going to church, but his folks would be upset if he stayed home. He yawned and stretched one arm over his head, holding tightly to the reins with the other hand as he guided his horse and buggy down the road in the direction of the Hiltys' place, where church would be held. Last night, he'd had a troubling dream about Mandy and hadn't slept well. In the dream, he and Mandy were riding in his buggy, chatting pleasantly as they headed down the road. Suddenly, she clasped his arm and said, "I've decided not to join the church. The Amish way of life isn't for me."

He'd pleaded with Mandy to change her mind, yet she stood firm, repeatedly saying the Amish life was not for her. The dream seemed so real. When Gideon woke up, he was drenched in sweat. He'd tried to calm himself by getting out of bed and opening the window for some fresh air, but it hadn't helped much. Even now, as he approached the Hiltys' home, Gideon felt apprehensive. *If Mandy hadn't gone to Hawaii, I wouldn't be having these fitful dreams and conflicting thoughts. If she was here right now, everything would be fine between us.* Even as the thought entered his head, Gideon wasn't sure it was true. He'd sensed an unrest in Mandy for some time and kept trying to convince himself she would eventually join the church. The dream he'd had last night only reaffirmed his fears.

"I need to stop thinking like this," he mumbled, guiding his horse, Dash, into the yard.

Soon after he stepped down from the buggy, he was greeted by his friend, Paul Miller. "Where's your Sunday *hut*?"

"My hat's right here." Gideon pointed to it.

Smirking, Paul reached up and snatched Gideon's hat off his head. "This isn't a Sunday hat. Looks more like something you'd wear to clean the barn."

Gideon jerked his head back and let out a yelp. "Ach! I was wearing my straw hat this morning while getting my horse. Guess I forgot it was on my head when I left home to come here." His cheeks felt like they were on fire. "This old hat will stay in my buggy, 'cause I don't want anyone else knowing I forgot to wear my black Sunday hat."

Just then, Mandy's dad, Isaac, stopped by. "Have you heard about Mandy?" he asked Gideon.

Quickly tossing his hat into the buggy, Gideon shook his head. "Heard what? Is she okay?" Fear rose in his chest.

"She's fine, physically." Deep lines formed at the corners of Isaac's brown eyes when he frowned. "She and Ellen are stranded on the island of Kauai."

Gideon opened his mouth. "How can they be stranded? I thought the cruise ship she and her friends were on was taking them from island to island."

"It has been, but they missed the boat when it was leaving Kauai to go to the Big Island."

"What about Sadie and Barbara?" Paul questioned. "Didn't they go on the trip to Hawaii, too?"

"Jah." Isaac rubbed his forehead. "Unfortunately, my daughter and Ellen went off by themselves when the ship docked that morning. If they'd been with the tour group, they wouldn't have been left behind."

In an effort to calm himself, Gideon drew

a deep breath. "How's Mandy going to get home?"

"They're working on it. I'm guessing they'll try to book passage on the next cruise ship coming to Kauai. Of course, it could be expensive."

"If she needs money for her ticket, I'd be willing to chip in."

Isaac gave Gideon's shoulder a squeeze. "We'll let you know."

"I tried calling her yesterday but only got her voice mail." Gideon groaned.

"Mandy had more troubles. She lost her cell phone on a sightseeing excursion. When they found a place to stay, she called us. Said she and Ellen are staying at a bed-and-breakfast run by some nice Christian folks."

Gideon felt a little better hearing Mandy had a place to stay. "Could I have the number there so I can give her a call?"

"Sorry, but I don't have it with me right now. If you drop by our place sometime tomorrow, I'll see you get it." Isaac pointed to the large shop, where the service would be held. "Right now, though, we'd better be going inside."

As Gideon turned his horse over to Barbara Hilty's brother Crist, he made a decision. As soon as he got the number of the place where Mandy and Ellen were staying, he'd call and let her know he'd be willing to pay part, or even all, of her fare.

Kapaa

A few minutes before 9:00 a.m., Mandy and Ellen entered a church building with Luana and Makaio. The Andersons were on their way home, having checked out after an early breakfast.

It was nice of the Palus to invite us to join them for church today, Mandy thought as they signed the guest book. Since she and Ellen had washed their Amish dresses the day before, they were able to wear them to services. Mandy was glad, because she would have felt funny wearing a muumuu to church, even though many other worshipers were dressed in Hawaiian-style clothing.

But if we had worn muumuus, we'd look less conspicuous, Mandy thought, observing the sanctuary as she followed Makaio and Luana to a seat. Several people had already greeted them, and one lady gave Mandy and Ellen each a shell lei, which looked a bit strange over their dresses; especially since the Amish didn't wear jewelry. A few others glanced their way with strange expressions. *Amish people have probably never visited this church before.*

It wasn't all that common for the Amish

116

to visit Hawaii. The village of Pinecraft in Sarasota, Florida, was more of a possibility, since they could travel there by bus or train. Mandy knew a few people from her community who had gone there for vacation during the winter months, but the only person she knew personally who'd visited any of the Hawaiian Islands was her cousin Ruth.

Her muscles relaxed a bit as she took in a few easy breaths. *Well, it's a new experience for us as well, because this is my first time in an English church.*

Mandy was about to sit down when she spotted a tall young man with thick, shoulder-length blond hair on the platform, holding a ukulele. Several other people also sat on the platform with musical instruments. This seemed strange to her, since no instruments were ever played during an Amish church service. Sometimes at home or for family gatherings, Mandy's dad would play his guitar, which added to the pleasure of singing songs for fun or private worship.

Returning her focus to the young man with the ukulele, she thought she'd seen him before — not from back home, but someone she'd met on their trip. As the music and singing started, it all came back to her. He was the same man she'd talked to when she and Ellen visited Spouting Horn on Friday. *What a coincidence. I wonder if I'll get the chance to speak to him after church. If so, will he remember me?*

Later in the afternoon as Mandy and Ellen sat in the Palus' living room, chatting, she thought about the young man again and wished she'd had the opportunity to at least say hello. But he'd been busy talking to several others after church, and she didn't want to interrupt.

"So how did you two young women like our service today?" Makaio's question drove Mandy's thoughts aside.

"It was certainly different." She reached for the glass of guava juice Luana had brought out earlier. "Nothing like our church services at home."

"What are they like?" Luana questioned.

Mandy glanced at Ellen, who sat quietly beside her on the sofa. When her friend remained quiet, Mandy answered. "Our services are held bi-weekly in the home, barn, or shop of church members who take turns hosting the service. We sit on back-less, wooden benches for three hours, and there are no musical instruments."

"That's interesting." Luana tapped her

lips with a finger. "Think I'd have a hard time sitting that long on any bench or chair."

"Another thing different from your church is the women and girls sit on one side of the building during our services, while the men and boys sit on the other," Ellen spoke up.

"And also," Mandy interjected, "our sermons are preached in German, not English."

Makaio's thick brows furrowed. "I wouldn't be able to understand the message, since I've never learned the German language. I can speak our native Hawaiian language fluently, though."

"Would you teach us a few words?" Mandy asked. She was interested in learning new things. And since the Hawaiian word book Ellen had bought was in her suitcase on the ship, they had no guide to teach them any of the words they may want to know.

He nodded. "You may already know the word *Aloha.* It's a familiar Hawaiian greeting and farewell."

Mandy and Ellen bobbed their heads.

"Our alphabet consists of only twelve letters," Luana explained. "There are five vowels — *a, e, i, o, u,* and seven consonants — *h, k, l, m, n, p,* and *w.*"

"Here are a few common words," Makaio said: "*Hana,* which means work; *nani,* meaning beautiful; *kāne,* man; *wahini,* woman; and *keiki,* child."

"I'm a wahini." Mandy pointed to herself and chuckled. "When we get home I can't wait to tell my dad he's a kāne."

"If you're interested, I'll teach you some more Hawaiian words while you're here." Makaio picked up his ukulele. "Right now, why don't we sing a few songs? Afterward, maybe we can talk my dear wahini into serving some snacks."

"You won't have to talk me into it." Luana patted her husband's knee. "I'd planned all along to bring out some special treats."

As Makaio began to play the ukulele, Mandy became almost mesmerized. "I have a battery-operated keyboard at home, and my dad plays the guitar, but playing the ukulele would be even more fun." She clapped after he finished the first song.

"If you stay here long enough, I'd be happy to teach you." Makaio's grin stretched ear to ear.

On the Cruise Ship
"I should call Mandy," Barbara announced as she sat with Sadie in their cabin that evening. "Since I have the number of the

120

place they are staying, I want to find out how she and Ellen are doing."

Sadie set her book aside and leaned forward. "Good idea. Let them know we've been praying for them, too."

Barbara grabbed her purse and took out her cell phone, as well as the slip of paper with the number for the B&B. A few seconds later, a pleasant-sounding woman answered. "Aloha. This is the Palms Bed-and-Breakfast."

"Is Mandy Frey there? This is Barbara Hilty. I was one of her traveling companions on the cruise ship."

"Yes, she and Ellen are both here. I'll put Mandy on."

After a minute, an excited voice came on. "Barbara, is it really you?"

"Jah, and it's sure good to hear your voice. I got this number from my mamm, who got it from your mamm. How are you and Ellen doing?"

"Were both fine. Did your mother explain how we missed the boat and ended up staying here?"

"She sure did. I bet you were frightened when you realized you'd missed the ship."

"We were."

"Tell them we were frightened, too," Sadie whispered.

Barbara repeated what her friend had said.

"Did you realize what had happened?" Mandy asked.

"Not at first, but as the evening progressed, it didn't take long for us to figure out you'd been left behind. Up until then, we thought you might be somewhere on the ship. It seemed strange you didn't show up at dinner, but we figured you may have had a late lunch and weren't hungry. So many thoughts ran through our heads it was hard not to *druwwle*."

"Sorry for causing you to worry. Ellen and I have no luggage, of course."

"It's here in the room. Sadie and I will make sure both your suitcases go with us on the train when we reach Los Angeles."

"Danki, we appreciate it."

"How are you managing with only one dress?" Barbara questioned.

"Luana, the lady who runs the B&B with her husband, bought us each a muumuu."

Barbara pursed her lips. "A what?"

"A muumuu. It's a Hawaiian dress. Mine is purple with pretty flowers on it."

Barbara pressed her palm against her mouth to keep from gasping. She couldn't imagine how her two friends would look wearing Hawaiian dresses.

"Remember when we talked about how

we wished we could spend more time on each of the Hawaiian Islands?"

"Jah."

"Well, now Ellen and I are able to do it."

Barbara grimaced. Being stranded on an island was not what she would have wanted for herself or her friends. "Have you talked to Gideon yet? I'm sure he'd like to know what happened."

"No, and I forgot to ask Mom to tell him. I'll say something the next time I call home."

Wow! Barbara cringed. *If Gideon were my boyfriend, he'd have been the first person I would have called to let him know what happened. What is Mandy thinking?*

CHAPTER 11

Monday morning as Barbara and Sadie reclined on chairs near the pool, they talked about how they would arrive at Ensenada, Mexico, within the next few days.

Sadie yawned. "The sun feels so warm. I'm feeling sleepy all of a sudden. Think I'll take a nap."

"Go right ahead. I may end up falling asleep, too." Barbara watched some of the people by the pool. By the time she and Sadie had arrived, nearly every chair had been taken. They'd been fortunate to find two lounge chairs together. A young couple with a small child took the last three seats. The curly haired boy threw his towel down and bounced on his chair. He sat only a few minutes, then jumped into the pool, splashing a good amount of water onto the deck, sending a spray of water on Sadie.

Her eyes snapped open, and she leaped out of her chair like she'd been stung by an angry hornet. The boy's mother walked quickly over to Sadie. "I'm so sorry. My son gets pretty excited whenever he has a chance to be in a pool. I'll make sure he stops splashing."

"It's okay. No harm done. The warm sun will dry my dress in no time." Sadie sat back in her chair. "What a full trip this has been." She looked at Barbara. "We've been fortunate to visit four of the Hawaiian Islands, and now we'll get to see a bit of Mexico before returning to Los Angeles."

Barbara nodded. "I only wish Mandy and Ellen were with us. They're missing out on so much."

"When they book their tickets on another cruise ship, I'm sure they will go from there to the Big Island, like we did."

"Maybe so, but by then, we'll either be home or close to arriving." Barbara slipped her sunglasses on. The frames felt warm from being in the direct sunlight. "I still can't believe Mandy didn't call Gideon right away. You would think she'd want him to know what happened."

"She was probably upset when they got stranded and wasn't thinking clearly." Sadie grabbed her glass of pineapple juice and took a sip. "Our friends are bound to be stressed out."

"True. I'm glad it wasn't us who missed the ship, because I'd be a basket case."

"Me too."

Barbara leaned her head back and closed her eyes. "When we get to Mexico, I'll give Mandy another call. I'd like an update on how they are doing."

Middlebury

Gideon left the upholstery shop and headed straight for the Freys' house. His stomach churned as he thought about getting the phone number for the bed-and-breakfast. He needed to know how Mandy was doing. "Sure don't understand why she hasn't called me, though," he muttered, pedaling as fast as he could. Since it wasn't raining or snowing today, he'd ridden his bike to work.

It was hard to think positive thoughts right now, with his girlfriend being so far away. Once he talked to Mandy, Gideon hoped he would feel a little better.

Approaching the house, he parked his bike near the porch and set the kickstand. Then taking the steps two at a time, he knocked on the door. Several minutes went by. When no one answered, he knocked again. He figured Mandy's father, who managed a meat-and-cheese store, would be home from work by now. Even if he wasn't, Mandy's mother should be around.

Gideon knocked again, with a bit more force. "Hello! Anyone at home?"

Still no answer.

Thinking someone might be in the barn, he headed in that direction. When he stepped inside, he saw Mandy's brothers, Mark and Melvin, mucking out the horses' stalls. It seemed a little odd that Isaac and Miriam had given all their children names beginning with *M.* But then he remembered Mandy saying her dad wanted their daughter and son's names to start with *M* because his wife's name began with that letter.

Redirecting his thoughts, Gideon walked toward the stalls. "Hey, Mark. Hey, Melvin. Are your folks around?"

Mark, the older boy, crossed his arms. "Nope. Dad's workin' late this evening, and Mom went to see the chiropractor."

"Oh, I see." Gideon leaned against the stall door. "I came by to get the phone number of the place where Mandy and Ellen are staying in Hawaii. Would either of you know it?"

Both boys shook their heads.

"Sorry," Melvin said. "Guess you'll have to come back tomorrow."

"Oh, great," Gideon muttered under his breath.

Mark moved closer. "What was that?"

"Nothing. Tell your folks I stopped by and I'll drop by again when I get off work tomorrow."

"You okay?" Melvin asked. "You look kinda down-in-the-mouth."

"I'm disappointed." Gideon turned to go, calling over his shoulder, "See you boys later."

After mounting his bike, Gideon gripped the handlebars so tight his fingers began to ache. *This is ridiculous. I wouldn't have to get the number if Mandy had called me.*

Kapaa

"You have a beautiful garden, Luana." Mandy knelt on the grass beside a healthy-looking tomato plant. It seemed almost unbelievable all these vegetables could be growing in the middle of November. "It must be nice to be able to garden throughout the year."

Luana smiled. "I suppose we take it for granted."

"Have you always lived here on Kauai?" Mandy asked.

"No. Makaio and I were born and raised on the Big Island. We moved here to open the bed-and-breakfast a few years ago." Luana checked the leaves of a bean plant.

"Why didn't you open one there?"

"I suppose we could have, but after visiting Kauai several times, we fell in love with the island. And when the opportunity to buy this place came up, we couldn't resist." She moved over to the tomato plants and knelt down.

"It is beautiful here." Ellen spoke for the first time since they'd come outside. She'd been awfully quiet this afternoon. Mandy suspected her friend might be homesick.

"We do get some rain here, of course, but without it, the flowers wouldn't be so beautiful and it wouldn't be this lush and green." Luana pulled a few weeds. "If I had the choice of living any place on earth, I believe it would be here. In addition to liking the island, my husband and I love the opportunity to meet people from all over who come to stay at our B&B."

"I'm sure the people enjoy getting to know you, as well." Mandy held her hands loosely behind her back.

"I hope so. We do all we can to make our guests feel welcome."

The roar of a vehicle interrupted their conversation. An SUV with camouflage paint pulled into the parking area for guests.

Mandy picked some grass off her bare foot, then stood at the same time as Ellen.

A few minutes later, a young man got out, carrying three egg cartons. Her mouth fell open. It was the same young man she'd met at Spouting Horn and seen again on Sunday at church.

Luana waved him over. "Aloha, Ken. I'd like you to meet Mandy and Ellen. They'll be staying with us until they're able to purchase tickets on a cruise ship to take them back to the mainland." She gestured to him. "Girls, this is Ken Williams. He and his family live nearby. They own an organic chicken farm, and they supply all the eggs and chicken meat we need."

"We've met before, haven't we?" Ken looked at Mandy and tipped his head. "I talked to you at Spouting Horn last week."

Mandy nodded, feeling unexplainably shy. Ellen remained quiet.

"I didn't recognize you when I first got out of my rig, because when we met before, you wore an Amish dress."

Mandy's cheeks burned as she stared at her flower-print Hawaiian dress. "My friend and I were late getting back to the ship, and it left without us. So with our luggage still on board in the cabin we shared with two other friends, it left us with only the clothes we were wearing."

"I took Mandy and Ellen shopping, and bought them both nice muumuus," Luana interjected.

"I see." Ken shuffled his feet a few times then handed Luana the eggs. "These are for you. When you need more, let me know."

"*Mahalo,* Ken." She smiled. "I'd better take these into the house and get them put in the refrigerator."

"Would you like me to do it for you?" Ellen offered.

"No, it's okay. I also want to check on Makaio. He's doing some work on the other side of the house." Luana gave Ken's shoulder a tap. "If you're still here when I get back, you're invited to sit on the lanai with us for some coconut cake and iced coffee."

He pulled his fingers through his thick, tousled hair and grinned. "I may take you up on that offer. Can't stay too long, though. I still have several more cartons of eggs to deliver."

When Luana headed into the house, Mandy stood with her hands clasped behind her back. It felt awkward not to say anything, so she asked if Ken would like to take a seat in one of the lawn chairs under the shade of a tree.

"Sure. It'll give us a chance to get better

acquainted," Ken replied.

Once they were all seated, Mandy glanced over at Ellen, hoping she would start a conversation, but she sat quietly, with a placid expression.

Mandy cleared her throat. "I — I saw you at church yesterday. You were on the platform, playing a ukulele."

"Yeah; I'm part of the worship team." Ken took his cell phone from his shorts' pocket and glanced at it, then put it back.

"Makaio plays the ukulele, too," she added. "I'm surprised he's not on the worship team."

"He used to be, but he wanted some time off for a while." Ken kept his gaze on Mandy so long it made her ears heat up.

He probably thinks I look strange wearing a Hawaiian dress, even though my normal head covering's been replaced with the scarf Luana gave us.

Just then, Luana dashed around the side of the house with a panicked expression. "Help! Help! Makaio fell off the roof!"

CHAPTER 12

Lihue

Luana paced the hospital waiting room, praying for patience. Her twenty-four-year-old daughter, Ailani, who was five months pregnant, sat in one of the chairs, picking at her cuticles — a nervous habit from her teen years.

Luana glanced at Ken, thankful he'd let Ailani know what had happened to her father. When the ambulance came and transported Makaio to the hospital, Luana rode along. Ailani's husband, Oke, was still at work, but he should be here soon.

"Tell me again, Mama." Ailani pursed her lips. "How did Papa fall off the roof?"

Luana stopped pacing and sat beside her daughter. "I'm not sure, but he was holding a Frisbee when he fell, so I assume he must have gone up there to get it." She glanced toward the nurses' station, wishing someone would come and tell them the extent of

Makaio's injuries.

"I'm sure we'll hear something soon." Ken reached over and clasped Luana's arm. He always seemed to know what to say and had become almost like a son to Luana and Makaio. She hoped his parents appreciated the fine young man he'd turned out to be — always willing to help others, tender-hearted, hard-working, and a Christian in every sense of the word. *I hope the Lord sends Ken the right woman someday — someone who will make him as happy as he makes others.*

Luana's contemplations were halted when a doctor came into the room. "Mrs. Palu?" He moved toward her.

She nodded, rising from her chair.

"Your husband's leg is badly broken. He also has a slight concussion and numerous bumps and bruises. His leg will require surgery as well as a full cast, which he will need to wear for six to eight weeks. When Makaio is released from the hospital in a few days, he'll need to use crutches and not put any weight on his foot until X-rays show it's healed enough for him to walk on it."

Luana's shoulders drooped as she stared at the doctor in disbelief. If her husband couldn't be on his feet, how would he be able to help out at the B&B? And because she would need to care for him, she wouldn't have time to do everything necessary for hosting their guests. Ailani could help some, but she'd been quite sick to her stomach with her pregnancy and often didn't feel up to working, even part-time. The idea of hiring help flitted through Luana's mind, but with hospital bills to pay now, money would be tight.

"When can I see my husband?" she asked the doctor.

"You can go in now, before we prep him for surgery." The doctor turned and went out the door.

Luana rose from her chair. "Ailani, would you like to go in with me?"

Her daughter's brown eyes swam with tears. "Yes, Mama. I want Papa to know I'll be praying for him."

Luana looked at Ken. "Would you mind going back to the B&B to let Mandy and Ellen know how Makaio is doing and that I'll be here at the hospital for the next several hours? I need to stay until he's out of surgery and settled into his room. So it could be late before I get home."

Nodding, Ken rose from his seat and gave her a hug. "I understand your concern, but try to keep the faith. I'll be praying for Makaio, and you, as well."

Her lips quivered. "Mahalo."

As soon as Ken left, a nurse arrived to lead Luana and Ailani down the hall to see Makaio. The two women took seats, while another nurse prepared an IV for him.

"How are you feeling?" Luana scooched her chair closer to his bed.

"I'm a little fuzzy but better now than when we first arrived. I'm gonna need to get some fixing done on that leg of mine, though." He frowned, tears seeping from the corners of his eyes. "Sorry I slipped off the roof."

She placed her hand on his. "It was an accident, so don't give it another thought. I'm grateful nothing worse happened to you."

The nurse took Makaio's vitals. "You're in good hands, Mr. Palu. The surgeon will do his best to see that your leg heals as it should."

The nurses moved in and out for a while, but then the family sat together with no interruptions. He was scheduled for surgery as soon as the patient ahead of him came out. Luana would be glad when it was over.

After a while, another nurse came in and announced it was time to wheel Makaio into surgery. Luana and Ailani said their goodbyes and walked back to the waiting room with one of the nurses.

"We'll call you back when he's in recovery." The nurse motioned to a table with hot beverages. "There's coffee and hot water for tea, so feel free to help yourselves."

"I don't like waiting and wondering." With a watery gaze, Ailani ran trembling fingers through her shiny, black, shoulder-length hair. "It's hard not to worry about Papa."

"We need to pray and ask God to guide the surgeon's hands." Luana closed her eyes. *Lord, please help the doctor repair the damage done to Makaio's leg. I'm thanking You in advance.*

Kapaa

Mandy glanced out the living-room window and frowned. It seemed like she and Ellen had been waiting for hours to hear from Luana. They didn't know how badly Makaio was hurt or why he'd been on the roof. "Sure wish Luana would call," she murmured, turning away from the window. "It's hard to wait. I feel like we should be doing something, but I'm not sure what."

"We have no choice except to wait." Ellen handed Mandy a glass of guava juice. "It's a *schee daag*. Why don't we go out on the lanai and enjoy it?"

It was a pretty day, but Mandy wasn't sure she could enjoy it. At least, not until she knew how Makaio was doing. She took the offered glass and sipped a little juice. "I guess we can go outside, but we need to keep the door open in case the phone rings."

"The lanai is screened in," Ellen reminded, "so we won't be in the yard and should be able to hear the telephone."

"Okay." Mandy followed her friend to the enclosed porch and took a seat in one of the wicker rocking chairs. The simple motion of moving back and forth helped her relax.

Ellen sat motionless in her chair. "I wonder what Sadie and Barbara are doing right now. I sure miss them." She looked out toward the yard, where palm leaves swayed in the breeze.

"They are probably on the ship somewhere, eating ice cream, reading a book, or lounging by the pool. I'll bet they're both getting quite tan by now."

Ellen snickered, pointing at Mandy. "Have you looked in the mirror lately? Your face and arms are much darker than when we left Los Angeles eleven days ago."

Despite her apprehension over Makaio, Mandy squeezed her eyes together and laughed. "You're right. We've both gotten some color." She drank the rest of her juice and set the empty glass on the table between them.

Glancing into the yard, Mandy spotted a colorful bird. It looked like one of the cardinals they had back home, but this one had a red head, and the feathers on its body were gray and white. She stepped off the lanai for a better look, but the bird flew over her head and into a tree.

"What if Luana's not back in time for supper?" Ellen asked when Mandy joined her again. "Do you think she would mind if we fix ourselves something to eat?"

"I'm sure she wouldn't. She told us to help ourselves to anything we needed the day after we arrived here." Mandy wiped some moisture from her face. "It's warm out here. Maybe we should go back inside and turn on the air conditioner."

"We don't have air-conditioning at home, but we all manage during the warm summer months."

"True. Since it's been made available to us, we may as well make use of it, though." Mandy rocked in her chair.

Ellen's brows pulled in. "Now don't get too reliant on modern things. We won't have them available to us forever."

Before Mandy could respond, she noticed Ken's SUV pull into the yard. She leaped out of her chair, flung the screen door open, and ran out to greet him. "Do you have any news on Makaio?"

"Yes, I do. Just came from the hospital." Ken gestured to the porch, where Ellen still sat. "Let's take a seat, and I'll bring you up to speed."

Mandy led the way, and when they were both seated, Ken gave them the details on Makaio's injuries.

"Oh my!" Mandy touched her lips. "That poor man. I can't imagine how badly he must hurt."

"I'm sure they've given him something for the pain, and when he's in surgery, he'll be completely out." Ken's forehead wrinkled a bit. "Luana's worried about him, and so is their daughter."

"She mentioned Ailani, but we haven't met her," Ellen spoke up.

"I'm not surprised. She's expecting her first baby and has been having a tough time with nausea and swollen feet." Ken waved his hands in front of his face. "Sure turned out to be a warm day — even hotter than what was forecasted."

"Would you like a glass of juice?" Mandy offered. "Or we could go inside where it's cooler."

"Some juice would be great."

Ellen stood, pulling her hands down the sides of her dress. "I'll get it. Would you like another glass, Mandy?"

"Jah, danki."

After Ellen went inside, Ken turned to Mandy. "Were you speaking German to her?"

"I said, 'Yes, thank you.' It's a form of German. We call it Pennsylvania Dutch. Some also refer to our everyday language as German Dutch."

He leaned forward, resting his elbows on his knees. "Interesting. Would you teach me some Amish words?"

"I'd be happy to. Is there anything specific you'd like to know?"

"In a minute. I need to do something first." Ken sat up straight and pulled a handkerchief from his back pocket. "Looks like one of our birds left its mark on the shoulder of your dress." He wiped off the mess.

"Oh no." Embarrassed, Mandy touched her hot cheeks. "I was in the yard, admiring a colorful bird before you got here."

Ken gently rubbed the area, while Mandy sat, stiff as a board. "Don't worry. Think I got most of it off. You might want to spray the area with a spot cleaner, though, so it doesn't leave a permanent stain."

"Thank you, Ken. I appreciate it." Mandy spoke quietly.

"Okay now. How do you say the word *pretty*?" He stuffed the hankie back in his pocket.

"Oh, that's right. You wanted to learn some Amish words." Mandy felt so flustered, she'd almost forgotten. "That's an easy one. It's *schee.*"

He smiled. "You look schee in that muu-muu you're wearing."

Mandy felt warmth start up the back of her neck, spreading promptly to her face, adding even more heat. She wasn't used to anyone other than Gideon saying she was pretty. Clearing her throat, she quickly changed the subject. "How long will Makaio be in the hospital?"

Ken shrugged. "I'm not sure. Probably a few days. When he gets home, he'll have to take it easy for several weeks. The doctor doesn't want him to put any weight on his leg until it's healed well enough."

"I wonder how Luana will manage without his help." She wiped at the moisture on her forehead.

Ken leaned farther back in his chair. "I don't know, but I'm sure the Lord will provide what they need."

Ellen returned to the lanai with three

glasses of juice on a tray. She'd no more than placed it on the small wicker table when another vehicle pulled in. A few minutes later, a middle-aged man and woman got out.

"Looks like you may have some guests. Was Luana expecting anyone to check in this afternoon?" Ken's question was directed at Mandy.

"She didn't say." Mandy swallowed hard. With Luana not here, she had no idea what to do. Running a bed-and-breakfast was different from waitressing. But apparently Ellen knew how to handle the situation, for she left the lanai and walked out to the couple. A few minutes later, she led them inside.

Mandy went over to assist her friend in welcoming the guests. *It's a good thing we're here,* she thought. *With Makaio unable to put any weight on his leg, Luana's going to need our help for a while.*

CHAPTER 13

After Ellen explained the situation to the guests who'd arrived, she picked up the guest book and asked them to sign it. In the meantime, she found their name in Luana's book, which also told what room the couple would be staying in. This wasn't much different than the routine of the B&B where she worked back home.

"We're sorry to hear Makaio's been hurt," said the woman, who identified herself as Sharon McIntire. "My husband and I stayed here last year and enjoyed getting to know him and his lovely wife." Her sincere expression revealed the depth of her concern. "If there's anything we can do, please let us know."

Ellen almost replied, "Danki," but answered instead, "Thank you. It's kind of you to offer."

"You must be new here." The man, who introduced himself as Carl, spoke up. "How long have you been working at the bed-and-breakfast?"

"I don't officially work here. My friend and I are filling in for the owners today." Ellen went on to explain how they'd missed the cruise ship and were staying here for the time being. "Luana and Makaio have been so kind to us. It's the least we can do to help them out."

They visited awhile longer, and then Ellen showed them to the Bird of Paradise Room. After leaving the couple alone to get settled in, she returned to the lanai.

Strange. I wonder where Mandy and Ken are. When Ellen peeked outside and saw Ken's vehicle, she knew he hadn't left. Opening the screen door and stepping into the yard, she spotted them crouched on the ground beside Luana's bountiful garden. They seemed to be deep in conversation, so she turned and went back into the house. Ellen couldn't help wondering how two people who barely knew each other could find much of anything to talk about.

"I can't get over all this garden produce." Mandy pointed to a head of butter lettuce. "It's November. Back home, our gardens are done for the year. We don't start planting again till spring."

"Do you enjoy gardening?" Ken tipped his head.

She nodded enthusiastically. "I like all the fresh produce we get in the summer, but it would be even nicer if we could grow it all year."

"It's one of the reasons I like living on this island so much." He fingered a cucumber. "Know what I wish?"

"What?"

"Wish I had my own organic produce business. I'd even like to try growing some things hydroponically." Ken let go of the cucumber. "I've never liked working on my folks' chicken farm that much. If my brother, Dan, was willing to take over the farm someday, I'd branch out and start my own business." Ken's eyes took on a faraway look.

"Isn't he interested in your family's business?"

Ken shrugged. "Dan's a surfer and likes to run off to the beach every chance he gets. Course I like to surf, too, but not till after my work is done each day. Speaking of the beach, have you had a chance to visit one of our beaches?"

"Not yet. Ellen and I have been busy with other things. But I would like to go when I get the chance." When Mandy rose from the grass, she lost her balance and fell back. "Oh, my legs fell asleep."

"Let me help you." Ken held out his hand. Easily and quickly he stood, pulling Mandy to her feet. "Now about the beach, I'd be happy to take you there on my next day off."

"It would be nice, but we'll have to wait and see how things go with Makaio. Luana may need Ellen's and my help — especially now, having guests at the B&B." Mandy glanced at the house. "Speaking of which, I should go inside and see if Ellen got the new guests settled into their room."

"Okay. I should get going myself. My folks will be anxious for a report. I called them from the hospital before the doctor came in and told us about Makaio's injuries."

"I still can't believe he fell off the roof."

"Accidents happen when we least expect."

Mandy walked with Ken to his vehicle. After saying goodbye, she hurried into the house to find Ellen. *It would be nice to go to the beach. I hope Ellen and I can make it there before it's time to head home.*

On the Cruise Ship

During dinner that evening, the woman who sat at Barbara's left kept bumping her arm every time she reached into her purse to check her cell phone. Barbara tried to be patient, but then the woman picked up Barbara's glass of iced tea and took a drink. "Oops. Sorry about that." She set Barbara's glass down and scooted her chair over a bit.

Barbara managed a smile. She was sure the woman hadn't drunk from her glass on purpose.

Their waiter came by about that time and asked if he could get them anything.

"I'd like another glass of iced tea," Barbara replied.

He nodded. "I'll bring it with your dessert."

The tea and slices of coconut cake arrived a short time later. As she and Sadie enjoyed their dessert, Barbara smacked her lips. "This was another delicious meal. Should we do some laundry when we're done with dessert, or would you rather go to the lounge where the ventriloquist is performing?"

Sadie jiggled her brows playfully. "Now who would choose washing clothes over seeing a young man throw his voice?"

Barbara laughed. They'd seen the ventriloquist once before, but it would be fun to see his performance again. She and Sadie certainly needed a few laughs. Since Ellen and Mandy got left behind on Kauai, their conversations had been much too serious.

"Okay, it's settled." She placed her fork on the empty dessert plate and finished her iced tea. "Let's head up to the lounge and prepare to have our funny bones tickled."

After saying goodbye to the other people at their table, Barbara and Sadie headed for the lounge. Sadie took a deep breath and exhaled. "It's hard to believe we'll be in Mexico tomorrow. Our trip has gone way too fast."

"At least we'll be able to tour a bit before the ship sails back to Los Angeles." Barbara paused. "It'll seem strange, riding home on the train without our friends. We should get Mandy and Ellen's things packed up this evening."

"Jah. The only good thing about them not being here is we have more space to spread out in our cabin."

"I'd prefer having Mandy and Ellen with us right now."

Kapaa

When Luana arrived home from the hospital, she was surprised to see a car parked outside the B&B. She sat in her vehicle a few minutes, trying to recall if any guests were supposed to check in. After the ordeal she'd been through with Makaio, it was hard to make sense of anything. He would

149

be out of commission for weeks — maybe months — making it difficult for them to run the bed-and-breakfast. But if they didn't remain open, it would hurt them financially — especially with hospital bills to pay.

Leaning her forehead against the steering wheel, she shut her eyes and prayed. *Lord, please help us through this difficult time.*

She lifted her head, remembering some repeat guests were scheduled to arrive. A middle-aged couple from Canada.

Luana pulled the visor down, checking in the mirror to see if there was a red mark from pressing her forehead on the wheel. Thankfully, there wasn't. *I need to get inside and check on things. I hope they're not sitting in the living room, waiting for me.*

When Luana entered the house, she found Mandy and Ellen in the kitchen. Ellen was preparing a pot of tea while Mandy put some macadamia-nut cookies on a serving tray.

"I'm glad you're back. How's your husband doing?" Mandy closed the cookie container.

"Surgery was done on his leg, and when I left the hospital, he was sleeping." Luana put her purse in the closet and leaned against the counter. She glanced toward the hallway leading to the living room. "Are Mr. and Mrs. McIntire here? I saw a car parked outside and remembered they had booked a room and would be arriving sometime today."

"They're here." Ellen placed the teapot on the tray beside the cookies. "I had them fill out the guest book, then made sure they were comfortable in their room." She gestured to the serving tray. "We asked them to join us in the living room for refreshments. I hope you don't mind."

"Not at all." Luana sank into a chair, feeling a wave of relief. "I appreciate you taking over in my absence. I couldn't leave before Makaio was out of surgery and settled into a room. The doctor was pleased with how the surgery went today. My husband will have a long road ahead of him, though." She glanced at her watch. "Ailani should be home by now. Her husband, Oke, came to the hospital to see how Makaio was doing and take his wife home. Oke worries now that Ailani is expecting a baby." Luana rubbed her forehead. "You two haven't had the opportunity to meet them yet. Maybe after Makaio gets home from the hospital, we can have Oke and Ailani here for supper."

"That will be nice. Oh, before I forget,

Ken came by earlier," Mandy said. "He told us about Makaio's injuries and that he'll need to stay off his feet for several weeks."

Nodding, Luana forced a smile. "But we'll get through this. The Lord will provide."

CHAPTER 14

The following day, Mandy entered the kitchen and found Luana sitting at the table, weeping. With a sinking feeling in the pit of her stomach, she hurried across the room, placing her hands on Luana's trembling shoulders. "Are you okay?"

"I thought I'd committed everything to God when I went to bed last night, but this morning our situation hit me full force." Luana sniffed. "With Makaio laid up and me having to take care of him, I'm not sure how I'll be able to handle things here by myself. Since our daughter is expecting a baby in the spring and has been having some difficulty with her pregnancy, the doctor says she shouldn't be on her feet too much. I won't do anything to jeopardize the health of Ailani or our future grandchild." She wiped her tears with a tissue. "Right now, we can't afford to hire any outside help, either."

Mandy took a seat next to her. "Ellen has experience working at a B&B back home, and we're both pretty good cooks. We could work for our room and board."

Luana sniffed. "I . . . I appreciate the offer, and it would help for the time being, but you'll be going home soon. Based on what the doctor stated about Makaio's condition, we're going to need help here for two or three months."

"We'll stay for as long as we're needed," Mandy blurted. Surely, Ellen wouldn't object. After all, it wouldn't be right to leave Luana and Makaio in the lurch.

Luana blinked. "But what about your families? They may not want you to stay here so long." She wiped at the tears still rolling down her cheeks.

"Once we explain the situation, I'm sure they'll understand." She gave Luana a tender hug.

Luana patted Mandy's back. "God bless you for your generosity. I feel better already."

"You're welcome." Mandy stood. "I'm going to our room to get Ellen now. Then we'll fix breakfast for your guests. After we eat, we'll call our folks and let them know we will be staying here longer."

Ellen was about to put her headscarf on when Mandy entered the room. "We need to talk." She flopped down on the end of the bed.

"What is it?" Ellen asked. "You appear to be *engschtlich.*"

"I'm not anxious, but I am concerned about Luana." Mandy clutched the folds of her muumuu. "When I went to the kitchen, she was crying."

"She's no doubt upset about Makaio."

"Jah, but it's more than that. When Makaio comes home, Luana is worried because the care he will need won't give her enough time to do everything here to keep the bed-and-breakfast running." Mandy paused and moistened her lips with the tip of her tongue. "So I said we would help out in exchange for room and board. I hope you're okay with it."

Ellen slowly nodded. "We can do it for a little while, but remember, we won't be here much longer. As soon as our folks send the money and we can book passage, we'll be going home."

"Makaio won't be able to help Luana for two to three months, so I told her we'd stay

155

as long as we're needed."

Ellen's mouth fell open. "But we can't, Mandy. Why would you commit to such a thing? We both have jobs back home. If we don't get there soon, our employers will find someone else to take our place — assuming they haven't already."

Mandy stared at her hands as she continued to fiddle with her dress. "If my job at the restaurant is gone when I get home, I'll look for something else." She lifted her chin, eyes wide and almost pleading. "You can go if you want to, Ellen, but I'm staying here until Makaio is back on his feet. He and Luana have been good to us, and I won't leave them during their time of need."

Ellen couldn't believe her friend was willing to risk losing her job for people she barely knew. Then again, Mandy had always tried to help anyone with a problem. *It wouldn't be right to leave my best friend here. Besides, staying to help Luana and her husband is the Christian thing to do.*

Ellen pressed her palm to her cheek. "Okay, you're right. I shouldn't have been so hasty."

"You mean you'll stay for as long as we're needed?"

"Jah, but if we're going to be here for an indefinite amount of time, I'd like to find a fabric store and look for a simple dress pattern and some plain material."

Mandy pointed to Ellen's dress. "What's wrong with what you are wearing? We can always buy more Hawaiian clothes, you know."

Ellen shook her head. "I'm not comfortable wearing a muumuu. The print is too bold. If Luana has a sewing machine, I'd feel better making a few plain dresses."

"If she doesn't, maybe the fabric store would let you borrow a sewing machine and make your dresses there."

"Maybe." She blinked. "What about you? Don't you want to make a dress like what we're used to wearing at home?"

Mandy shrugged. "I'm comfortable in the muumuu and don't see the need."

What's gotten into my friend? Has she forgotten her Amish roots? Ellen's muscles tightened.

"Let's go. We need to help Luana fix breakfast." Mandy hurried from the room.

Ellen started to follow but paused at the door, closing her eyes. *Heavenly Father, help Makaio to heal quickly so Mandy and I can go home.*

Middlebury
Gideon whistled as he headed for the phone

shack to call Mandy. He'd gone by her folks' house after work today and finally gotten the number where she and Ellen were staying. It seemed like forever since they'd been together. He could hardly wait to hear her voice. Even more, he couldn't wait for Mandy to come home.

When Gideon stepped into the small, chilly building, he took a seat on the wooden stool and quickly made the call. A woman's voice came on a few seconds later. "The Palms Bed-and-Breakfast."

"Is Mandy Frey there?" he asked.

"Gideon, is that you?"

"Sure is. Who am I speaking to?"

"It's Ellen. Mandy's upstairs, making one of the guest beds. Hang on. I'll get her."

Gideon doodled on the notepad next to the phone while he waited. It seemed strange Mandy would be making a guest bed. *Maybe Ellen meant she's making the bed she slept in last night. But if that's so, shouldn't the hired help do it?*

Finally, Mandy came on the phone. "Hello, Gideon. How are you?"

"I'm fine. More to the point, how are you? I heard from your daed that you and Ellen missed the boat."

"We did. The ship moved on, which left us stranded." She cleared her throat. "We're

158

thankful to be staying at a bed-and-breakfast with a nice Hawaiian couple who are Christians."

"So how come you didn't call me?" Gideon wrote Mandy's name on the notepad in front of him. "I had to get this number from your mamm."

"Things have been a bit hectic on our end." She paused. "But it's no excuse. I'm sorry, Gideon. I should have called you."

He leaned his head against his hand, releasing a soft breath. "It's fine. I'm relieved to hear your voice." Gideon's face felt uncomfortably warm. He liked hearing the sound of her voice, even if it wasn't as clear over the phone. "When are you coming home, Mandy?"

"Not for a while."

"I'd be happy to pay part of your passage."

"It's nice of you, Gideon, but we can't go anywhere right now."

"Why not?"

"The man who owns the B&B fell off the roof and broke his leg, which means he won't be able to help his wife manage the place. So Ellen and I volunteered to help out until he's back on his feet."

"It was kind of you to offer, but can't they find someone else?" Gideon gripped the receiver. This phone call was not going well at all.

"We're working for room and board, because they can't afford to hire anyone right now. Sorry, Gideon, but I need to go. Someone is knocking on the back door, and since I'm the only one in the kitchen, I need to answer it."

"Okay. I'll talk to you again soon, Mandy. Take care."

Gideon hung up but remained in the phone shack, rubbing the bridge of his nose as he reflected on their conversation. It was just like sweet Mandy to do a charitable deed, but now he had no idea when she'd be home. How were they supposed to keep their relationship going when she was thousands of miles away?

Kapaa

Ken pulled his motorbike up to the B&B, anxious to find out how Makaio was doing. When he stepped onto the lanai, where Mandy and Ellen sat snapping green beans, he smiled. "Looks like Luana put you to work. Is she here?"

"No. She got up early this morning and went to the hospital to see Makaio." Mandy motioned to the chair across from them. "You're welcome to sit and visit while we

160

snap beans."

"If you have an extra bowl, I'd be more than happy to help with that." He seated himself near Mandy and began rocking.

"I'll get one." Ellen rose from her seat and returned with a plastic bowl and more beans, which she handed to Ken. "Here you go."

He took the bowl and placed it in his lap. "Thanks, I think." He chuckled then reached into his pocket and pulled out a business card. "On a more serious note, if you two need anything while you're here, don't hesitate to get in touch with me. Here's my phone number in case you need to call."

"Actually, there is something," Ellen said as Mandy took the card. "We'd like to make a trip to a fabric store. Would you be able to give us a ride — maybe later, after Luana gets back?"

"I'd be glad to take you, but I don't have time today. Would tomorrow be soon enough? I'll have the day off."

Mandy nodded. "Of course. We can work it in around your schedule."

"How long do you plan to be here?" Ken asked as he began snapping the beans in half. He didn't work as quickly as she or Ellen, but Mandy figured Ken hadn't had as much practice.

"We'll stay for as long as we're needed," she replied. "I'm sure we won't be working all the time, though, so it will give us a chance to see more of this beautiful island during our free time."

"I'm glad you'll be staying longer." He rocked too far back, and when he let go of the bowl, his hands went for the arms of the chair. The plastic bowl slid off his lap and bounced on the tile floor. "Oh no! I'm sorry." He jumped up and crouched by the rocking chair, grabbing for the beans. Some had even gone under the rocker.

"It's okay." Ellen dropped down beside him and started picking up beans. Once they had them all, she stood and took the bowl inside to wash them.

Ken smiled at Mandy. "Well, that was sure an icebreaker. Now we can get better acquainted. As I mentioned yesterday, I'd like to show you some special places. We can go to the beach, and if you like flowers, there are some really nice tropical gardens."

"I would enjoy either of those places. This island feels like paradise to me." Mandy stretched her arms out wide. "I wish there was an Amish community on Kauai. I could get used to living here."

CHAPTER 15

The following day while Ellen walked through the fabric store to look at material and patterns, Mandy stood near the front door with Ken. "It was nice of you to take time out to bring us here. I'm sure you had other things to do on your day off."

"I can't think of anything I'd rather be doing than helping two friends." Grinning, he winked at Mandy. "One of these days, I'll take you and Ellen for a tour of our farm and to meet my folks. Oh, just a second. My phone is buzzing." Ken pulled it out of his pocket. "Yep. My friend Taavi is trying to call me." He stepped aside. "Hey, buddy. What's up? That sounds like fun, but I'm in the middle of something right now. I'll call ya back later." He hung up and moved closer to Mandy again. "Sorry for the interruption. Taavi's one of my friends. He's a good surfer and was letting me know there's gonna be some prime wave action today.

But I'd rather be here right now, getting to know you better."

Mandy felt the heat of a blush spread like fire across her cheeks. It was nice Ken wanted to know her better. Even though she'd known him less than a week, Mandy felt as though they were kindred spirits. *Maybe it's because he likes gardening and enjoys the beauty of God's creation,* she told herself. Of course, Gideon appreciated many things God created, but he had no interest in flowers, trees, or vegetable gardens. Whenever they were together, he talked more about his horse than anything. She shifted her purse to the other shoulder. *I shouldn't be comparing the two men.*

"Aren't you going to browse through the material?" Ken asked, pulling out a pack of gum.

"No, I'm not planning to make a dress." Mandy looked down at the green muumuu she'd bought with her own money yesterday. "I have two Hawaiian dresses now, and they work fine for me. I only came to the fabric store in case Ellen needs my opinion on anything."

Ken stared at her strangely, but made no comment. Several seconds passed before he spoke again. "Would you like a piece of gum?"

164

"No, thank you."

"Who's keeping an eye on the B&B this morning?"

"Ailani is there, but only to answer the phone. She won't be doing any physical work."

"Good to hear. What about Luana? Is she at the hospital with Makaio?"

"Yes. She left soon after we served our B&B guests their breakfast."

With wrinkled brows, Ken folded his arms and leaned against the wall. "Sure hope he won't have to be in the hospital too long. It will be better for Makaio and Luana once he's home. He'll be more comfortable in his own surroundings, and she won't have to run back and forth to the hospital."

Mandy shifted her weight to the other foot. "When my younger brother, Milo, got hit in the head with a baseball last year, he had a pretty severe concussion. Our folks had to hire a driver to take them to and from the hospital every day for a week."

"Is your brother okay now?"

"He's doing fine. No repercussions from the accident, and I'm grateful."

"Accidents happen so quickly." Ken sighed. "One minute, everything is fine, and the next minute something unexpected occurs. A person can become severely injured.

I like to surf, and it can be dangerous, too."

Mandy winced, fiddling with the straps on her purse. *Why would anyone choose to take part in a dangerous sport?*

"You need to know how to swim if you're gonna surf — or at least know how to tread water real well. It helps going to a beach that's patrolled by lifeguards. That's a stipulation my parents drummed into my brother and me." His mouth twisted grimly. "Another thing is watching out for other surfers in the water and trying not to get hit by someone or even by your own board. I've seen it happen many times."

"Surfing sounds exciting but also frightening."

Ken shifted his gaze away from her a few seconds, then looked back, clasping his chin with his fingers. "It can be, but the fun outweighs my fears." He took a step closer. "Say, I have a question."

"What is it?"

"I thought Amish people traveled by horse and buggy."

"We do." Mandy rested her hand on her hip. "Why do you ask?"

"When your brother got hurt, how come your parents hired a driver to take them to the hospital?"

"We usually only take the horse and buggies ten miles or so from our home. Farther away, and especially into the bigger cities, means we need to hire a driver."

"Interesting." He rubbed his chin.

She grew quiet as their conversation came to a lull. Ken kept looking at Mandy though, causing her face to warm. It was almost as though nothing existed except the two of them standing by the door. Even the sounds inside the store seemed to cease. Her throat constricted. For some reason, she couldn't look away.

It appeared as if Ken might be about to say something, but Ellen walked toward them with a bolt of beige material. "I found the color I want, but I need your opinion on a pattern."

"Okay." Mandy wiped moisture from her face.

"Think I'll wait outside in my rig while you two finish shopping." Ken looked toward the parking lot. "Take your time, though. I'm in no rush."

Mandy glanced over her shoulder, watching Ken go out the door. *He's such a nice person. I only wish . . .* She turned and followed Ellen to the back of the store, refusing to let her thoughts get carried away. *It must be the heat,* Mandy told herself. *I'm not thinking clearly today.*

"This is a nice enough hospital, but I'm anxious to go home." Luana's husband frowned. "I'll sleep a lot better in our own bed, too."

"It shouldn't be too much longer." Luana placed her hand on Makaio's arm. "You ought to enjoy all the attention you're getting here while you can, and don't forget all the good food they've been feeding you."

"Your cooking is much better than hospital food. Guess I shouldn't complain though. I'm happy to be alive." Makaio closed his eyes a few seconds, before opening them again. "How are we going to manage the B&B with me unable to walk right now?" He winced as he gripped the bedsheets and tried to sit up. "We're starting into our busiest time of the year. You'll need my help more than ever."

"What's done is done, so there's no need to fret." Luana asked him to lean forward a bit and plumped up his pillows. Then she took a seat in the chair beside his bed and reached out to clasp his hand. "I have some good news."

"Please share it with me. I've had enough negative news since I fell off the roof."

"Mandy and Ellen have agreed to help out in exchange for their room and board." She gave his fingers a reassuring squeeze. "You need to quit worrying and relax so you can get better. You're not doing yourself any good by getting upset."

"You're right, and the Amish women's help is appreciated, but they won't be here much longer. As soon as they're able to get tickets, they'll be on a ship taking them back to the mainland." He reached for his glass of water and took a drink.

"No they won't. Mandy and Ellen have agreed to stay with us for as long as we need them — until your leg has healed and you can take over your responsibilities again."

"Why would they do it, Luana? They barely know us."

"Because they care and want to help." She smiled. "They're putting their Christianity into practice."

Makaio fell back against the pillow and closed his eyes. When he opened them again, Luana saw tears. He looked at her and asked, "Remember, when you believed God sent those young women to us for a reason?"

Her throat constricted, and she could only manage a slow nod.

"I'm certain now that it was so they could

help us during our time of need."

Luana squeezed his fingers gently. "You may be right. But whatever the reason, I'm thankful Mandy and Ellen are staying with us."

Ensenada, Mexico

"Do you see the green, white, and red Mexican flag greeting us near the cruise terminal?" Sadie pointed at the huge flag waving in the breeze.

Barbara lifted her hands over her head to stretch her arms. "I could see it for some distance as we approached the harbor."

"I heard someone say Ensenada is a major cruise ship destination and thousands of tourists come here ever year." Sadie reached into her tote and removed her camera. Then she took a picture of the Mexican flag. "First Street is supposed to be another busy spot for tourists, so we ought to check it out."

"I'm glad we're sticking with a tour group today," Barbara commented. "I wouldn't want to be stranded in Mexico. The people speak a language we don't understand. It could be a little frightening."

"That wouldn't be a problem. Our tour guide mentioned most of the people who live here — especially those selling their wares — understand English."

"Even so, I'd be umgerrent if the ship left us behind, like what happened to Mandy and Ellen."

Sadie nodded. "You're right, so we shouldn't venture too far on our own today."

"I'm going to call Mandy when we get back to the ship and see how she and Ellen are doing," Barbara said as they began walking up Avenida Lopez Mateos, the main tourist street of Ensenada, lined with paved, red brick sidewalks. "I'll bet they're as eager to get home as we are."

"Jah, but unfortunately their luggage will reach their homes before they ever do."

"That's right. We're in charge of extra suitcases." Barbara's lips compressed. "Seeing that they make it off the ship and then onto the train could be a challenge, since we'll have our luggage to deal with as well."

"I'm sure we can manage." Sadie pointed to a store up ahead. "Let's go in there and see what souvenirs we can find." They paused to look at some colorful Mexican blankets and sombreros. "If nothing else, I'd like to buy a few postcards and maybe a handmade basket. After we finish shopping, I want to try one of those fish tacos I've heard others on the ship talking about."

Barbara's nose itched, so she paused to

rub it with her finger. She hoped she wasn't allergic to something in the air. "I'll pass. Don't think I'd enjoy eating fish in a soft-rolled taco shell. I may try a regular ground beef taco if we can find any."

"I'm sure they're available." Sadie's next step caused her to stumble on the slippery brick. Suddenly, she was flat on her back.

CHAPTER 16

Albuquerque, New Mexico

"How nice it is to finally be heading home." Sadie shifted in her seat, trying to find a comfortable position. "I only wish we could get there sooner." Normally, the *clickety-clack* of the train's wheels against the tracks would lull her to sleep, but not today. They'd only been riding the train since yesterday, and already she was tired of sitting. Her biggest problem was her bruised tailbone from the fall she'd taken in Ensenada. Fortunately, the only thing that had been seriously hurt was her pride. If she'd broken a bone, she may have ended up in the hospital and missed the ship when it left Mexico. Then she'd have been in the same predicament as her friends who were stuck on Kauai.

"Are you doing okay?" Barbara's anxious expression showed the extent of her concern. "You took a pretty hard fall on that brick sidewalk the other day. You must still be quite sore."

"I am, but I can deal with the pain. I'm having a hard time sitting, though."

"Should we go up to the café car and get a snack to eat? It might do you some good to walk awhile."

"Maybe in a little bit. Right now I'm trying to enjoy the scenery, even though my body is screaming to get up." Sadie pointed out the window. "I'm watching for some wildlife, like we saw on the train as we were heading to California near the beginning of our trip."

"We did see a lot of deer, as well as some turkeys, antelope, and coyote. I hope we spot some elk this time." Barbara leaned against the window and released a sigh. "I wonder what Mandy and Ellen are doing right now. Sure wish I could have talked to Mandy longer the other evening, but she said they were busy so she couldn't talk long. I'm still surprised they'll be staying longer than planned. I wonder how their families are dealing with this."

Kapaa

Ellen and Mandy had been working hard, keeping things at the B&B well organized and running smoothly. Makaio had come

174

home from the hospital, but since he couldn't be on his feet, he'd been watching a lot of TV. It bothered Ellen because she wasn't used to having a television in the house, much less dealing with the blaring noise. Luana kept after Makaio to keep the volume down — especially when they had B&B guests. But the sound crept up as soon as she left the room, like it had this afternoon.

Ellen peeked into the living room and saw Makaio sleeping with the remote in his hands. She wouldn't dare take it from him, as she'd seen Luana do last night when Makaio fell asleep in his chair. He wasn't too thrilled when his wife woke him, either, and Ellen didn't want to upset him.

Since all their guests had gone out for the day and wouldn't be bothered by the noise, Ellen closed the living-room door and went to the kitchen, where Luana was showing Mandy how to make Hawaiian teriyaki burgers.

"Yum. It smells good in here." Ellen moved close to the counter, watching as Luana mixed soy sauce, sesame oil, ginger, and several other ingredients into the ground beef.

Luana looked at Ellen and smiled. "My husband loves this kind of burger."

"Speaking of Makaio, he's asleep right now."

"With the TV on, no doubt."

Ellen nodded, and Mandy, who stood nearby, winked at her.

"I'm not surprised." Luana lifted her gaze to the ceiling, while making a little clucking sound. "Normally he doesn't watch much TV. But now he has nothing else to do but sit, and I fear he will become addicted to it."

Mandy leaned toward the bowl and sniffed. "If these burgers taste half as good as they smell, then I may end up with an addiction."

They sat down to eat lunch a short time later and enjoyed pleasant conversation during the meal. Luana seemed a bit more relaxed since Makaio was now home. She even told them about some silly things he'd done years ago. "My husband can be a character at times." Luana laughed.

They had no sooner finished the meal than Ken showed up. Grinning from ear to ear, he asked if Mandy and Ellen would like to go watch the surfers with him.

"I would," Mandy responded with an eager expression. "It sounds like fun."

"How about you, Ellen?" Ken asked.

"Actually, if Luana doesn't need me for

anything, I'd planned to get started on making my new dress this afternoon."

"You girls have been busy here all morning," Luana said, "so you deserve some time off to do your own thing."

"Why don't you and Ken go without me?" Ellen suggested.

Mandy's forehead wrinkled. "Are you sure?"

Ellen nodded.

"Okay then. Give me a few seconds while I get some things from my room to take along." Mandy hurried off but returned promptly with her sunglasses and a bottle of sunscreen.

"Why don't you put your things in here?" Luana handed Mandy a colorful tote decorated with palm trees.

"Thanks." Mandy and Ken said their goodbyes and headed out the door.

Ellen turned to Luana. "Would you mind if I use your dining-room table to cut out my dress pattern?"

"Not at all. While you're working on the pattern, I'll get Makaio some coffee and a burger. I looked in on him a while ago, and he's awake now."

On the way to the beach, Mandy and Ken pulled into the drive-through at a fast-food place, ordered drinks and some Maui onion chips, and then continued on their way. It was fun riding in Ken's camouflaged SUV.

As they approached the beach, Mandy's heart raced with excitement. Frothing white waves rolled in over the aqua-blue ocean, which in places appeared to be a beautiful turquoise. Being on an island, where the water could be seen from most places, was truly amazing.

Ken parked the car and shut off the engine. "Are you ready to watch some action?"

"Oh yes! I'm sure it will be exciting." Mandy hopped out and grabbed the floral-print tote she'd borrowed from Luana, while Ken took out a blanket and their snacks.

As they walked toward the water, Mandy's sandals sank into the soft sand, and she noticed the pretty golden color.

Ken pulled off his flip-flops. "Ah, now this feels more like it." He picked them up and pointed at Mandy's feet. "How 'bout you?"

Smiling, she did the same. The sand felt warm as the grains sifted between her toes. "I couldn't agree more."

"Let's pick a spot to sit and relax. My buddy, Taavi, is out there right now in the blue." Ken pointed to one of the surfers.

They walked farther down the beach to get a better view of the ocean. It was difficult for Mandy to walk properly, since her bare feet kept sinking in the sand. She lowered her head. *I probably look foolish, wobbling with every step.*

"How about here? This looks like a good spot for us to sit." Ken spread the blanket on the sand, and they both took a seat.

Watching the action on the water, Mandy was spellbound. Some surfers disappeared in the tube of a wave, then reappeared at the other end. She couldn't imagine how they kept upright on a surfboard, nearly swallowed up by the ocean, and seemed to have no fear.

A young Hawaiian man paddled in toward shore, lying on his stomach on a colorful surfboard. "Hey, how's it going, Ken?" he shouted after stepping out of the water and setting the board down.

"Not bad. The waves are lookin' pretty good today. Come on over! I wanna introduce you to my friend."

Hauling his board up the beach a ways, the young man came over to where they sat.

"Taavi, this is Mandy."

"Hey, it's nice to meet you." He knelt beside Mandy and shook her hand.

"Hi, Taavi. It's nice meeting you, too."

"I take it you aren't going out there today?" he asked, looking at Ken.

Ken shook his head.

Taavi snickered. "It's okay. Leaves more waves for me to enjoy."

"Yep. You can have all the waves you want today." Ken looked at Mandy and winked.

They talked for a while, and then Taavi picked up his board and headed back into the surf. He paddled a good distance, and when the wave began, he was up on his feet, moving swiftly along in front of it. The way he sliced through the water, with the ocean's momentum, was incredible.

They continued to watch Taavi and others who were surfing the huge breaks in the water. *I wonder what Ellen is doing right now,* Mandy mused. *She's missing out on everything.*

"A nickel for your thoughts." Ken nudged her arm gently.

"I was thinking how Ellen is missing out on this beautiful beach and the fun going on in the water."

"I never get tired of coming to the beach. Makes me glad I'm living in Hawaii." He reached into his pocket and pulled out a pack of gum. "Would you like a piece?"

Smiling, she took one. "Thank you, and thanks again for paying for the drinks and chips we got at the drive-through."

"You're welcome." He put the gum back in his pocket.

Mandy watched as two surfers rode a wave a little too close to each other. It was one of the largest waves she'd seen so far. Neither guy seemed willing to give up his spot.

"Boy, they're too close!" Ken stood about the time the two guys collided with each other. They both splashed into the water and disappeared in the waves. Unfortunately, one of the surfers was Taavi.

"Sure hope no one got hurt. I'd better go check." Ken raced toward the water.

Mandy's heart pounded. She got up from the blanket, hoping for a better view. Holding her hands tightly against her sides, she prayed, *Lord, please help Ken's friend and the other fellow to be okay.*

Both guys surfaced. The people on shore seemed relieved, as everyone clapped. Taavi and the other surfer paddled to shore on their boards. When the fellow Taavi had collided with came out of the water, it appeared that his nose was bleeding. Ken took a look at him, then Taavi and turned to wave at Mandy.

A few minutes later, Ken ran back to her. "The other guy must have gotten clipped in the nose by his board, but it's not serious."

Relieved, Mandy took her seat again. She was glad no serious injuries had occurred. She directed her gaze toward the water, watching the young guy lying on the sand pinching his nose. Someone handed Taavi some tissues, and he took them over to the injured fellow. Then he headed in their direction.

"A great day for this sport." Taavi grimaced. "As you can see, accidents occur, no matter how much practice one's had."

"Does this happen a lot out here?" Mandy adjusted her scarf, keeping it from slipping off her head.

"It's random. Some people can go a long time and not get hurt. But sometimes it can sneak up on you, like it did for us today."

"Is his nose broken?" she questioned.

"Didn't look like it. He'd know if it was, since he's had it broken before." Taavi plopped down on the sand.

Ken sat on the other side of Mandy, pulled out his cell phone, and brought his knees up to his elbows. "Looks like I missed a call from my mom. Guess I'd better see what she wanted." He hopped up from the blanket and began to pace, kicking the sand a few times while he walked. "Hi, Mom. Yeah, we're still at the beach. Umm . . . I'm not sure when I'll be there."

Mandy tried not to eavesdrop, but it was hard not to hear what Ken was saying, with him only a few feet away.

"How are you liking Hawaii, Mandy?" Taavi asked.

"It's nice. You live on a beautiful island."

"Yeah, it's great. So where ya from?" He combed back his wet hair with his fingers.

"My friend Ellen and I are from Middlebury, Indiana. We're staying with Makaio and Luana Palu and helping out at their B&B until he's back on his feet again."

"Yeah, I heard about his accident. Makaio's a nice guy. Too bad it happened."

Mandy nodded.

"You're a long way from home. It's nice of you to hang around so you can help out. Wouldn't be easy on Luana, tryin' to do everything by herself."

"We're glad to do it, and I'm hoping during our free time we can see a few places on the island."

"Where's your friend today? Didn't she want to come to the beach?"

"Ellen had something she wanted to get done."

"Did I miss much?" Ken plopped down beside Mandy again.

"Not really. Mandy and I have been getting acquainted." Taavi pointed toward the water. "Now would ya look at that? The guy I collided with is already in the water and up on another wave."

They visited awhile longer, until Taavi said goodbye and headed back out to the water with his board.

Ken glanced briefly at Mandy and smiled, before leaning back and resting his elbows behind him.

She returned his smile, and as a gentle breeze blew across her face, she found herself savoring the moment and wishing she could freeze time so she could remain here forever.

CHAPTER 17

Elkhart, Indiana

On Monday, November 18, as the train pulled into the station, Barbara's heart began to race. They'd only been gone twenty-one days, but it seemed so much longer. "Oh look! It's snowing." She pointed out the window. "Now, that's a pretty homecoming."

Other passengers commented on the snow. Two young boys had their faces pressed against the window, fogging up the glass. One of them drew a smiley face with his finger.

"What a contrast from the blue skies and sunshine we had in Hawaii," Sadie commented. "All the hardwood trees have their winter look — gray and bare of leaves."

"Jah," Barbara agreed. "But the white pines are sure pretty. Their soft green needles, with a light sprinkle of snow, reminds me of the holidays fast approaching."

Sadie grunted, rising from her seat. "It's gonna be hard to get used to cold weather again. In some ways, Mandy and Ellen are lucky they got stranded on Kauai."

"I can't believe you would say such a thing." Barbara stood and reached for her carry-ons. "I'm glad to be here, and I bet they're missing home as much as we were."

"I'm happy to be here, too. I only meant I'll miss the nicer weather and our friends get to enjoy it longer than we do." Sadie pulled on her heavy shawl and picked up her tote bags and purse. "For me, it will seem more like the season, especially with Thanksgiving and Christmas around the corner. I can't imagine those holidays without cold temperatures and a bit of snow."

"I suppose you're right," Barbara agreed, pulling her jacket closed at the neck. When they'd left Indiana at the beginning of their trip, it had been chilly, so they'd taken their jackets and sweaters along. But they'd never worn them in Hawaii except on the Big Island when they visited the volcano and a few times on the ship. The colder weather would take some getting used to.

The two boys Barbara had been watching earlier tried to get around Sadie in their eagerness to get off the train. Their mother called out to them, but one of them managed to squeeze past. In the middle of trying to collect all their things, his mother hollered for him to wait. Barbara and Sadie moved aside so the boy's mother and younger brother could join him.

When Barbara stepped off the train, she spotted her parents right away. Sadie's mother and father were there, too. Hugs and smiles were given all around, and more than a few tears were shed. Once their suitcases, as well as Mandy's and Ellen's, were taken off the train, they loaded everything into their driver's van.

"It's a shame Mandy and Ellen aren't with you." Barbara's mother wiped at the tears beneath her eyes. "I talked to Mandy's mamm the other day, and she misses her daughter."

Before they climbed into the van to leave for home, Barbara squeezed her mother's hand. "I'm sure they miss their folks, too." Snowflakes fell onto her eyelashes, and she had the urge to stick out her tongue to catch a few of the crystals. "It's good to be back. I had a great vacation, but there's no place like home."

Middlebury
I can't believe Barbara and Sadie are getting

home today, but Mandy won't be with them.
Gideon fretted as he headed down the road
with his horse and buggy toward his mother's store. *Maybe calling her and explaining
how hard it is to be without her would get
Mandy home sooner. I should be at the train
station right now, greeting my* aldi, *instead of
here, wishing it were so.*

"Wow!" Gideon nearly jumped out of his
skin when a car coming up on him tooted
its horn. Being deep in thought, he'd allowed his horse to drift over into the other
lane. He redirected the animal to the right
side of the road.

After the car drove by, Gideon leaned
back in his seat and tried to relax. But the
knowledge of Mandy still being in Hawaii
stuck in his craw.

"I need to quit stewing about this," Gideon mumbled. *Complaining and rehashing
won't bring Mandy back any sooner. I
shouldn't be thinking so much when I'm driv-
ing my horse and buggy, either. If I'm not careful, I could end up in the hospital, seriously
injured.*

The roads were still bare, even though it
had started snowing. He felt safe giving his
horse the freedom to trot and was soon pulling up to the hitching rail at the quilt-and-
fabric store.

When Gideon entered the building, he found his mother behind the counter cutting material for Ellen's mother, Nora. He figured she probably missed her daughter and wished she had arrived home today, too. Gideon wanted to say something but decided it might be best to keep quiet. No point pouring vinegar on the wound. Nora wouldn't want to be reminded of her daughter's situation any more than he did Mandy's.

"I'm heading to the back room to unload those boxes you mentioned would be coming in today," he announced when Mom glanced at him.

She smiled and gave a quick nod, then kept right on cutting.

Gideon hurried to the back of the store, nearly bumping his elbow on one of the shelves. As he stepped into the storage room, he spotted four large boxes filled with bolts of material. With Barbara gone almost a month, and Mom being shorthanded, Gideon often came by the store after he got off work to help out. Mom had mentioned hiring someone during Barbara's absence but in the end decided to try and get by. If Gideon hadn't been helping a few hours each day, Mom may have changed her mind.

Focused on the task at hand, he opened

the first box and pulled out several bolts of material, all in different shades of green. After placing them vertically on the proper shelf, he went back and got some more. Soon every box was empty, so he headed up front to see what else Mom wanted him to do. As he approached the counter, the front door opened, and Barbara stepped in.

"Wie gehts?" he asked, surprised to see her. He hadn't expected she'd be at the store so soon. "How was your trip?"

Barbara's blue eyes twinkled like fireflies dancing on a sultry summer night. "It was amazing! I can't begin to describe the beauty of Hawaii."

"Welcome back." Mom stepped around the counter and gave Barbara a hug. "Was it hard to leave the warm weather and return home to snow?"

"A little." Deep dimples formed in Barbara's cheeks when she smiled. "I did enjoy my vacation but missed my family, so I was ready to come home." Her shoulders drooped a bit. "I'm only sorry Ellen and Mandy couldn't be with Sadie and me today. It was exciting to have our parents waiting for us at the train station this morning."

Gideon's jaw clenched. *Mandy should have been with you, and I ought to have been there*

190

waiting to greet her. He was giving in to self-pity again but couldn't seem to help himself.

Mom gave Barbara's shoulder a pat. "I missed you. Not only for your help here at the store, but for the enjoyment we have when we visit during slow times."

"I agree." Barbara glanced at Gideon, then quickly back at his mother. "Is my job still waiting for me, or have I been replaced?"

Mom shook her head. "You're too good of a worker to be replaced."

"Can I start back tomorrow, or would you rather I wait till Monday?"

"If you're up to it, tomorrow would be fine." Mom looked at Gideon. "Did you get all those bolts of material put out?" Shifting her weight, she rested her hand on the counter.

"Jah. Came up to see what else you might want me to do."

She reached under her glasses and rubbed the bridge of her nose. "Let's see. I suppose you could stay behind the counter while I take a much-needed break."

"I don't mind, as long as no one comes in needing material cut." Gideon's forehead wrinkled. "I wouldn't be any good at that."

Barbara chuckled. "For goodness' sake, you work with upholstery all day. I would

191

think you'd be an expert at cutting material."

"Nope. I don't do the cutting. That's Aaron's job. I take care of doing the books and waiting on customers, 'cause I'm the one good with numbers."

Mom tapped her foot, the way she did when her patience grew thin. "I'll tell you what, Son, if someone comes in needing material cut, you can come get me."

"Okay." Gideon waited for his mother to head to the back room, then he stepped behind the counter in her place.

"Would you like me to stay until she comes back?" Barbara offered. "If a customer comes in and wants some material cut, I'll do it for you."

"Are ya sure? I mean . . ."

She held up her hand. "I'm more than happy to do it."

"Danki." Gideon grinned. *Barbara's sure nice. No wonder she and Mandy are friends.*

Kapaa
As Mandy checked each of the rooms in the B&B, making sure they were prepared for the next guests' arrival, she thought about similarities between the Amish and Hawaiian people, such as their family values and desire to live a simpler life. She was

fascinated, too, with Luana's beautiful quilts, displayed throughout the bed-and-breakfast. Every guest room had a different quilt on the bed and a lovely wall hanging. The Hawaiian quilt patterns were different from Amish quilts, but similar in some ways.

She leaned over and touched the pretty green-and-white quilt on the king-sized bed in the Bird of Paradise Room. Like most Amish quilts, the tiny hand-stitches were evenly spaced and barely visible. Once again, she found herself wishing she could take one of these magnificent quilts home.

Maybe Luana would like to have an Amish quilt, Mandy thought. *I could ask Gideon's mother to make one for her when I get home. In exchange, perhaps Luana would part with one of her quilts or even a quilted wall hanging.* She shook her head. *No, I shouldn't expect too much. Most likely, each of the quilts here at the B&B are special to Luana. It wouldn't be right to ask her to part with any of them.*

Pushing her thoughts aside, Mandy left the room and shut the door. Luana's daughter and son-in-law would be coming for dinner soon, and she needed to help Luana and Ellen in the kitchen.

That evening, everyone sat around the dinner table, enjoying the chicken chowder and haystack Mandy and Ellen had prepared for them. The delicious aromas reminded Mandy of home. *I wonder what Gideon's doing right now.* Chicken chowder was one of his favorite soups. Mandy had fixed it for him several times since they'd begun courting. *I should make the soup again when I get home and invite him over for a meal.* She placed her napkin in her lap and bowed her head for silent prayer.

"This chowder is good." Ailani and her husband, Oke, spoke at the same time.

"We're glad you like it." Mandy looked at her friend and smiled. When they'd been putting the chowder together this afternoon, she'd told Ellen she was sure everyone would enjoy it. Since it was a traditional Pennsylvania Dutch recipe, Ellen wasn't sure the Hawaiian family would like it as much as they did.

Makaio, who had insisted he hobble to the table on his crutches unassisted, was gulping down his second bowl. "This is different from what I'm used to, but I have to say, it's sure good."

"Don't eat too much," Mandy teased. "There's still a Dutch apple pie coming for dessert."

"Yes, and Makaio, where are your table

manners?" Luana scolded, shaking her finger. "You sound like a puppy lapping milk."

Everyone laughed, including Makaio. "Sorry. The soup is so tasty, I couldn't help it. Bet the pie you made will also be good." He looked at Luana and grinned before taking another bite.

"You two young women are spoiling us with your good cooking. I won't know what to do when you leave — except maybe put my husband on a diet." Luana laughed, then reached over and touched Mandy's arm. "I can't begin to tell you how much I appreciate you both being here and helping out."

Mandy sighed. As much as she wanted Makaio's leg to get well, she was in no hurry to leave Kauai. She wondered if God had a special reason for allowing them to become stranded on this island.

CHAPTER 18

Middlebury

"I don't know what to do anymore," Gideon mumbled, clutching his shirt to his heart. "I feel like I'm losing her." He left the phone shack and headed up to the house. It was the second day of December, and Barbara and Sadie had been back two weeks, but in all those days, he'd only talked to Mandy once. Each time he called, she was either busy doing something at the bed-and-breakfast or had gone someplace. He'd finally gotten ahold of her, but it hadn't gone well. Mandy seemed distant — like her mind was someplace else. When he'd asked when she might be coming home, she wasted no time telling him she and Ellen were still needed there. It almost seemed as if she didn't want to come home.

I need to quit dwelling on this. He kicked a clump of snow with the toe of his boot. *Think I'll head over to Mom's store and see if she needs help with anything.*

"I've said this before, but I'll say it again, Barbara, I'm glad you're back working in the store again."

Barbara chuckled as she carried a bolt of material to the counter for a customer who was still shopping. "It's good to be back, Peggy. I enjoy my work here." She glanced around the room. "I haven't seen any sign of Gideon today. Do you know if he's planning to come by?"

"I'm not sure." Peggy looked toward the battery-operated clock on the far wall. "Maybe he had to work later than usual at the upholstery shop. When he does come by, it's usually earlier than this."

"I'm hoping to get the chance to talk to him about Mandy." Barbara folded some material from a customer who had changed her mind.

Peggy's eyebrows rose. "Is something wrong with Mandy?"

"No, nothing like that. She's fine physically. I'm worried about her attitude."

"What do you mean?"

"Well, I spoke to her last night, and —" Barbara stopped talking when another customer came in.

"We can talk later," Peggy whispered. "I'll

197

take care of the counter, if you don't mind putting some more white thread on the notions shelf. I can't believe how many spools we've sold in the last two weeks."

"I'll take care of it right away." Barbara headed to the back room to get the box of thread. As she turned to leave the room, Gideon stepped in, bumping her shoulder.

"Oops, sorry. Didn't realize anyone was in here," he apologized.

"It's okay. No harm done." Barbara's face warmed as she stepped aside so he could enter the room. "Mind if I ask you something?"

"Sure." Gideon took off his hat and tossed it aside.

"Have you heard from Mandy lately?"

"Jah. Talked to her this morning." He dropped his gaze. "The conversation didn't go well."

"I'm sorry to hear that. I spoke with her last night." She ran her hands down the sides of her dress. "I'm worried about her, Gideon."

"Same here." Frowning, he looked up. "She won't be coming home for Christmas."

"She told me the same thing." Barbara leaned against the cabinet where some of the extra notions were stored. "Mandy and Ellen are doing a good deed by helping out at the B&B while the Hawaiian man is recuperating." She drew in a quick breath, wondering if she should share her concerns with Gideon.

"You're right. It's a charitable thing they're doing, but it seems as if Mandy likes being there a little too much."

"I agree. All she wanted to talk about was all the wonderful things she's seen so far on the island, and Mandy even mentioned . . ."

Gideon took a step toward her. "What else were you going to say?"

"Mandy admitted she wished she could stay on Kauai forever. Of course, I'm sure she didn't mean it. She's probably caught up in the excitement of being there, where the weather is warm and all the tropical flowers and trees are so pretty. I felt the same way when I was there, although I did miss home and looked forward to returning."

"You don't think Mandy will decide to stay in Hawaii, do you?" Gideon clasped Barbara's wrist, sending a strange tingling sensation all the way up her arm.

Disappointed when he let go, she tried to reassure him. "I'm sure she and Ellen will come home as soon as Makaio is better. From what Mandy said, his leg is slowly healing, but he needs to stay off it right now."

"Sure hope you're right. I hate to say this, but Mandy seems different. When we talked this afternoon, I had a horrible feeling she's forgotten where she belongs."

"With all she and Ellen have gone through, they've had to adjust to a new environment. Once she gets home, things will go back to what they were before our trip." Barbara moved back toward the door. "Guess I'd better get the spools of thread put out. Don't lose hope, Gideon. Mandy will be home soon."

As Barbara headed for the notions aisle, she glanced back and saw Gideon carrying a larger box out of the room. *How could Mandy treat her boyfriend like this? Doesn't she realize how worried he is and how much he misses her?* She placed the box of thread on the floor. *If Gideon was my boyfriend, I would have come home by now. Mandy and Ellen are doing a good deed, but I'm sure the Hawaiian couple could have found someone else to help out at their bed-and-breakfast.*

Kapaa

"Where are you going?" Ken's mother asked when he grabbed a cardboard box and started for the back door.

"Over to the B&B. I'm taking them more eggs and poultry. Remember when Luana called and asked for those?"

Mom nodded. "You've been over there quite a bit lately, Son, and staying longer than normal. What's grabbed your interest all of a sudden at Luana and Makaio's place?"

Heat crept up the back of Ken's neck. "Nothing, Mom. I'll be back as soon as I can." It was one thing to admit he was looking for excuses to go there, but another thing to acknowledge the reason why. Ken was not going to admit he was interested in Mandy or that he looked for any excuse to see her. Not that it mattered. She'd be leaving as soon as Makaio's leg healed, and then he'd probably never see her again. Besides, they were worlds apart. She'd return to her plain Amish life in Indiana, and he would remain here on Kauai, taking care of chickens. So there was no point in telling Mandy how he'd begun to feel about her.

"Whew! It sure can get humid here." Mandy wiped the perspiration from her forehead with a handkerchief. "I wonder if it's going to rain." She and Ellen had spent most of the afternoon pulling weeds in Luana's garden. It hadn't been so bad when they'd first come out, but as the sun grew higher, the heat increased, along with the muggy air. "This isn't the kind of weather they're having back home. Isn't it strange to be doing this type of work in December?"

Ellen nodded.

"Think how nice it would be if we could garden all year. Our lives would be a lot different, jah?"

"You're right." Ellen paused for a drink of water. "Speaking of home, how did your conversation with Gideon go?"

Mandy swatted at a pesky fly buzzing her head. "Not well. I could hear the disappointment in his voice, and he seemed offended. In fact, when I told him we wouldn't be back for Christmas, he got kind of huffy."

"It's no wonder, Mandy. He misses you."

"I miss him, too, but we're needed here right now."

Ellen sighed. "The hardest part of being gone from home for me is missing Christmas with my family."

"I'll miss my family, as well, but we can celebrate the holiday with Luana and Makaio, like we did Thanksgiving. To me, they're starting to feel like family." Mandy thought about the delicious turkey dinner Luana had prepared with their help. In addition to Ailani and Oke joining them,

Luana had invited the four guests at the bed-and-breakfast to enjoy the holiday meal with them. Mandy was impressed with her hospitality and kindness. It was one more similarity to the way her Amish family and friends reacted to those who visited their homes.

"I don't know about you, but I'm more than ready to take a break." Ellen set her small shovel aside, stood, and flexed her back. "Let's go inside and see if Luana needs us to do anything else."

"If not, maybe we can do something fun before supper."

"What do you want to do?"

"Why don't we go to the beach? You haven't been there yet, and it's a perfect day with no wind at all."

"I don't know." Ellen's eyes blinked rapidly as she tapped her chin. "With the sun being so hot, we might get burned."

"We have our sunscreen." Mandy gathered up her weeding utensils and was almost to the house when Ken's rig pulled in.

"Aloha!" he called after he got out of his SUV. "I brought some eggs and poultry."

Mandy waited for him to join them on the grass. "Luana will be glad, because we're getting low on eggs."

"I can take the box inside to her," Ellen offered.

"You don't have to. I'll take it myself." Ken smiled. "What have you two been up to this afternoon?"

"Weeding, but now we're ready for a break." Mandy returned his smile.

"I could use one myself. How'd you like to join me for a hot dog and some shave ice?"

"Is it really called *shave ice,* or did you leave off the *d*?" Mandy questioned.

"Nope. Here in Hawaii, it's known as shave ice."

Mandy smiled at Ellen. "Seems like we learn new things about Hawaii all the time."

Ellen nodded quickly before making her way to the house.

"So do you want to get something to eat with me?" Ken asked.

Mandy nodded. "Could we go to the beach for a bit when we're done eating? Ellen hasn't been there yet since we arrived on Kauai."

"Not a problem. As soon as I give the eggs to Luana, I'd be happy to take you both there."

As Ellen walked barefoot along the shoreline with Ken and Mandy, she noticed how well they got along. The way they laughed and talked nonstop, walking close to each other, made it almost seem as if they were a courting couple. Of course, how could it be? Mandy's boyfriend was waiting for her back home.

When Ellen stepped into the water, she couldn't get over how warm it felt. The waves lapped against her ankles as the sand moved slowly away, tickling her bare feet.

"Hey, look at the seal over there!" Ken pointed as the creature swam out of the water and came onto the beach.

"Do you see many seals here?" Mandy asked, reaching into her satchel for her camera.

"Not all the time, so it's worth a few pictures."

They watched the seal awhile, then moved down the beach, visiting and walking in the surf. The edge of Mandy's dress had gotten wet, and Ellen noticed hers had, too. It was hard to guess where the water would hit her legs as it rolled onto the beach. The breeze blowing on her face felt good, as the sun warmed her exposed skin.

"Hey, come take a look at this." Ken stopped walking and bent down to scoop something off the sand.

"What is it?" Ellen moved closer.

"It's a piece of coral." Ken held it out. "You'll find pieces like this in many places on the beach."

"It reminds me of a head of cauliflower, only it's tan instead of white." Ellen reached out to touch it.

"We should each take a small piece," Mandy suggested. "Then, when we return home, we can have part of the island with us."

Ellen felt a bit of relief. *At least Mandy is talking about going home. I hope this means she has no crazy ideas about staying here on Kauai. If she did, there would be a lot of disappointed people back home.*

CHAPTER 19

"I've said this before, but I can't begin to tell you how much I appreciate your help." Luana examined a vase as she, Mandy, and Ellen went through some things she planned to sell at her two-day yard sale, which would start the next day. "You both have been a God-send to us."

"We're glad to do it." Mandy hoped they would make enough money to help with Makaio's hospital bills. He had health insurance, but it didn't cover all his medical expenses. Luana had mentioned they'd also receive some aid from their church, and several people had brought things over for them to sell at the yard sale. It did Mandy's heart good to see how the people from Makaio and Luana's church had rallied to help them out financially. It reminded her of how things were done at home when an Amish church member had a need.

"You have a lot of nice items here." Ellen

held a photo of pink primroses.

"The picture you're holding used to hang in one of our guest rooms, but we replaced it sometime ago with a painting a friend made for us." Luana sighed. "Unfortunately, we can't keep everything. Since the primrose picture is a reproduction I found at our local thrift store, it doesn't have any real sentimental value." She picked up a small photograph. "This, on the other hand, has a lot of sentimental value."

"What is it?" Mandy leaned toward Luana as she handed her the photo.

"It's a picture of the quilt Makaio and I received as a wedding present from my parents." Sighing, she lifted her hands and let them fall into her lap. "It's been missing since we moved here from the Big Island."

"It looks like a beautiful quilt." Mandy looked closer at the picture. "The detail is beautiful, and I like the blue and white colors."

Tears welled in Luana's dark eyes as she nodded. "My mother made it. She even sewed Makaio's and my initials in one corner of the quilt." After Mandy handed the picture back to her, Luana stared at it with a somber expression. "I fear my mother's precious wedding gift may have been thrown out or accidentally given to charity before our move."

Mandy clasped Luana's hand, gently squeezing her fingers. "It's hard to lose something meaningful."

"It is, but life moves on, and I try to remember not to focus on *things.*" Luana smiled. "Our relationship to God and people is what truly counts."

Friday morning, things were hectic at the B&B. Every room was booked, and Luana had to make sure breakfast was ready for her guests, as well as check that everything was set up as it should be for the yard sale later on. Fortunately, it wouldn't be open to the public until ten, which gave her enough time to feed her guests first. She was thankful Ellen and Mandy had offered to go outside right after breakfast, in case anyone showed up early.

When Makaio first woke up, he'd complained about his leg bothering him, but now, as they sat down for their morning meal, he shared with their guests some information about Kauai and said he'd be willing to answer any questions about island living.

"One thing you should be aware of is the vog," Makaio announced, reaching for his cup of coffee.

"What's a vog?" Ellen asked, as she served more coffee to their guests.

"I'd like to hear about this, as well," a middle-aged woman from Oregon said.

"The vog is sort of like fog, only it's from the volcanic ash on the Big Island." Makaio's nose twitched. "Depending on the intensity of the ash, it can bother some people, causing sneezing, congestion, and burning eyes."

"I hope it doesn't occur during our time here," the woman said. "I have enough problems with allergies and such."

"Hopefully, you won't have to deal with it." Luana gestured to the bowl of miso soup, along with some chopped green onions, small cubed tofu, and steamed white rice. "Miso soup is from Japan. Some people on this island enjoy having it for breakfast."

"Not me," Makaio announced with a shake of his head. "I prefer Spam and eggs."

Luana rolled her eyes. *Some things never change.*

From the minute the yard sale opened, until a few minutes before it was time to close up for the day, things had been busy.

"We did well today. I think there were some tourists browsing the tables. They seemed interested in the jewelry and wooden knickknacks I had for sale." Luana smiled. "Thank you, Ellen and Mandy. I couldn't have done it without your help. I'm glad Ailani was up to staying with her father while we were out here in the yard today, too."

"We were happy to help." Ellen picked up a roll of plastic. Then she and Mandy covered everything on the tables and furniture in case it rained during the night.

"Luana, I have a question. What kind of birds are those?" Mandy pointed to several small birds on the lawn. "They look like miniature doves."

"You're right, they are. They're zebra doves, and you'll find them all over the Hawaiian Islands."

"They sure are cute," Ellen commented.

"Yes, but they can be quite brazen — especially when there's food around. When we eat outside, I've seen them swoop right down and, if we're not looking, steal whatever's on our plates." Luana yawned. "Oh my. This is one night I wish I didn't have to fix supper." She rubbed a sore spot on her back. "I'm exhausted."

"Don't worry about supper," Mandy said. "Ellen and I will take care of it. Why don't you go inside and put up your feet? We'll be in to get things started as soon as we gather up the empty boxes."

"Mahalo." Luana gave them both a hug and hurried into the house, thankful yet again for everything the young women had done.

"Do you have a problem with me staying over at the B&B awhile and joining them for supper?" Ken asked when his mother handed him a box of food she'd prepared for him to take over. "No doubt, they'll ask me to stay."

With hands on her hips, the small wrinkles around her eyes deepened. "Really, Ken? I thought we talked the other day about you spending so much time over there."

"I'm not a kid, Mom." Ken raised his voice slightly, to make a point. "In case you forgot, I'm twenty-three years old."

"No, I haven't forgotten."

"And it's not like I'll be shirking my duties here, 'cause I'm done for the day. It's Dan's turn to feed and water the chickens this evening." He shifted the box in his arms.

"I'm well aware of that. I just think —"

"Go ahead and say it, Mom; you think I'm spending too much time at the B&B."

"Is it about those Amish girls? Are you interested in one of them?"

"I've gotta go, Mom. This food will be getting cold if I don't head out now."

"All right. We can discuss this some other time." Mom reached out and touched Ken's hair. "When are you planning to get a haircut? You're starting to look like a shaggy dog."

"I like my hair this way." Ken swung his head side to side, hoping to make a point. "See you later." He turned and hurried out the door.

The sun felt intense on his shoulders as he headed to his vehicle. *I shouldn't have gotten defensive with Mom. I'll apologize when I get home. Are my feelings for Mandy so obvious? If I had admitted the way I've begun to feel about her, what would Mom have said?*

Ken's parents had only spoken to Mandy and Ellen a few times at church. Maybe it was time they got to know them better.

"This chicken casserole your *makuahine* made for us sure hits the spot." Makaio licked his lips. "Be sure to tell her mahalo."

"I will." Ken reached for a piece of bread and spread some guava jelly over it.

Having learned a few Hawaiian words, Mandy understood *makuahine* meant "mother," and *mahalo* was the word for saying "Thank you." Thanks to Luana, Makaio, and Ken's teaching, she'd learned how to count to ten in Hawaiian, as well as say the days of the week and months of the year. When she returned home, it would be fun to teach these words to her family.

"How'd the yard sale go today?" Ken asked Luana, before glancing briefly at Mandy.

"It went well. We made several hundred dollars and are hoping to do equally well tomorrow. I opened a hall closet a while ago and found a few more things to add to one of the tables for tomorrow's sale. I might look around the house some more after dinner and see if there's anything else I can get rid of." Luana looked at Makaio. "How about selling some of the Hawaiian shirts you've outgrown?"

He shook his head. "No way! I'm not parting with any of my shirts. I can still wear most of them, you know." Makaio stuffed a fork full of casserole in his mouth and winked at her.

"Back home, our yard sales draw a lot of folks, too." Ellen reached for her glass of mango flavored lemonade. "It's amazing what people will often buy."

Mandy nodded. "Some folks' unwanted stuff ends up becoming someone else's treasure," she added.

"Wish I could have been here to help, but I had deliveries to make and was gone most of the day." Ken picked up his glass.

"We're glad you're here now and could join us for the evening meal." Luana handed Ken the bowl of fruit salad Mandy and Ellen had made.

"Same here." He grinned at Mandy, and she felt the heat of a blush cascade over her face.

Every time Ken looked at her, she felt something undeniable pass between them. *Maybe it's my imagination or wishful thinking.* She glanced at Ellen, wondering why she'd been so quiet. Except for the comment about yard sales, she'd been rather silent since they'd sat down at the table. *Maybe she's tired. We did have a pretty full day.*

Ken leaned closer to Mandy as he passed her the dish of purple sweet potatoes. "I was wondering if you and Ellen would like to take a tour of my parents' chicken farm after church on Sunday. Afterward, you can stay for dinner."

"Seeing how the chickens are raised would be interesting." Mandy looked at Ellen. "Don't you think so?"

"I suppose, but we might be needed here to help Luana with the Sunday meal."

"It won't be necessary," Luana was quick to say. "You two have been working hard lately; you deserve to enjoy a meal at the Williamses' place." Luana fingered the yellow plumeria tucked in her hair. "I want you to go and have a good time. We'll be fine on our own a few hours."

"It's settled then." Ken took a drink. "I'll look forward to seeing you both on Sunday."

Mandy looked forward to it as well — more than she cared to admit.

"How's your leg feeling, Makaio?" Ken asked.

"Not so bad, but I'll be glad when the cast comes off." His nose scrunched as he looked down at his leg. "I'm gettin' awful tired of sitting around, doing nothin' but watching TV all day."

"You don't have to watch TV." Luana's eyebrows raised.

"What else is there for me to do? I sure can't do any work."

"You could work on a word search or crossword puzzle." Smiling, Luana squeezed his arm. "I read somewhere those are good for stimulating a person's brain."

"It's my leg needing help, not my brain. And to make matters worse, my leg itches like crazy."

As Mandy ate the rest of her meal, Luana

and Makaio's playful bickering caused her to think about her parents. *Dad can be stubborn and sometimes moody whenever he's faced with a challenge or when Mom wants him to do something he doesn't want to do. But they love each other, and as Dad sometimes says, "It's okay to disagree."*

There'd been times when Gideon acted moody, like the last time they'd spoken on the phone. *He's upset because I'm still in Hawaii.* Mandy's gaze went from Makaio to Luana. *If he could meet these wonderful people, maybe he'd understand.*

CHAPTER 20

"Look at the glorious sunrise God has given us this beautiful Sunday morning!" Mandy exclaimed as she stood at the bedroom window. "You won't see anything at home comparable to this."

Ellen moved over to stand beside her. "It is lovely, but we have sunrises in Indiana, too."

"Not rising from the ocean." Mandy opened the window. "I wish we had a view of the water from here. But then, it might be hard to get anything done. I'd want to stay at the window and admire the ocean all day." She drew a deep breath. "You can even smell the lovely fragrance of the flowers on the breeze. How much more *fehlerfrei* can it get?"

"You know, Mandy, not everything in Hawaii is perfect." Ellen's sharp tone was a surprise.

Raising her eyebrows, Mandy looked at

her friend. "Course not, but it's what I dreamed of, and even more. Ever since my cousin told me about her trip to Hawaii, I've wanted to come. I like it here on Kauai." Hugging her arms around herself, Mandy moved away from the window and flopped down on her freshly made bed. "I'd love to live here, in fact."

"You're not serious, I hope."

"Jah, I am."

"Well, I hope your fancy for this island fades in the near future, because we'll be heading back home as soon as Makaio is in good shape again."

"I'm well aware." Mandy pulled her long hair aside, but instead of securing it into a bun, she let it hang loosely across her back. "I wish I could wear my hair down sometimes."

"You mean like when you're going to bed?"

"Jah."

Ellen stared. "Are you forgetting our Amish customs?"

"Of course not, but . . ." Mandy stood. "Never mind. I was only thinking out loud." She quickly pulled her hair into a bun at the back of her head and set her head covering in place. "Guess we'd better help Luana with breakfast so we'll be ready for church when Ken picks us up."

Ellen followed Mandy across the room, stepping in front of her. "Before we go, there's something I'd like to ask you."

Mandy halted, nearly colliding with her friend. "What is it?"

"Is it the island you've fallen in love with, or is it Ken?"

"I'm not acquainted well enough with Ken to declare any love for him, but . . ." Mandy turned her head to the side, unable to look at Ellen. "In all honesty, I do enjoy being around him. And if he were Amish . . ." Her voice trailed off. "Never mind. You wouldn't understand."

"You're right, I don't understand. But I do understand one thing. You're not the same person who began this journey with me. You rarely talk about home or Gideon anymore. And now you're wishing to live in some fantasy world, imagining what it would be like to live here on Kauai." Ellen paused, "Whether you're willing to admit it or not, I believe you have feelings for Ken, and they go beyond friendship."

Mandy's throat tightened as tears welled in her eyes. "It doesn't matter how I feel about him, because once we leave here I'll probably never see Ken again."

■ ■ ■ ■

"Too bad Luana and Makaio couldn't join us for church," Ellen whispered as she and Mandy took seats inside the sanctuary. "When Makaio said he wasn't feeling up to going, one of us should have volunteered to stay with him so Luana could go."

"Maybe, but he'd probably rather have his wife stay with him instead of one of us." Mandy glanced at the platform at the front of the church, where Ken had gone to tune his ukulele. This morning he wore a pair of tan-colored slacks and a blue shirt with white palm trees on it.

Most of the men attending this church dressed casually, in lightweight clothes, such as shorts and Hawaiian-print shirts. Even some of the women wore shorts or capris. Mandy felt out of place in her Amish dress and white head covering. Of course, she would have been uncomfortable wearing a muumuu, since she'd never worn anything other than her traditional Amish dress while attending church at home. For some reason, though, here on Kauai, she felt like stepping out of her comfort zone.

When the musicians started playing at the front of the church, she focused on learning the new song the worship team sang. It still seemed strange not to sing traditional Amish hymns found in the *Ausbund.* However, she enjoyed many of the choruses she'd already learned at this church. A couple of times, Mandy tapped her foot in time with the music, until Ellen looked at her in disapproval.

Mandy had been away from home so long, she'd lost track of which weeks were off-Sundays for her home church district. On those days, her family usually visited a neighboring district, and on a few occasions stayed home and had private devotions. *I wonder what church district my family will attend today. If Mom and Dad were here right now, I bet they'd feel out of place — especially with the music and the casual way people dress.*

Ellen felt a bit uncomfortable with the loud music, but she enjoyed the message the pastor preached near the end of the church service. He mentioned how sometimes God provides for His people in surprising ways, as He did the Israelites when they were hungry. He sent them manna from heaven.

When the ship left without us, God provided for Mandy and me by guiding us to a place we could stay and giving us the privilege of helping Luana and Makaio in their time of need. Ellen shifted on her seat. *I need to stop feeling sorry for myself because I'm so far from home and do whatever I can to make the best of my time here on Kauai.*

They would be going with Ken to his parents' home after church for a meal and a tour of their poultry farm. It would be interesting, and another opportunity to do something fun. At times, Ellen felt as if she were intruding, but she was glad he'd invited both of them, and not Mandy alone. It would give her a chance to keep an eye on things and make sure a serious relationship wasn't developing between Ken and Mandy.

"Thank you for a delicious meal, Mrs. Williams." Mandy leaned back in her chair after they'd finished eating dinner.

"Yes, thank you." Ellen placed her napkin on the plate.

Ken's mother smiled. "You're welcome. Oh, and please call me Vickie."

"And I'm Charles, but you can call me Chuck." Ken's father reached over and affectionately patted his wife's arm. "We don't stand on formalities around here. I'm only sorry you didn't get to meet our youngest son. He's having dinner at a friend's house today."

"No worries. You can meet Dan some other time." Ken pushed away from the table. "Are you two ready for a tour of our poultry farm?"

"You can show it to us after we help your mother with the dishes." Ellen stood, reaching for her plate.

Vickie waved her hand. "It's okay. Charles will help me. He's always been good about doing the dishes."

He smiled and nodded. "Go ahead, Son. Show your guests around the place."

Ken escorted Mandy and Ellen outside and immediately began to explain about poultry farming. "You're probably aware of this already, but the chickens we raise for eggs are called 'layer chickens,' and the chickens which are raised for their meat production are called 'broiler chickens.' Literally billions of chickens are being raised throughout the world as a good source of food from their eggs and meat." He gestured to the chickens roaming about their acreage. "Here, we grow our chickens organically, using the free-range method. Commercial hens generally start laying eggs at the age of twelve to twenty weeks. By the time they are twenty-five weeks, they are laying eggs regularly."

Fascinated, Mandy watched the chickens run around, squawking and pecking at the ground. "Do they stay out all night?"

"Nope. Only during the day. At night, they're kept inside our chicken houses to keep them safe from predators and unfavorable weather. Our indoor facilities need to have an adequate drainage system, good ventilation, and appropriate protection from winds, all types of predators, and excessive cold, heat, or dampness. This system also requires less feed than cage and barn systems." Ken pointed to the buildings they housed the chickens in. "The poultry manure from the free-range chickens is used as fertilizer for our garden and fruit trees."

"Is there something specific that sets organic poultry growing and traditional growing apart?" Ellen questioned.

"Yes. The main differences between the traditional free-range poultry farming and organic farming is that with the organic method, a certain species of poultry bird are raised in small groups with low stocking density. The organic system also has some restrictions in the use of synthetic yolk colorants, water, feed, medications, and other feed additives. We feed our chickens high quality, fresh, and nutritious food to ensure their good health, proper growth, and high production."

"In addition to providing Luana and Makaio's B&B with eggs and poultry, who else buys what you raise?" Mandy lifted her head to meet Ken's gaze.

"We sell to the local farmers' markets, and also some of the bigger supermarkets on the island." He smiled. "People are always looking for locally raised, organic eggs and poultry."

"Thanks for explaining everything, Ken." Mandy wiped her forehead. The day had turned out to be quite warm.

"We'd better go back inside where it's cooler," Ken suggested. "But before we go, would you like to see our swimming pool?"

"With the ocean so near, I'm surprised you have a pool," Ellen stated.

"I actually prefer to swim in the ocean, but Mom likes the pool because there's no sand." Ken led them to the pool on the other side of the house. "You two are welcome to come use it any time."

"The water looks inviting, but I'd rather not."

"Really? How come?"

"Mandy doesn't know how to swim," Ellen interjected.

Mandy's heart beat rapidly as she turned

to Ellen. She couldn't believe her friend had blurted that out. "Ellen . . ."

"No problem there. I'd be more than happy to give you a swimming lesson. I'm not bragging, but if anyone can teach you how to swim, it's me." Ken pointed to himself. "I've had lifeguard training, so I promise I won't let you drown. Oh, and if either of you needs a swimsuit, I'd be happy to take you shopping." As if the matter was settled, he started walking toward the house.

Mandy swallowed a couple of times as she scanned the outlying areas of the pool. It was stunningly landscaped with a different array of flowers, thick with blossoms. They formed a private border, cut off from the rest of the Williames's property. There was no grass in this section of the yard. Instead, large pieces of slate in different shapes and sizes covered the entire area, right up to the water's edge. A table and chairs sat in the far corner, and in the other was an open fire-pit, surrounded by several more chairs. The kidney-shaped pool and its aqua-blue color looked inviting, with the sparkling water so clear, she could see the bottom. On the end where the water was a deeper blue, a diving board jutted out. Even as nice as it was, Mandy wasn't sure she had the nerve to let Ken teach her how to swim.

Just thinking about being in the water, especially over her head, sent a chill up her spine.

Middlebury

Gideon wasn't sure how he'd made it through church or the meal afterward. One thing he was certain of: he couldn't wait to get home. For the last two days he'd felt fatigued and irritable, but figured it was due to missing Mandy. Today, however, he realized he might be coming down with something. His forehead felt unusually hot, and his throat had a twinge of soreness.

As soon as I get home, I'm going to take a nap, because I'll bet I've got the flu, he told himself as he climbed into his buggy and gathered up the reins.

Gideon was glad church had been held at a neighboring farm, so he didn't have far to go. As crummy as he felt right now, he wasn't sure he could go more than a mile.

His horse picked up speed as soon as they approached his folks' house. Gideon didn't have to direct the animal down the driveway, because Dash galloped there by himself.

Gideon unhitched the horse, using all the strength he could muster, and let him run free in the pasture. Since they hadn't gone far, the horse hadn't worked up a lather. He would put the buggy away later on.

Plodding through what snow was left in the yard, Gideon made his way to the house. He stopped and leaned against the porch post, listening to a woodpecker tapping nearby. After scanning the yard, he located the bird in a dead tree.

Gideon's head pounded. Still, he remained where he was, watching the woodpecker at work. The red-headed bird skillfully tapped at the loose bark, searching for bugs underneath. As a chunk of the tree's bark broke away, Gideon looked a little closer, realizing the bird must have worked on this particular tree before. Not only were there pieces of bark scattered all around, but small piles of wood particles covered the ground like sawdust on a lumberyard's floor.

Gideon jumped when his mother's voice startled him. "I'm surprised to see you back already." Since Mom had stayed home with a cold this morning, she greeted him at the door. "Ach, Gideon, what's on your face?"

"What is it?" He pressed his palms against his warm cheeks. "I'm not feeling well. I need to go lay down."

She touched his forehead. "You're running a *fiewer,* and from the looks of those little bumps on your face, I'm sure you have the *wasserpareble.*"

"The chicken pox? Oh, no! This is not what I need!"

CHAPTER 21

Kapaa

After all the rooms had been cleaned and the beds were made, Ellen took a walk outside to enjoy the sun for a bit. As she moved around the yard, breathing in the fragrance of the plumeria, with their pretty yellow petals, she smiled. The birds were happy, singing and fluttering overhead in the palms and other trees in the Palus' yard.

Moving toward Luana's vegetable garden, she watched the bees buzzing busily around the toppling cherry tomato plants. Ellen couldn't help reaching out to pluck a perfectly ripe piece of fruit. She looked at it a few seconds, enjoying the feel of the sun-warmed tomato in her hand, before popping it in her mouth and savoring the fresh, rich flavor. *Nothing compares to homegrown food from the garden,* she thought, heading back to the house.

Ellen entered the kitchen and went to look

at the wall calendar. It was hard to believe, but in eleven days it would be Christmas. Never had she felt so homesick. Being away from her family this time of the year made it even harder. She had to admit, though, Thanksgiving hadn't turned out too bad.

She groaned inwardly, trying to convince herself to make the best of the situation. *Christmas will probably be nice, but it won't seem like the holidays without snow. I'm sure back home they'll have a beautiful white Christmas.*

Heaving a sigh, she moved away from the calendar and poured herself a cup of herbal tea. The delicious aroma of macadamia nut wafted up to her nose as she brought the mug to her lips.

I need to quit feeling sorry for myself and get busy on the Christmas cards I want to send to my friends and family back home. Ellen set her teacup down. She had a few letters to write, as well.

Ken had invited them to see some sights on the island after he'd gotten off work this afternoon, but Ellen didn't want to go. She'd promised to help Luana decorate the B&B for Christmas, which she planned on doing as soon as she finished her cards and letters.

Ellen went to her room and found the

supplies she'd picked up at the craft store the other day. Mandy had bought some, too, and they'd decided to use the same colors and rubber stamps to create their cards.

At the kitchen table, Ellen set everything out. She began by cutting the different-sized colored papers to stamp and glue together. *I hope Mandy works on hers soon, or she won't get them sent out in time. I know she enjoys seeing the sights with Ken, but she's been shirking her duties lately.*

Ellen liked helping Luana and meeting the guests. It reminded her of being at the B&B where she'd worked at home. Plus, she had established a friendship with Luana and enjoyed their talks. It was the one thing she would miss the most when they returned to Indiana.

"I can't wait for you to see Opaekaa Falls," Ken said as he drove Mandy up Kuamoo Road. "From the overlook, you'll have a spectacular view. The falls are at their best in full sunlight, so I'm glad you were free to go with me this afternoon."

"I'm looking forward to seeing it." Mandy didn't know if her enthusiasm was for seeing the falls or even more of being with Ken. He sure loved the islands, and she was falling in love with Hawaii, too. Mandy felt energized here. Every morning when she awoke, she could hardly contain her eagerness to see what new discoveries awaited.

"Oh, and if you're wondering about the fall's name," Ken added, "*Opae* is the Hawaiian word for shrimp, and *ka'a* means 'rolling'. It dates back to days when shrimp roamed the river and were seen rolling in the raging waters at the base of the falls. Also, across the road from the falls overlook is another lookout over the Wailua River Valley. From there you can get a good look at where *Raiders of the Lost Ark* was filmed."

Mandy's forehead wrinkled. *"Raiders of the Lost Ark?"*

"Yeah. It's a movie. You do go to movies, right?"

She shook her head. "Some Amish young people go to movies during their *rumschpringe,* but —"

"What's a rumschpringe?"

"It's a time of running around, before we make a decision about whether we want to join the Amish church or not."

Ken crossed his arms. "What if you don't join the church? Would you be shunned?"

"No." Ken's question caught Mandy off guard. She couldn't blame him for not knowing how shunning worked in the Amish community, but it was a bit unsettling to talk about because many English people had the wrong idea.

"Shunning is a form of church discipline," she explained. "It's meant to bring a wayward member back into fellowship with the church and body of believers." She clasped her hands together, struggling with her own desires. "I have not yet joined the church. If I decide not to, I won't be shunned."

"How come you haven't joined?" He glanced at her quickly, then back at the road ahead.

"I'm not sure it's the right thing for me." Mandy struggled for words, but as Ken pulled his rig into the fall's parking lot, she spoke again. "My parents are expecting me to join, and they'll be disappointed if I don't, but in the end, the final decision is mine."

"I see. Well, I hope you make the right decision." Ken turned off the engine, hopped out, and came around to open the door for her. "When we leave here, I'll drive you up to Wailua Falls. It's a double-tiered waterfall, and if we're lucky and the sun is at the right angle, we'll see a beautiful rainbow extending from the base of the falls in the mist. Wailua Falls is about eighty-five feet high — although some people say it's twice that height — and it drops into a thirty-foot-deep pool. During high flow, the falls often have a third tier."

Mandy took a deep breath. "There's so much I didn't know about Kauai, but I'm excited to find out."

She followed Ken over to where several others stood along a chainlink fence, and peered out toward the falling waters. "It's so beautiful." Mandy readied her camera to take some snapshots.

A lady next to them turned and asked if they'd like a picture together with the falls behind them. Before Mandy could reply, Ken spoke up. "Thanks. That'd be great."

The woman took a few pictures, then handed the camera back to Mandy and moved aside.

I wonder how the photos will turn out. Mandy gazed at the falls spilling over the ledge behind them. *Does that lady think Ken and I are a courting couple? Do I dare admit, even to myself, that I wish it were so?*

"I appreciate you helping me with this." Luana took another ornament from the box as Ellen helped her decorate the Christmas tree. "I'd meant to do it sooner, but with the yard sale and taking care of Makaio, there hasn't been time."

"Believe me, I'm enjoying myself." Carefully, Ellen touched the needles of the tree. "What kind of tree is this, Luana?"

"It's a Norfolk Island pine. In Hawaii, some people order trees from the mainland, but we've always gotten ours here on the island, where they grow."

"Mandy doesn't realize what she's missing out on today." Ellen frowned. "Too bad she didn't stay and help us. But then, she hasn't been acting herself lately."

"It's all right. Ken was anxious to show her some sights, and you could certainly have joined them if you'd wanted to."

"Someone needed to stay and help with this." Ellen picked up a shiny glass ornament and hung it on the tree. "I've never decorated for Christmas before, so this all seems a bit strange to me."

Luana's mouth opened slightly. "You don't put out any decorations?"

"Only the Christmas cards we receive, and a few candles. Our focus at Christmas is on Jesus and how God sent His only Son to earth as a baby so He could later die on the cross to become our Savior."

"It's our focus, too, which is why I display this in a prominent place." Luana gestured to the Nativity set she'd placed on one end of the check-in table.

Ellen touched the baby Jesus figurine, running her finger across the smooth porcelain surface. "It's lovely."

"Do you get together with family and friends to share a meal on Christmas Day?"

"Yes, but sometimes we have to choose other days, close to the holiday, to have our family meal. Since our families are large, we can't always be together at the same time."

Luana smiled, reaching for an antique star ornament to hang on the tree. "It doesn't matter what day we celebrate, as long as we spend time with our *ohana*."

"*Ohana* means 'family,' right?"

"That's correct. Our family is important to us."

"Mine is to me, as well." Ellen stepped back to see how the tree looked. "I can smell the pine scent," she murmured.

"I like putting the tree in here for our guests to enjoy. I imagine my husband will come in and check things out when we're finished decorating. He's like a big kid at Christmas." Luana chuckled. "Normally, Makaio helps me decorate the B&B. He usually gets a new ornament for our tree every year, too. The reason he didn't come into the living room while we're doing this is because it's hard for him to sit and watch when there's work to be done. He's quite comfortable sitting on the lanai this afternoon, drinking iced tea and reading the paper." She plugged in the string of lights, then stood off to one side, no doubt to admire their work. "I love the pretty colors and how the lights play off the shiny ornaments."

"It looks very nice, and the lights do make it stand out." Ellen added another wooden ornament to the tree — this one had palm trees painted on it. "I've never had a broken bone, but I imagine it's hard for Makaio to sit around when he was used to being so active."

"Yes. Makaio is not a patient man when it comes to being idle."

They continued to visit as the room was transformed. "You may have noticed," Luana said, "there are poinsettias blooming in many yards in our area. They're not potted, but grow quite large and bloom around this time of the year."

"Actually, I haven't noticed." Ellen smiled. "But I did observe the red-and-green leis you've put around the candles."

After they finished decorating, Luana suggested they go to the kitchen and bake some special Christmas cookies her mother used to make when she was a girl.

Mandy's heartbeat picked up speed when

she and Ken climbed aboard the small boat that would take them up the Wailua River to see Fern Grotto. She had worn her lavender muumuu. It blended well with the tropical flowers she'd seen near one of the waterfalls.

"I think you're gonna enjoy the ride up to the grotto," Ken said as they sat on one of the wooden benches on the right side of the boat. "The scenery is beautiful."

"I can already see that," she responded as the boat pulled away from the dock.

"This is the only navigable river in Hawaii. It's fed by Mt. Waialeale, one of the wettest spots in the world. During the two-mile trip upstream, we'll be entertained with songs and stories of old Hawaii." He raised his eyebrows playfully. "You can even participate in a hula lesson if you like."

Mandy's face heated. "I don't think so. It's not something I'd be comfortable doing."

"It's okay. I was only teasing."

As they started up the river, Mandy was amazed at the beautiful mangrove trees lining the river's banks, as well as the colorful foliage. *If only we had something like this back home.*

When the boat reached the Fern Grotto landing, they took a short nature walk through a lovely rainforest. As they approached a fern-covered lava cave, the highlight of their tour, Mandy's breath caught in her throat. Colorful tropical plants grew in and around the cave. Their tour guide explained the grotto was one of Kauai's geological wonders and had formed millions of years ago. At one time the cave was open to the public, but it was no longer accessible.

They stood admiring the grotto for several minutes as the musicians who'd also ridden on the boat sang a few songs. Mandy felt as though she was in the middle of a fairytale.

As they began the walk back to the boat, Ken halted and leaned close to her ear. "You look nice in that dress, but there's something missing."

"Oh? What's missing?"

Mandy's heart beat a little faster, and her face warmed when he picked a Hibiscus flower and stuck it behind her right ear.

"Wearing it this way means you're not married." Unexpectedly, he reached out and took hold of her hand.

At a loss for words, all she could do was manage a smile. She'd had a fantastic time and wished the day didn't have to end. *Does Ken have feelings for me? Does he suspect how I've begun to feel about him? It would be wrong for us to become involved when we live so far apart — not to mention, he's English and I'm Amish. Besides, I don't think Mom and Dad would approve. Then there's Gideon — how would he feel if I broke up with him and didn't join the church? Oh, so many questions.*

CHAPTER 22

Middlebury

Except for a few remaining scabs on his arms, Gideon was pretty much over the chicken pox. He'd hated being sick and missing time from work, but at least he didn't have to deal with the itching anymore. When the pox had flared, he'd given in to the temptation to scratch on more than one occasion. Remembering the ordeal made his skin crawl. *I'll probably be left with some scars.* He let out a snort as he sat at a table in the back of the upholstery shop to eat his lunch.

"It's good to see you working again." Jim Nicolson sat beside Gideon and opened his lunch pail. He was the only English man working at the shop.

Gideon nodded. "The morning went by fast. Can't believe it's time for lunch already."

"So you're feeling all right now?"

"Physically, I'm fine, but emotionally, I'm a wreck."

"What's the problem?" Jim took out a sandwich and pulled off the cellophane wrap.

"My girlfriend, Mandy. She's still in Hawaii." Gideon grunted, slowly shaking his head.

"Is that so? Figured she'd be back by now."

Gideon poured coffee from his thermos into a cup. "She and her friend Ellen got stranded on the island of Kauai, so now they're helping out at a bed-and-breakfast there."

"To earn some money for their trip home?"

"No. The man who owns the B&B fell off the roof and broke his leg. Mandy and Ellen are helping the man's wife run the place while he's laid up." Gideon finished his coffee then dug into his lunch container and removed his tuna sandwich. Not one of his favorites, but busy as she was, Mom had taken time to make lunch for him this morning, so he would eat it without complaint.

"Sounds like a charitable thing they're doing."

"Yes, and I can't fault her for it. But she

won't be here for the holidays, and it won't seem like Christmas without her."

"Any idea when she'll come home?"

"Nope. It's hard enough I haven't seen Mandy in a long time, not to mention we missed being together at Thanksgiving. But there's something else that's been nagging me even more."

"Oh?" Jim bit into his bologna sandwich.

Gideon poured another cup of coffee. "Mandy rarely ever calls me."

"Why don't you call her? Do you have the number there?"

"I have called, but she's usually too busy to say more than a few words. Sometimes she's not there at all." He frowned, rubbing his arm where a few scabs remained. "Once when I called, I was told she was out with someone named Ken, who was showing her around. Do you think she's avoiding me?"

"I wouldn't worry too much, Gideon. Your girlfriend probably wants to enjoy the beautiful island." Jim stared off for a moment. "Years ago, I was on Oahu for a short while. I'm sure it's changed a lot since then. It was a nice place to visit, but the cost of living is high — at least, compared to what we're used to here in Middlebury." He leaned back in his chair, sipping from his can of soda. "When do you expect your girlfriend to come home?"

Gideon shrugged, turning his palms up. "All I know is when she finally gets here, I'll be relieved." He couldn't help thinking about this fellow, Ken. Was he merely a friend showing them around the island, or could he be interested in one of the girls? If so, he hoped it wasn't Mandy.

Better not let my thoughts get carried away, he scolded himself. *Jim's probably right. I shouldn't be worried.*

Peggy and Barbara had kept busy at the fabric store from the time it opened until well past noon. Now it was time to take a break.

"It's nice we've slowed down for a while," Barbara commented. "This morning was so hectic we could hardly catch our breath."

"You're right. When the tourists locate this store, they spread the word and others come in. They take their time looking around, too, and often find plenty of trinkets to take home." Peggy pointed to the nearest shelf. "That's why I've added more variety in the store, like purses, shoes, and some small home decor."

"I have to agree. In fact, I've been eyeing a purse over there myself."

Peggy tilted her head. "Oh? Which one?"

"The black purse with a little tan on it."

Peggy left for a moment and returned with the handbag. "Consider it yours. It'll be a bonus for the hard work you've been doing around here." She handed the purse to Barbara and gave her a hug.

"Danki." Grinning, Barbara put the purse straps over her arm.

"You're welcome to eat your lunch in the back room or sit here with me." Peggy motioned to the stools behind the counter. "One of us needs to stay up front in case any customers come in."

"I'll put my new purse away then get my sandwich and join you. It's not much fun to eat alone."

"I agree." Peggy pulled her lunch box out from under the counter while Barbara went to the back room to get hers. When she returned, they sat at the small table behind them, keeping the counter free for customers' purchases.

"How is Gideon doing these days?" Barbara asked after their silent prayer.

"He's feeling much better. In fact, today is his first day back at work."

"I had the wasserpareble when I was a child." Barbara crinkled her nose. "My mamm put stockings over my hands at night so I wouldn't scratch those itchy pox. One time, my arms itched so intensely I took the stockings off and scratched." She lifted her right arm and pointed to a scar. "Here's proof I should have listened to Mom."

Peggy sighed. "Even though Gideon is old enough to know better, he did his share of scratching, too. I'm sure he'll have at least one bad *moler* to prove he scratched."

Barbara unwrapped her sandwich. "It's strange he never came down with the chickenpox when he was a boy."

"It is odd, especially because my other five *kinner* all had them. Walter and I always figured he must be immune." Peggy shook her head slowly. "Boy, were we ever wrong."

"Since Gideon is older now, I'll bet he was a lot sicker with the pox."

"Jah. He was one sick puppy the first week or so."

"I've been praying for him." Barbara's tone was sincere. She had asked about Gideon every day since he came down with the chicken pox.

Peggy frowned. *Then there's Mandy, stranded on an island and rarely bothering to call my son. Yet Gideon seems determined to talk her into joining the church and marrying him. I wish he'd reconsider.*

"Your sandwich looks good." Peggy blew on the chicken noodle soup still steaming in her thermos.

"It's chicken salad." Barbara took another bite. "If you like, I'll bring you some tomorrow."

"Sounds good. And I'll have some molasses cookies for us, too. I plan to make a few batches this evening for our bishop's wife. There'll be plenty to share."

"I'm looking forward to taking classes in the spring so I can join the church," Barbara added. "Will Gideon be joining, too?"

"He wants to, but I believe he's waiting on Mandy so they can be married."

"I thought so." Barbara's shoulders slouched a bit as she ate her sandwich.

Peggy touched her arm. "You mentioned awhile back that you were worried about Mandy, but our conversation was interrupted. Is this something you'd like to talk about now?"

Barbara shook her head. "It was nothing, really. I just wish she and Ellen were home."

Peggy didn't pursue the conversation, but she had an inkling Barbara was holding something back. *Could she possibly have feelings for Gideon herself, or is she missing her friend?*

Massaging the back of her neck where it felt a bit stiff, she continued to reflect on things. *Why couldn't my son have taken an interest in someone like Barbara? Sure wish mothers could pick out their son's wives. This girl is so caring and sweet. She's almost like a daughter to me.*

Kapaa

Mandy stood near the edge of the pool, trembling and breathing hard. She couldn't believe she'd let Ken talk her into this. Worse yet, it was awkward wearing a skirted lavender swimsuit. For modesty, she'd put a T-shirt over the top, but that didn't help her nerves. Ellen wore a similar swimsuit, only hers was dark blue. Yesterday, Ken drove them to one of the shops in town, and they'd bought the most simple-looking, modest swimsuits they could find.

Ellen was able to swim quite well and had already gotten into the water and begun doing the backstroke. While they were on the cruise ship with their friends, she would effortlessly skim through the water. Mandy envied her friend for making it look easy. She wasn't sure she could even get in the pool. All she could think about was when she'd struggled for air after her brother pulled her into the water when she was a girl. Her fear of drowning was almost paralyzing, and to this day, the trepidation gripped her. Mandy would never forget feeling certain she would drown. If not for their dad coming along and rescuing her, she probably wouldn't be here right now.

"Ready to give this a try?" Ken's deep voice, up close to Mandy's ear, caused her to jump back.

This is so embarrassing. Maybe agreeing to let him teach me to swim wasn't the best idea. She coughed, cleared her throat, and coughed again. *Maybe I should have told Ken why I'm afraid of the water.*

"You okay?" Squinting, he looked at her with obvious concern. "Are you coming down with a cold?"

"No, I . . . I'm a bit nervous right now."

"You have nothing to fear. I've taught people how to swim before, so I know what I'm doing." Ken jumped in the pool. "Hold onto the ladder and come on in. The water on this end of the pool isn't over your head."

Mandy's legs shook as she stepped onto the ladder. *Lord, help me be able to do this.*

As her feet touched the water, Ken's strong hands grasped her waist. "Easy now . . . You're doing fine."

Mandy wasn't sure if it was the nearness of him or the cool water on her legs, but a shiver went up her spine. When her feet touched the bottom, the water was as high as her waist. She turned her head toward

Ken, but for assurance, kept one hand behind her, touching the ladder.

"Okay, now." Ken looked at her with an air of confidence. "Let yourself get used to the water."

All Mandy could do was shake her head as she gripped the ladder tightly.

"See there." Ken pointed to the middle of the pool. "Those markers painted on the side of the pool are to let us know where it starts getting deeper. The pool slopes downward and then levels off to a depth of eight feet."

"I don't want to go there," Mandy whispered.

"Don't worry, we have all this area to work in, and we'll stay at this end as long as you like." Ken pointed to the shallow end where they stood. "For now, though, why don't you walk around and put your arms out to the sides? Then move them in front of you, back and forth, letting the water roll over your hands and through your fingers. Keep repeating the motion until you feel more comfortable."

Mandy did as Ken instructed. All the while, he stayed beside her, doing the same motion.

The water felt almost like velvet as it softly whooshed through her fingers. After a while,

Mandy smiled at Ken, feeling a little more at ease.

"Would you mind telling me why you never learned to swim?"

She drew a quick breath and looked away from him. One of her greatest dislikes was expressing any form of weakness, yet with Ken she felt vulnerable. Mandy tried sorting out her thoughts, but they kept getting scrambled by *what if*s. She didn't want Ken to think her reason for not wanting to swim was silly. Even though the incident happened when she was a child, it still greatly affected her.

"You don't have to tell me if you'd rather not." Ken's voice penetrated her thoughts. "I figured talking about it might help calm your nerves."

A wave of heat rushed through Mandy's body, yet it wasn't from being flustered. It was more pleasant and comforting, like sipping on warm cocoa during a cold winter's evening. The familiar sensation briefly reminded her of being back home with her family. Mandy wasn't one to vent about her problems, but her family was always there for her whenever she needed someone to talk to. Having this sort of feeling around a person she'd only known a little while was odd. *Do I trust Ken enough to share my thoughts? Perhaps telling him would be the right thing to do.* "Well, the truth is . . . I'm afraid of the water."

Mandy waited for him to respond and was surprised when he gently nudged her shoulder. "Then what made you decide to visit Hawaii, with so much water around?"

Heat flooded her cheeks. Ken was obviously confused by such a contradiction. "Just because I can't swim doesn't mean I don't enjoy staring out at the ocean. I'm okay with being around water, as long as I'm not expected to swim in it."

"All right. Makes sense." Ken looked directly at her, but the smile he wore seconds ago slowly diminished. "So why are you afraid of the water, if you don't mind me asking?"

It was difficult, but Mandy managed to explain the event that took place during her childhood. She stumbled a bit while she spoke and had a difficult time finding the right words to use, mostly because she was worried what Ken would think after she finished. Her gaze met his, but he wasn't laughing. His eyes appeared relaxed, reflecting somberness and concern.

"I'm sorry you went through that, Mandy." His voice was soft, and he spoke slowly, which was unusual since he was always so energetic. "It's frightening to think you could have drowned."

"It was, and I should've told you earlier why I didn't want to try swimming again."

"If you're having second thoughts about this, you don't have to do it. I won't force you to learn how to swim."

Mandy turned her head, noticing Ellen in the water, still swimming on her back. *I've gone plenty of years without swimming. Am I really going to let my fear stop me from learning now?*

The muscles tightened in her arms as she looked up at Ken. "No, I want to do this. I need to overcome my fear."

"Okay. You did well with the first part. Now we're gonna try something else."

"What do you mean?" Mandy eyed the ladder on the other side of the pool, wishing she had it for support.

"You need to trust me on this," Ken urged. "Take my hands and let me guide you around, only when I start walking backward, I want you to let your feet float behind you and start kicking."

"You won't go to the deep end, will you?" Mandy's eyes widened.

"Trust me, Mandy. We're only staying in the shallow end. And if you feel uncomfortable, we can stop anytime."

She did as Ken asked. Before long, as he pulled her from one side of the pool to the other, she found herself rather enjoying the feeling of gliding along on her stomach. *This isn't so bad. In fact, it's kind of fun.*

"Now, I want you to go one step further." Ken reassuringly squeezed her hands, keeping his backward motion. "As I pull you, keep kicking your feet, but also lower your head a bit more so your chin is skimming the water."

Nervously, Mandy complied. She was used to the water's coolness now, and it actually felt good as the bright sun shone down on them.

"You'll be a fish in no time, Mandy." Ellen smiled and waved as she stood on the end of the diving board.

"Be careful, Ellen." Mandy glanced at Ken after watching Ellen dive and go beneath the surface, hardly splashing any water at all. "I'll probably never be able to dive like Ellen, let alone feel comfortable if my feet can't touch."

"Never say never," Ken encouraged. "Look how good you're already doing."

"I have to admit, this is the first I've been in water this deep since I was a little girl."

"I have great confidence in you." Ken stopped while Mandy let her feet touch the bottom. Wiping the water from her chin, she missed Ken's touch when he let go of her hands. "That's why I'm going to ask you to keep trusting me. I wouldn't suggest you do anything I didn't think you could do."

"Okay. I . . . I trust you, Ken." Mandy took a deep breath. "You're good at this. Did you ever think of giving swimming lessons fulltime?"

"I taught children at one of the resorts here on the island for a while, but it took a lot of time away from helping my family at the chicken farm. So I only taught for one summer. It was fun, though."

"I know from experience, it's best to learn to swim when you're young. And I regret not pursuing it when I had the chance to learn from my dad."

"Don't look back Mandy. You're here now, and that's what counts. The next thing I'm going to ask you to do is lean over and put your face in the water."

Mandy gulped. "But . . . but I won't be able to breathe."

"You'll hold your breath while your face is in the water, then count to ten and lift your head to take a breath. Once you're able to put your face in the water, you can learn to float without assistance."

"I–I'm not sure I can." Mandy glanced at the other side of the pool, where Ellen continued to swim, this time with her face in the water. She made it look so easy as she kicked her feet and lifted her arms easily in and out of the water. It was the first time since they'd become stranded on Kauai that Mandy had seen Ellen enjoying herself so much.

"It may help if you hold on to me again." Ken grasped Mandy's hand. "Now take a deep breath, close your eyes if you're more comfortable, and put your face in the water."

Mandy grimaced. *That's easy for you to say. You already know how to swim, and you're not afraid of the water.*

Wanting to please Ken and hoping he wouldn't think she was a fraidy-cat, she took a deep breath and dunked her head under the water. But she couldn't muster the courage to open her eyes.

"Good job!" Ken grinned when she lifted her face out of the water. She noticed his face was wet, too. "Now do it again; only this time, try opening your eyes."

Mandy did as he asked. Once her eyes got used to the stinging sensation, it wasn't so bad. She grinned when she saw Ken under the water, looking right at her. Then quickly, they surfaced together.

"Okay, now, I want you to grab the edge of the pool. When you put your face in the water, stretch out your legs and kick."

Again, Mandy did as Ken instructed. After she'd done it awhile, he showed her how to float on her back while stabilizing her head. If not for his gentle coaching, she never could have done as he asked. Mandy trusted Ken and felt sure she was in good hands.

"You're getting the hang of it, Mandy. Great job!" Ellen shouted.

Mandy was pleased with her friend's compliment. It made it easier to press on with the lesson.

"Ellen's right. You're doing very well." Ken gave her a thumbs-up. "A few more visits to my folks' pool, and you'll be swimming like a mermaid."

Mandy wasn't sure, but with Ken teaching her, she felt hopeful about learning to swim. In fact, she was beginning to think she could do almost anything with him at her side. Even though she had fought it, she was beginning to see Ken as more than a friend, and home filled her thoughts less often.

CHAPTER 23

Middlebury

Christmas didn't often fall on a Sunday, but today was one of those years it did. As Barbara sat on a church bench inside her uncle Nate's barn, she glanced at her friend Sadie, who sat to her left, and then to her sister Libby, on the right. The weather was quite chilly this morning, but the barn was kept warm by her uncle's woodstove. It was good to be with the people closest to her. *Too bad Mandy and Ellen aren't here.*

Sadie must have been deep in thought, starring into space, while drumming her fingers on the inside of her arm. Was she, too, wondering about their friends?

Ever since she'd arrived home, a day hadn't gone by when Barbara's thoughts didn't end up hundreds of miles away. It was hard enough to believe she'd been to Hawaii, let alone to think about Mandy and Ellen on a tropical island without any family. *I wonder what our two friends are doing right now. Are they wishing they were home with their families?* Barbara glanced out the window and saw it was beginning to snow. *Are Mandy and Ellen missing the cold, snowy weather, or are they content to be where it's warm?*

Barbara reflected on the last conversation she'd had with Ellen, when she'd mentioned how she and Mandy attended a church on Kauai. No doubt, they would attend services there today and then take part in whatever kind of celebration the Hawaiian couple had in their home.

I wonder if my friends feel out of place. I sure would. It must be hard for Miriam and Isaac, having their daughter so far away — especially during the holidays. I'm sure Mandy's brothers miss her, too, since it's the first Christmas their entire family isn't together. Same for Ellen's parents and her siblings. I'm thankful I can be with my family for Christmas. I can't imagine being stuck on an island, far from home, with people I'd only met a little over a month ago.

She glanced at the men's side of the room and spotted Gideon, wearing a grim expression. Barbara's heart clenched. *I wish he didn't look so sad. He must miss Mandy something awful today.*

■ ■ ■ ■

Gideon had a hard time concentrating on the bishop's message. Christmas was supposed to be a joyful occasion, but he wasn't in the holiday spirit, even with the pleasure of seeing a few snowflakes falling this morning. Going to church and celebrating with his family afterward wasn't the same without Mandy. He'd called her the night before to wish her a Merry Christmas, but like before, she was busy and couldn't talk long. She'd been polite, of course, and explained they had company at the B&B, but it almost seemed as if she was looking for an excuse not to talk to him.

Maybe I'm being paranoid. With Mandy so far away and me not knowing when she's coming home, it's easy to conjure things up in my mind that may not even be true. I miss her so much, I can't think straight anymore.

The bench Gideon sat upon seemed more uncomfortable than usual. Or was it only because he felt so miserable? Scooching around to find a comfortable position didn't help, nor did stretching his legs out in front of him.

He sighed and instinctively reached up to touch the small indentation on his right cheek, caused from scratching an infected pox. This was not going to be one of his better Christmases.

Kapaa

"I'm glad we were able to go to church today," Ellen whispered as she and Mandy took seats in the sanctuary. "But it would have been nice if Luana and Makaio could have come with us."

"They wanted to, but Makaio still isn't doing well with his crutches, so he figured it would be better to stay home."

Ellen's stomach tensed as she heard the word *home.* Every year she looked forward to spending Christmas with her family. Not being with them today was heartbreaking. She turned to her friend. "Do you think he's ever going to be well enough to help Luana again so we can go home?"

"Of course he will. But is going home all you ever think about?" Mandy's brows furrowed. "Can't you enjoy our time here on Kauai for as long as it lasts?"

Ellen bristled. "The things you say shock me sometimes. It's Christmas, Mandy, and I miss my family. You should miss your family, too."

"How can you even suggest such a thing?" A pained expression gathered on Mandy's face, and then she lowered her head. "I do miss everyone back home, but I'm trying to make the best of our situation." She slowly lifted her head. "And what about Luana? Would you want to leave her in a bind? I would hope not. It isn't the way we were taught."

"No, of course not. I only meant —"

"*Shh.* It's time to get quiet." Mandy motioned to the front, where the worship team had assembled.

The pastor stepped up to the podium and tapped on the microphone. The sound boomed through the speakers. Startled, many people jumped.

Red-faced, he grinned sheepishly. "Sorry. I didn't mean for that to happen. Would everyone please stand for a word of prayer?"

Luana sat on the sofa, gazing at the twinkling lights on their Christmas tree. Makaio was asleep in his recliner, with his Bible in his lap. He'd had a restless night, and soon after they'd read scripture together this morning, his eyelids had grown heavy. It was all right. He needed his rest. Luana's only regret was they couldn't go to church with Ellen and Mandy. Makaio was disappointed, too, and had become impatient, complaining about not being able to climb a ladder to decorate the outside of the house with colored lights.

She understood her husband's edginess. After six weeks of wearing the cast, he had been excited to get the thing off. But when he'd seen the doctor two days ago, he was told he would need to wear it another two weeks to be sure the leg healed properly. Luana never let on, but she'd been hopeful for Makaio. Eight weeks was a long time to be wearing a cast.

She leaned her head back and let her mind drift to the many Christmases she'd spent as a young girl on the Big Island. Some years, her parents got together with other family members in one of their homes. Other times, they would gather at one of the beaches for a picnic. Anywhere with her loved ones felt like home.

She laughed faintly, thinking about her uncle Randy. He always showed up wearing a shell lei around his neck and a Santa hat on his head. Of course, he made sure it was his job to hand out all the Christmas presents to the children who were there. He used to tell them stories about how Santa Claus rode in a red canoe pulled by dolphins, and then they all sang, "Here comes Santa in a Red Canoe." Songs such as "Christmas in Hawaii" and the Hawaiian version of "The Twelve Days of Christmas" were accompanied by ukulele or a guitar.

As soon as Ailani and Oke came over and Mandy and Ellen returned from church, they would share a meal. Afterward, if Makaio felt up to it, he would play his ukulele while they sang Christmas songs for their holiday gathering.

Sighing, Luana stood and headed for the kitchen. The tantalizing smell of ham slowly heating in the oven reached her nose and caused her stomach to growl. It was tradition to have coconut pudding for dessert, but instead, she'd made a pineapple upside-down cake.

I'll miss those young Amish women when they return to the mainland, Luana thought. Even though she hadn't known them long, they'd become almost like family to her. *Maybe someday, if we can find someone to take over the bed-and-breakfast for a few weeks, we can go to Indiana to meet Mandy and Ellen's families. Visiting Amish country would be an interesting way to spend a vacation. We'd have to make sure we went during the warm summer months, because I don't think I could get used to the cold or snow.*

"Who's ready for dessert?" Luana asked, carrying a pineapple-upside-down cake into the living room shortly after their afternoon meal.

Oke smacked his lips. "It looks *'ono,*"

"I agree. It does look delicious."

Ellen turned her head and gave Mandy a strange look. "You understood what 'ono means?"

Mandy smiled. "In addition to the Hawaiian Makaio's taught me, Ken's also shared a few more words and phrases."

"I should have guessed." Ellen got up from her chair. "Would you like some help serving the cake, Luana?"

"I can manage, but if you'd like to bring in the coffee and hot tea, I'd appreciate it."

"I'll come with you." Mandy hopped up and followed Ellen into the kitchen. Then she tapped Ellen's shoulder. "What did you mean in there, when you said you should have guessed Ken taught me some Hawaiian words?"

Ellen picked up the teapot and turned to face her. "I only meant that since you've been seeing him so much lately, I wasn't surprised he'd taught you to say the Hawaiian word. Why are you so touchy?"

"It's the way you sounded, I guess. Ken's been very helpful, and he's become a good friend. And may I remind you, he's been kind to you, too." She set the coffeepot on a tray and got out the cups. "I never expected when we began our trip to Hawaii that I'd come to understand so many Hawaiian words, much less learn how to swim. I didn't think I'd ever conquer my fear of the water, but I'm grateful to Ken for making it happen."

Ellen gave her a hug. "Believe me, I'm happy for you. Getting over your fear of the water was a huge step. Trusting Ken to teach you how to swim was even greater. Now when we go on picnics during warmer weather at home, we can swim in the pond near the back of my folks' property. I'm looking forward to enjoying the summer months next year."

"Jah, and I can't wait to surprise my brothers."

A knock sounded on the back door, so Mandy went to answer it. She was surprised to see Ken on the lanai, holding a large paper sack.

"Mele Kalikimaka." Grinning, Ken stepped inside. "I come bearing gifts."

"Merry Christmas to you, too." Mandy's heartbeat picked up speed, as it always did when she was with Ken. "I'll tell Luana and Makaio you're here, and that you've brought gifts for them."

Ken set the sack on the table. "The presents are for you and Ellen. Since this is your first Christmas on Kauai, and you're no doubt missing home, I wanted to do something special for you."

"Mahalo. It was a thoughtful gesture." Mandy looked at Ellen, raising her eyebrows to stress her point of Ken being good to Ellen, too.

Ellen moved over to the table. "Yes, thank you, Ken, for thinking of us."

Mandy felt bad when he pulled two wrapped packages from the bag. "I wish I had something to give you."

"Your friendship is the only gift I need." Ken's sincere smile nearly melted Mandy's heart.

"Go ahead, open it." He handed her one of the gifts and gave the other one to Ellen.

Mandy's fingers trembled as she tore the wrapping paper off and opened the box. Her breath caught in her throat when she discovered a framed photo of a gorgeous sunrise. "Oh, Ken, did you take this picture?"

"Sure did." He beamed.

Mandy wanted to shout at the top of her lungs how much she appreciated the gift, but she spoke softly instead. "It's wonderful. Thank you so much."

"You're welcome." Ken pointed to the other present. "Ellen, your gift is almost the same, except it's a sunset. I took them both the same day."

Smiling, Ellen opened her gift. "Thank you, Ken. Now when we go home, we'll have another slice of Hawaii to take with us, along with the coral you found for us on the beach."

I wish I didn't have to go home, Mandy thought for the umpteenth time. *But at least I'll have the picture the woman at the falls took of Ken and me. I'll keep it hidden in one of my drawers to remind me of what I'm missing.*

CHAPTER 24

"I'm glad my husband got his cast off yesterday," Luana commented as she, Mandy, and Ellen got breakfast ready for their guests the second Saturday of January. "Unfortunately, he's like a crab with sore pinchers, because now he's faced with several weeks of physical therapy. He commented right away in the doctor's office how nice it was to finally have it off." Her forehead creased. "That man of mine grinned and said, 'Now I can scratch where I couldn't before, and it feels so good to have that added weight gone.' "

"Hopefully, it won't be long before his leg is good as new." Ellen placed a pitcher of pineapple juice on the tray, which she set on the table.

Mandy glanced at the calendar, wondering how much longer it would be before Makaio could resume his duties at the B&B. She wanted his leg to get better, but oh, how she would miss this wonderful place. In all her life she'd never been anywhere like Kauai, where she felt such peace.

"How are your swimming lessons going?" Luana asked, scattering Mandy's thoughts.

"Fairly well." Mandy smiled. "I'm getting more confident in the water and can even do the sidestroke and tread water a bit. Oh, and I'm getting used to putting my face under water, which is one thing I could never imagine being able to do. My family back home will be surprised at this accomplishment. They've tried to coax me to try swimming, but I've always refused."

Luana stirred the steaming eggs she'd begun cooking in a large frying pan. "If anyone could teach you to swim and feel confident in the water, it would be Ken. Besides being a good swimmer himself, he's kind and patient."

Mandy agreed wholeheartedly. Ken had never once pushed her to do anything she didn't feel comfortable with. He seemed to spread kindness to everyone he met.

"Are you two looking forward to the luau Ken is taking you to tonight?" Luana asked as she filled a platter with scrambled eggs.

"I certainly am." Excitement bubbled in Mandy's chest. "It should be quite interesting."

Ellen, looking less enthused, placed a pitcher of orange juice on the platter beside the pineapple juice. "I had planned to stay here and write some letters to family back home, but Mandy and Ken talked me into going."

"You won't be sorry." Luana stepped to the middle of the kitchen and did a little dance. "You'll see hula dancers, a fire dancer, and lots more great entertainment. And the food at a luau is downright delicious." Her eyes sparkled.

Watching Luana, Mandy and Ellen both giggled. "Did you ever hula dance?" Mandy asked.

"When I was a little girl I used to practice dancing in front of my bedroom mirror; with the door closed, of course. Then, during my teen years I took lessons and got pretty good, if I do say so myself." Luana chuckled and did a few hand motions to one side and then the other.

Mandy looked forward to attending the event, but even more, she was eager to spend time with Ken again.

Shipshewana, Indiana

Saturday was Gideon's day off, and he'd been running errands for his mother all morning. It was twelve o'clock and time to stop for lunch.

After entering the café inside Yoder's Complex and placing his order at the counter, he spotted Barbara sitting by herself. Stepping up to her table, he placed his hand gently on her shoulder. "Mind if I join ya, or is this seat taken?"

Turning her head quickly, Barbara gasped. "Ach, Gideon, I hadn't realized you were here."

"I've been running errands for my mamm this morning and decided to stop for something to eat. Sorry if I startled you." He gestured to the empty chair. "Is it okay if I sit at your table?"

She smiled. "I'd be pleased if you joined me."

Gideon took a seat. "Have you eaten already?" He noted she only had a glass of iced tea in front of her.

"No, I'm waiting for my order." She rested her hands on the table.

"Same here. I just put mine in." Gideon leaned forward. "Were you shopping, too?"

"Jah. I was looking for a birthday present for my sister Fern."

"Any luck?"

Barbara nodded before taking a sip of her drink. "I found a puzzle for her, featuring a beautiful black horse. All she talks about is raising horses when she grows up."

"It's good Fern knows what she wants, especially at her young age."

"I like horses, too, but not enough to raise them."

"Same here, although I've never considered giving up my job to do something like that. It would be an adventure."

"It certainly would." Barbara smiled.

Gideon sat quietly, suddenly at a loss for words.

"Have you heard anything from Mandy lately?" Barbara asked.

"I had a conversation with her on Christmas Eve. She was busy, though, so we didn't talk long." Gideon's posture sagged. "I can't help wondering if she's forgotten what we had. If a girl cares for a guy, she should be eager to talk to him." Frowning, he placed his straw hat on the table.

"Mandy may have been busy. There's a lot involved in running a bed-and-breakfast. No doubt she and Ellen have plenty of work to do." Barbara reached over and touched Gideon's arm.

"I suppose, but she can't be working all the time. You'd think on Christmas Eve . . ." Gideon's voice trailed off when both his and Barbara's meals were brought to the table. Was there any point in talking about this right now? It wouldn't change the facts. He appreciated Barbara's sympathy, but he wasn't sure she fully understand how badly he felt.

"Why don't we stop for a bite to eat?" Sadie suggested when she and her mother finished shopping at Yoder's Hardware.

"Good idea," Mom responded warmly. "I'm hungerich."

When they entered the restaurant, they placed their orders, then moved into the room where all the tables were set up. Sadie glanced at a table on the other side of the room and drew in a sharp breath. Gideon and Barbara sat together, and Barbara's hand was on his arm. *What? Why are they here together?* Her skin tingled as she wondered how Mandy would feel about this.

"Go ahead and find a table, Mom. Anywhere is fine with me. I'm going over to say hello to Gideon and Barbara, but I'll join you soon."

"Oh, okay. Don't be too long, though. I'm sure our food will be here shortly."

Sadie hurried across the room and stopped in front of her friend's table. When she said hello, Barbara pulled her hand away from Gideon's arm and stared at her with a wide-eyed expression.

"I'm surprised to see you," Sadie said. "Don't you usually work at the quilt-and-fabric shop most Saturdays?"

Barbara nodded. "I worked this morning, but surprisingly, things were slow, so Peggy said I could take the afternoon off."

Sadie glanced at Gideon. "Have you heard anything from Mandy recently?"

"Talked with her briefly on Christmas Eve but haven't heard from her since. How about you?"

"No. My plan was to call her on Christmas Day, but we had a big family gathering and time got away from me."

"The last time I spoke with Mandy was yesterday." Barbara spoke up. "She told me she's been learning to swim. She also mentioned that she and Ellen would be attending a luau this evening."

Gideon looked at Barbara and frowned. "Guess you were wrong about her workin' all the time." He leaned his elbows on the table. "I'm happy she's learned to swim, but Mandy seems like she has plenty of time for all kinds of things — except talking to me."

Sadie felt bad for Gideon, but at the same time, she hoped nothing was occurring between him and Barbara. Mandy would be devastated if she came home and found out he'd become interested in one of her friends while she was gone.

I wonder if I should talk to Barbara about this. Sadie bit her lip. *Regardless, now is not the time.*

Lihue

"Are you two ready to experience an evening you won't forget?" Ken asked as he led Mandy and Ellen to a table near the stage. He'd upgraded their reservations so they could have better seats.

"Yes, definitely!" Mandy looked down at the lovely flower leis she and Ellen had received when they'd entered the grounds. She was glad they'd both worn a muumuu tonight, rather than their Amish dresses. It made them blend in more with the crowd, even with the scarves they wore pinned at the back of their heads.

"The *imu* ceremony was interesting," Ellen commented.

Ken nodded. "Yes, and you'll enjoy eating some of the tasty pork during the meal we'll be eating soon. Since we have VIP seats, our table and the others closest to the stage will be called to the buffet table first."

"You shouldn't have spent the extra money." Mandy spoke softly. "We would have been satisfied to sit at any table."

Ken leaned closer to Mandy, touching her arm. "I wanted you to have the best seats so you could see the show up close and be transported to ancient Polynesia during the time of their migration to the islands." He pushed his seat back and stood. "Now, can I get either of you a glass of Hawaiian fruit punch while we wait for our meal?"

"I'd like one," Mandy replied. "But if you show me where to go, I can get it myself."

"Nope. You two are my guests this evening, and I'm going to wait on you." He looked at Ellen. "Does some punch sound good to you?"

"Yes, please."

Ken left the table and returned with two glasses of punch, which he handed to Ellen and Mandy. Then he went back and got one for himself.

A short time later, someone came and told them it was time to go to the buffet table.

"This reminds me of the buffet we serve at the restaurant where I work in Middlebury," Mandy whispered to Ellen as they took their plates and began dishing up. "Only the food's a lot different here."

"Be sure you try some of this to go with your kalua pork." Ken pointed to the container marked *Poi.* "It's made from the taro plant."

Mandy wrinkled her nose. "Luana told me about poi. She said it tastes rather bland."

"It's more of an acquired taste, but I think it's pretty good; especially when I dip the pork into it."

"Think I'll pass and have some purple sweet potatoes."

They continued down the line, filling their plates with stir-fried vegetables, teriyaki chicken, pan-seared filet of ono fish, tossed green salad with papaya dressing, taro rolls, and steamed jasmine rice. Mandy's mouth watered thinking how good it would all taste. As they passed the dessert bar, she noticed rice pudding, coconut cake, and pineapple upside-down cake, as well as several kinds of tropical fruits. She would wait until she'd eaten the main meal to get dessert, in case she was too full to enjoy it.

When they returned to the table, they bowed their heads for a silent prayer. As they ate their meal, Ken told them about the Kilohana Plantation, where the luau was being held. "There's a train ride you can take around the 105-acre historic plantation," he explained. "We could have ridden it this evening if we'd gotten here earlier, but I wasn't able to quit work in time."

"It's okay." Mandy forked a piece of pork.

"What we're doing now is exciting enough."

"Maybe we can take the train ride another time." He pointed to the poi on Ellen's plate. "What do you think of it?"

"It is rather tasteless but not too bad. You should have tried some, Mandy."

"I might some other time." Mandy put another piece of pork into her mouth, enjoying the tender, succulent morsel. "Right now, I'm enjoying this moist, delicious meat."

When the meal was over and they'd finished dessert, the lights lowered and the entertainment began. Mandy sat mesmerized as an incredible tale unfolded through dance, song, and the rhythm of Tahitian drums. The story showed the depths of one family's great effort as they sought courage and vision to carry them on a voyage from Tahiti to Hawaii.

She sat in rapt attention as the theatrical luau ended with a dream scene featuring fire poi balls and the traditional fire knife dance. The world seemed to slow down as she thought about the difficulty of leaving the only home they'd ever known and traveling to a land far away to begin a new life. She'd been away from her family more than two months. Could she remain on Kauai, knowing she may only see them on rare occasions? It was a question never far from her thoughts these days.

CHAPTER 25

Saturday, January 16

I am sitting here on the beach with Ellen, watching Ken surf. It's frightening to see him out there in those giant waves, yet it's exciting, too. How he manages to stand up and keep his balance on the board is beyond me. If I tried that, I'd be knocked into the water for sure.

Mandy placed her journal inside the tote bag she'd brought along and drew a deep breath. It had been several days since she'd written anything in it because they'd been so busy at the B&B. It felt wonderful to sit here now, enjoying all the sights and smells around her. This morning, when Ken stopped by and asked if she and Ellen would like to watch him surf, Luana had insisted they go, saying she could manage on her own for a few hours.

Turning to face Ellen, sitting on the

blanket beside her, Mandy observed the plain dress Ellen had made. Except for church, Mandy hardly wore her Amish clothes anymore. The muumuu was comfortable and modest. Wearing it made her feel as if she belonged on Kauai. She had to admit, even though Ellen didn't have the exact pattern for an Amish dress, she'd done a good job with what she'd had to work with. She hoped her friend wouldn't hold it against her because she'd strayed from their traditional dress. Sooner or later, Mandy would have to change back to her customary clothing. If she were to arrive home wearing a muumuu, her family would be stunned and no doubt displeased.

"Luana's such a nice lady," she said, setting aside her thoughts. "Just think, if we hadn't missed the ship, we'd never have met her and Makaio."

Ellen nodded.

"It was good of her to let us have time off this afternoon to spend time on the beach. And look at the beautiful water. It stretches out as far as the eye can see." Mandy adjusted her sunglasses so they wouldn't keep slipping on her nose where she'd put sunscreen.

She focused her attention on Ken when she noticed him talking with two young women on the beach. She assumed he must know them fairly well, for the dark-haired woman wearing a navy-blue swimsuit stood close to Ken, with her hand resting on his arm. Mandy felt a twinge of jealousy but reminded herself that she had no claim on him. They were only friends and would be saying goodbye, most likely for good, when she left Hawaii.

Refocusing, she noticed that Ellen's mind seemed to be elsewhere as she watched a stray dog digging frantically in the sand close to the surf.

"What's the crazy *hund* doing?" Mandy chuckled as the shaggy mutt continued to dig and spin around in circles.

"I don't know, but he's certainly energetic. Determined, too." Ellen laughed as the critter threw clods of wet sand into the air.

"The dog's not the only energetic one." Mandy pointed to the frothy water. Ken was paddling out from the shore. "It amazes me the way he paddles out with his board, then stands up and rides those big waves back in. I'd be exhausted if I tried that, not to mention making a fool of myself."

"But now you could swim, or at least stay afloat."

"No way! I'm not a strong enough swimmer yet. Even if I was, I wouldn't have the strength or nerve to do what Ken does."

"Me neither. It takes a lot of practice to master the art of surfing. Fortunately, where we live, we don't have to worry about such things. Swimming in my folks' pond is good enough for me." Ellen grabbed a handful of sand and let it sift through her fingers.

Swimming in a little pond won't be near as exciting as paddling around in the ocean, Mandy thought, but she didn't voice the sentiment to her friend. She looked back at Ken and the enormous wave forming behind him. She sat up straight as the current swelled like a huge wall coming up from the ocean floor. This was the biggest wave she had seen. Ken turned and obviously saw it as he readied himself on the board. She instinctively stood up, watching Ken use his arms to paddle as the wave approached. In no time he was on his feet, riding the water's crest as if it was as easy as riding a bike. Ken rode the wave beautifully and crouched a bit on his board as a huge curl formed alongside of him. Then quickly, he disappeared, as if the water had swallowed him up.

Not far from where Ken was last seen, another surfer was engulfed in a separate tube of water. Mandy covered her eyes, peeking through her fingers to watch as the surfer lost his balance. The power of the water flipped him into the air, and then he landed on the backside of the swell. He seemed to be okay after retrieving his board and simply waited for another wave to ride.

Mandy kept watching and silently said a prayer. *Please Lord, keep Ken safe and don't let him fall off the board.*

Ellen stood up, too. "I can't see Ken anymore, can you?"

"No." Mandy held her breath for what seemed like many minutes, looking for any sign of him. It wasn't like she hadn't seen this type of surfing when Ken took her to the beach a while back, but this was different. It was Ken out there in the unrelenting ocean.

She was about to run down to the water's edge — to do what, she didn't know. A sigh of relief escaped her lips as Ken, still on his board, emerged, skimming skillfully out of the curling wave. She watched in awe as he continued surfing the swell until it weakened and brought him in to shallower water.

Ellen sat back down and Mandy followed. "Wow, he had me scared for a minute." She smiled when Ken raised his hand to wave at them. Then he turned back toward the ocean.

"He seems to know what he's doing," Ellen said. "Look at him. He's going back out for more. I have to say, a huge wave like the one he rode would have been enough for me. Imagine being in a wall of water like he was. Makes me shudder, even thinking about it."

"Me, too."

"Do you think that silly hund belongs to anyone?" Ellen pointed to the dog again. "I don't see his master anywhere."

"Maybe whoever he belongs to is up the beach a ways and the dog wandered off." Right now, the animal was of little interest to Mandy, as she breathed deeply to quell her rapidly beating heart. She watched Ken float casually on his board to wait for another wave to swell. A short time later, he came out of the water, laying his surfboard on the sand. The dog raced over to him, barking and wagging his tail.

"What do ya want, boy? Wanna play?" Ken bent down, grabbed a stick, and flung it into the water.

The dog bounded in after it, swam back, and dropped it at Ken's feet. *Woof! Woof!*

"So you do wanna play, huh?" He picked up the stick and threw it again, a little farther out in the water.

Once again, the dog retrieved it, looking up at Ken as if begging for more.

"Okay, one more time, boy, and then I'm done. I need to go rest awhile." He tossed the stick, and as the dog swam out to it, Ken plodded up the beach and dropped onto the blanket beside Mandy.

"Do you know who owns the dog?" she asked.

"Nope. I'm guessing he's a stray."

"He was digging furiously in the sand a while ago," Ellen spoke up. "It was comical to watch him — especially when he looked over this way, with sand on his nose."

"For sure, he has a lot of energy." Ken chuckled.

"After watching you in those waves, I'd say the dog isn't the only one with a lot of energy." Mandy tilted her head. "What kind of dog do you think it is?"

He shrugged. "Hard to tell. Looks like a mixture of terrier and spaniel."

"Did you enjoy riding the big waves?" Ellen asked.

"Yeah. It's me at the mercy of the ocean. It's a rush — kind of hard to describe."

All Mandy could do was shake her head. She didn't want to let on how scared she'd been when Ken got lost for a few seconds in the wave.

"Would you like a glass of cold hibiscus tea?" Ellen reached for the cooler they'd brought along. "I imagine you're pretty thirsty by now."

"Sure. I'd appreciate something cold to drink."

"How about something to eat?" Mandy offered, relieved Ken was back on dry land. "We brought along some Maui onion chips, as well as some of Luana's macadamia nut cookies."

"They both sound good."

Ellen poured the iced tea, while Mandy got out the food. When they started to eat, the dog bounded up, barking and wagging his tail.

"The poor pooch looks hungry." Mandy broke off a piece of her cookie and held it out.

"Oh, oh, now you've done it. We'll never get rid of the mutt." Ken smirked as he reached out and scratched behind the critter's ears. "We're gonna have a friend for life."

"I guess so." Mandy giggled. "Maybe we should ask some of the people here on the beach if the dog belongs to anyone."

"I'll do it as soon as I finish my snack." He gave the dog a few chips. Although there was nothing left in Ken's hand, the mutt continued to lick the salt off his fingers. "From the way the pooch gobbled it up,

I'm guessing he hasn't eaten in a while. One more reason to believe he's a stray." He stood and wiped his hand against his black tank top before Mandy could think to hand him a napkin. "Wouldn't be surprised if someone didn't drop the dog off somewhere and he wandered down to the beach in search of food."

Mandy hated to think anyone would do such a thing, but even back home some dogs ended up to be strays, abandoned by their masters. If this dog was homeless, it was a shame, because he seemed so smart, not to mention friendly and playful. She wished they could take him back to the B&B, but Luana didn't have any pets and probably wouldn't appreciate having a dog hanging around pestering her guests.

As if he could read Mandy's mind, Ken looked over at her and smiled. "If I don't find the dog's owner, I'll take him with me — at least till I can find him a good home."

She smiled, too, thinking once more what a nice person he was.

"Oh, great. Looks like the vog is creeping in." Ken pointed to the haze blowing toward them.

"Could that be why my eyes are itching all of a sudden?" Mandy asked.

"Wouldn't be a bit surprised. I'll go ask

around about the dog, and then we should probably get going before the vog becomes any worse." Ken stood and started down the beach, with the dog trailing along.

"If the hund doesn't already have a home, I bet he'll find one with Ken," Ellen remarked.

Mandy was about to comment, when a round of sneezing overtook her. *Achoo! Achoo! Achoo!* "Oh, dear, my eyes itch worse now, too." She reached into her tote for a tissue.

When Ken returned, he took one look at Mandy and suggested he ought to take her home. He pointed to the dog. "Guess the mutt's coming with me for now, 'cause nobody I talked to knows where he belongs."

Mandy smiled, despite how miserable she felt. She was glad Ken would be taking the dog. It wouldn't be right to leave the poor animal alone on the beach.

Luana went out to the lanai to visit with Makaio awhile, but the telephone rang. "I'd better get it." She handed him a glass of freshly made lemonade. "It could be Ailani calling about the doctor's appointment she went to this morning."

She hurried back to the kitchen and

picked up the receiver. "The Palms Bed-and-Breakfast." When she realized it was someone asking about the availability of a room next month, she grabbed the guest book to check for vacancies. She gave the woman the available dates and details, then took down her information, including a credit card number to hold the reservation.

After Luana hung up, she returned to the lanai with a glass of lemonade for herself. "It wasn't our daughter, but we do have another guest scheduled for the first weekend in February."

"Good to hear. We need all the business we can get, especially with many of my hospital bills still unpaid." Makaio's brows furrowed. "I'll be glad when the doctor says my leg's healed sufficiently and I can resume my regular duties here. I feel like a burden to you when all I do is sit around. Think I've put on a few extra pounds, too." Patting his stomach, he took a sip of lemonade. "Good tasting. You make it just the way I like."

"Mahalo." She leaned over and kissed his cheek. "And you're not a burden. You'd do the same for me if I were the one laid up. It's part of the commitment we made to each other when we got married."

"True. I only wish —"

"And don't you worry. You'll lose those extra pounds when you're up and about again." Luana patted his cheeks. "I'll see that you do." The phone rang again, and she stood. "Hold your thoughts. I'll be right back."

Middlebury

Gideon hoped when he called Mandy this time, she'd be free to talk. He missed her and wanted to know she was missing him, too. Right now, he felt insecure feelings creeping in — the ones that told him Mandy wasn't his girlfriend anymore.

He chided himself for thinking this way and took a moment to shake off his doubts before making the call. After pausing at the door of the phone shack a few seconds, Gideon stepped inside and took a seat on the wooden stool. Then he punched in the number for the B&B. Mandy's birthday was coming up soon, and he wanted to tell her that he'd sent a gift and a card. The phone rang several times before a woman's voice came on the line. "Aloha! This is the Palms Bed-and-Breakfast."

"This is Gideon Eash. Is Mandy there? I'd like to speak with her, please."

"Oh, I'm sorry. Mandy isn't here right now. She's at the beach with Ken. She mentioned something about surfing."

"What did you say?" Gideon was sure he must have misunderstood. No way would Mandy have gone surfing. She couldn't even swim.

"I said, Mandy's at the beach. Ken took them surfing."

A chill shot up his spine. If she'd been foolish enough to try surfing, then her life could be in danger. The sport was dangerous — even for a strong swimmer, which Mandy definitely was not. Then another thought popped into his head. *Mandy's with that guy named Ken again. Just who is this fellow, and how close have they become?*

"Would you please tell her Gideon called and that I'll try to call again on her birthday? Oh, and let her know to expect a card and a gift from me."

"What day is Mandy's birthday?" the woman asked.

"January twenty-eighth. She'll be twenty-one years old."

"Thanks for letting me know. We'll be sure to do something special to help Mandy celebrate her birthday."

Gideon's jaw clenched. *It should be me helping Mandy celebrate, not people she barely knows. She was off someplace with him before when I called.* A rush of adrenaline coursed through his body. *Seems like she spends a lot of time with this fellow. Sure hope I have nothing to worry about.*

Kapaa

By the time Mandy and Ellen arrived back at the B&B, Mandy's nose was sore from blowing it so many times. She'd been sneezing a lot, and her eyes had become even itchier than they were at the beach.

"Is something wrong, Mandy?" Luana asked when they entered the kitchen. "You look like you've been crying."

"I've been sneezing, and my eyes are red and itchy." She brought her hand up to her right eye and rubbed it. "This started while we were on the beach and got worse as Ken drove us back here."

"I'll bet it's the vog." Luana handed Mandy a tissue. "I'll give you an allergy pill and then you should go lie down for a while."

Ellen gave Mandy's shoulder a tender squeeze. "See, not all things in Hawaii are perfect. You'd have to deal with the vog all the time if you lived here."

"Not all the time," Luana corrected. "Only when the wind blows the ash over from the Big Island."

Mandy sighed. "Guess there's good and

bad in everything. Wherever you go, no place is perfect." She pushed her shoulders back and smiled. "Even with the vog, I still enjoy being here on Kauai."

CHAPTER 26

"Oh my, this is a surprise!" Mandy exclaimed when she entered Luana's dining room and saw a decorated cake with her name on it. A pink tablecloth, with brightly colored balloons and the words *Happy Birthday* printed around the edge, covered the table. Paper plates and matching napkins had also been added. "How did you know today was my birthday?" Before Luana could respond, Mandy nudged Ellen's arm. "I'll bet you spilled the beans."

"Nope. It wasn't me."

"It was the young man who calls to speak with you so often." Luana covered her mouth. "Sorry, but I forgot to tell you he called the day you and Ellen went to the beach with Ken. He wanted to let you know he was sending a card and gift for your birthday."

Mandy scratched at her cheek where a mosquito had taken a bite. "That's strange.

I haven't received anything from Gideon in the mail. The only birthday cards I've gotten were from my parents and from Barbara and Sadie." She sighed. "I wish you could have met our other two friends who made the trip to Hawaii with us. I'm sure you would have liked them."

"If they're anything like you two, we definitely would have liked them." Makaio motioned to the birthday cake in the middle of the table. "Mandy, why don't you make a wish and blow out your candles so we can all eat some of my wife's yummy coconut cake?"

"Not yet." Luana shook her head. "We won't cut the cake until Ken gets here."

"Ken's coming over?" Mandy couldn't hide her pleasure.

"Yes. He'll be here as soon as he's done eating supper." Luana gave a playful wink. "I believe he has something for you."

Mandy grinned. She looked forward to seeing Ken.

She thought about the dog they'd found on the beach and how Ken had taken it home. He'd named the mutt Rusty, and it had taken a liking to Ken's mother right away. Now the critter was her constant companion.

"I have a present for you." Ellen handed

Mandy a floral gift bag. "Happy birthday."

Mandy reached inside and felt some fabric between her fingers. She raised it up and discovered a green, Amish-style dress. It wasn't what she'd expected, and it was difficult to show appreciation — especially when she'd told Ellen previously how content she was wearing a muumuu.

"It's for our trip home," Ellen explained. "Since you have only one Amish dress, you'll need a change of clothes."

Mandy hadn't even thought about her clothing for the trip. Ellen was right. She would need more than one plain dress. She hugged her friend. "Danki for your thoughtfulness in making the dress for me. It must have been hard to sew it without me finding out."

"Not really." Ellen smiled. "Whenever you went shopping with Luana or somewhere with Ken, I worked on it. I'm thankful she has a sewing machine."

"Here's our gift to you." Luana handed Mandy a large box covered with paper in a design of tropical birds. "There are actually two gifts inside — one from Makaio and one from me."

Mandy tore off the paper and pulled the lid aside. The first thing she saw was a set of lovely potholders and an apron to match.

Each had different Hawaiian flowers on them. "Mahalo, Luana. Did you make these?"

"Yes, I did. When Ellen began working on her dresses, it put me in the mood to sew."

"Keep looking, Mandy." Makaio motioned to the box. "There's something from me."

She pulled a layer of tissue aside and gasped when a beautiful ukulele came into view. "Oh, my . . . This is too much!" She stared at the instrument in amazement.

"It's not brand new," he explained. "It's a used one I picked up at a yard sale a few years ago, but it's in great shape, and I thought you might like it."

"I certainly do. Thank you both so much." Mandy gave Luana and Makaio a hug. Then she picked up the ukulele and started strumming the strings. Even though musical instruments were not used during an Amish church service, some Plain people, including her father, played the harmonica or guitar for personal enjoyment. She looked forward to many hours learning to play this wonderful birthday present.

"Sorry I haven't shown you how before," Makaio apologized. "Either I've not felt up to it or you've been busy. But I would like to teach you before you return to your home on the mainland."

"Oh, would you? I'd like that so much. Maybe we could make some time for it each evening."

"Good idea." He glanced at the cake and then at Luana. "Are you sure we can't cut the cake and eat it now?"

"Don't even think about it." Luana shook her finger at him. "Why don't you give Mandy a ukulele lesson while we're waiting for Ken? Then maybe you won't think about dessert."

Makaio and Mandy took seats on the living-room couch, and he showed her the three main chords used for playing the ukulele. "They are C, F, and G7," he explained, demonstrating with his own instrument, as Mandy held hers.

She positioned her fingertips on the strings in the way he showed her and was soon strumming a short tune.

"I'm impressed," Makaio said. "You catch on quick."

"I do have a bit of music experience from playing my battery-operated keyboard."

"Mandy caught on quickly to swimming, too." Ellen took a seat beside her. "But then, she's always been good at whatever she sets her mind to do."

"You're good at whatever you do, as well." Mandy gestured to the dress Ellen made for her. "I've never been able to sew as well as you."

"We all have our talents," Luana remarked. "God made everyone special, and each of us is unique."

A knock sounded on the door, and Luana went to answer it. When she returned to the living room, Ken was with her. He wasn't carrying a gift, and she wondered if Luana had been mistaken when she'd mentioned he might give her something. It didn't matter, though. His presence was gift enough.

"Happy birthday, Mandy." Ken smiled and moved toward the couch.

"I guess Luana must have told you I was turning twenty-one today."

"She sure did, which is why I wanted you to have something special for your birthday." Ken swung out the hand he'd been holding behind his back. It was holding a beautiful garland of flowers that he draped around Mandy's neck.

She touched the soft pink-and-white orchid petals. "Mahalo, Ken." She'd never received a bouquet of flowers before, and this was even more special.

"I have something else for you." Ken reached into his shirt pocket and pulled out a brochure, which he handed to her.

"What's this about?" she asked, eyeing it

curiously.

"It's information on a whale-watching cruise." He smiled widely. "I booked us to go on one tomorrow, early afternoon. You're invited, too, Ellen," he quickly added.

"Oh my!" Excitement swelled in Mandy's chest as she studied the brochure. "I never thought I'd get to see any whales while I'm here." She looked over at Luana, who sat in the wicker rocking chair across from her. "Won't you need Ellen and me to help out tomorrow? It wouldn't be fair if we left you with all the work to do."

"It's okay," Luana assured her. "You can take care of any work needing to be done in the morning. Going on a whale-watching cruise is special, and I wouldn't want either of you to miss it."

Tears welled in Mandy's eyes, and she blinked to keep them from spilling over. "This has been a special birthday. Thank you all so much."

"You're welcome," everyone responded.

"So now, let's head on back to the dining room and have some of Mandy's birthday cake." Makaio rose from his seat. "After waiting so long, I may even have two pieces."

Mandy snickered, and Luana poked her husband's belly. "If you don't watch it, you'll have no choice but to get rid of some of the shirts you've outgrown when we have another yard sale."

Makaio slipped his arm around her waist as he grabbed his cane. "Well, if you weren't such a good cook, I wouldn't have so many temptations."

Thank You, Lord, for my special Hawaiian friends, Mandy prayed, *and for allowing me to be here on my twenty-first birthday.*

Middlebury

Gideon had awakened during the night and realized he'd forgotten to call Mandy in the evening to wish her a happy birthday. He'd tried earlier today, but all he'd gotten was the B&B's answering machine. He couldn't leave a message, though, because their mailbox was full. He'd planned to call before going to bed, thinking it would be around dinnertime on the island, but exhausted after a long day at work, he'd fallen asleep on the sofa.

He pushed himself up and rubbed his face. "Why didn't Mom or Dad wake me before they went to bed?" he muttered, running his fingers through his hair.

Swinging his feet over the couch, Gideon thought about Mandy. *Sure hope she isn't upset with me for not wishing her a happy birthday. What if she thinks I forgot?* He massaged his forehead and groaned. *Maybe she's been too busy to notice.*

Port Allen

The following day, Mandy's heart pounded as Ken helped her and Ellen board the catamaran that would take them on the whale-watching tour. This was one of the most exciting things she'd done since leaving home. She'd brought her camera along, and if they saw any whales, she hoped to get some good shots.

"I hope the water doesn't get choppy," Ellen commented as she took a seat. "I don't do well on a boat in rough weather."

"You should be okay." Ken patted Ellen's shoulder. "If things get a little rough, remember to keep your focus on land, not the waves."

Before they set sail, the captain and his crew asked all the passengers on board to give their full attention to a safety briefing, letting everyone know where the life jackets were located and how to put them on. A member of the crew explained that the vests had a light attached, and when it got wet, the light would come on to help the Coast Guard locate the person in the water. This bit of information frightened Mandy somewhat. The thought of being in the middle of the ocean, even with a life jacket, made her tremble. Being in a swimming pool with her feet touching the bottom was different than being in the big ocean and not being able to see what was under her.

Another crew member let everyone know where the galley was and said snacks, as well as fresh water and soda, would be available.

Mandy whispered to Ken that she and Ellen had been through a similar safety briefing when they'd first boarded the cruise ship. "It was on a much larger scale, of course," she added, "because there were so many passengers."

As the boat moved out, things went along well. Mandy enjoyed the warmth on her skin and beautiful scenery along the way.

"Over there is the Na Pali Coast." Ken pointed to the emerald-green pinnacles towering above the shoreline. "The only land access to this rugged terrain is through an eleven-mile trail. The path crosses five different valleys and ends at a secluded beach. It's one of the most challenging hikes, with narrow sections and muddy soil from so much rainfall. Also, when the streams get high, they're extremely dangerous to cross."

The splendor of it all almost took Mandy's

breath away. "It's amazing."

"Look, there!" Ellen shouted.

Mandy turned in the direction her friend pointed and saw an enormous whale surface, thrusting its tail into the air. "Wow! Look how big it is!"

Soon, more whales appeared. Mandy pulled her camera from the tote bag and started snapping one picture after the other. "Without pictures to show, no one back home would ever believe this," she told Ellen.

"The whales come to our warm waters from Alaska this time of the year. They reproduce and give birth," Ken explained. "It's the reason you see so many of them."

"It makes good sense." Mandy chuckled. "Even the whales want to get out of the cold and come where the waters are warmer."

"What kind of whales are they?" Ellen asked.

"They're humpback whales," Ken replied. "They can grow up to sixty feet in length, and their lifespan averages fifty years."

Everyone on the catamaran grew silent. Mandy watched a gray whale with a white underbelly breach suddenly to the surface then fall heavily back below the water's depth. Another whale broke smoothly out of the ocean, spouting before it started under again. Before disappearing, the whale slapped its huge tail, as if it was waving to them. Cameras started clicking to capture the special moment.

"Humpback whales can be quite entertaining." Ken grinned. "Here in Hawaii, when they arrive, it's regarded as a homecoming, because they're considered the original locals."

As the boat continued on, the ocean became a bit choppy. It didn't take Mandy long to realize Ellen wasn't doing well.

"I feel nauseous, like I did on the cruise ship when the water became rough." Ellen moaned, holding her stomach.

Mandy looked over at Ken, then back to Ellen, who was beginning to cough.

"Oh, no, I'm going to vomit." Immediately, Ellen leaned over the railing and emptied her stomach.

Mandy stood close by, gently patting her friend's back. She wished she had some motion-sickness drops to put behind Ellen's ears. Of course, they hadn't helped her much when she'd become seasick on the cruise ship.

"I'll get a bottle of water to rinse her mouth," Ken volunteered.

"Thank you." Until now, Mandy had forgotten how sick her friend had been before. But that morning in the cabin with Ellen rushed back to her, like it was yesterday.

Ken returned with a bottle of water. "I'll give her this whenever she's ready."

Another whale showed itself, this one quite close to the boat. In her excitement to capture a picture of it, Mandy leaned over the rail. She was on the verge of snapping the photo when a wave hit the catamaran, causing Mandy to lose her footing. She nearly lost her balance, but Ken caught her in time. "That was close." He placed his hand around Mandy's waist and held her to his side. "Are you okay?"

Her face radiated with heat. "I'm fine."

Just then, Ellen got sick again. When Mandy reached out to comfort her, she loosened her grip on the camera and it plunged into the water. "Oh, no! My camera!" she wailed. "I've lost all the wonderful pictures I've taken on this trip."

What started out to be a glorious day and had suddenly turned sour. Not only was poor Ellen pale and trembling, but now Mandy had no photos of Hawaii to show her family or friends back home. What a disappointment. The only pictures she would have of Hawaii were her memories.

She stared at the choppy waters, struggling not to give in to tears. *I guess the memories I've made here are something to be thankful for. It's more than I would have had if Sadie, Barbara, Ellen, and I had never made this trip.*

CHAPTER 27

The last Sunday in February, Mandy was awakened by a fierce whooshing sound coming from outside. Something hit the outside of the window. Wind gusted hard against the B&B. Nature whistled as a storm held firm over the area.

"Is it windy out?" Ellen sat up in bed, yawning and rubbing her eyes.

"Jah, sounds like the wind to me." Mandy clambered out of bed and pulled the curtains aside. "Oh my! Come look at this, Ellen. You should see how the trees are swaying. Some are bending so much I'm afraid they might split. And look, palm branches are scattered everywhere."

Ellen joined her at the window. "I've never witnessed such strong winds before. The rain is actually blowing sideways!"

"It should be fully light out by now, but see how dark it still is. Those clouds look nasty." Mandy shivered. "You don't sup-

312

pose it's a hurricane?"

"It could be, I guess. Maybe we should see if Luana and Makaio are up. If so, they may be in the kitchen by now."

The girls hurried to get dressed, and by the time they entered the kitchen, the lights in the B&B had gone out.

"We have no power, and how long it'll be out, I can only guess," Makaio grumbled from where he sat at the table. "I can't watch TV now, either."

Luana looked over at the girls and winked. "No television playing in the background most of the day . . . How sad is that?"

Mandy stifled a giggle.

Makaio drummed his fingers on the table. "So much for the Spam-and-egg breakfast I was hoping for this morning. And what are we supposed to serve our guests, who no doubt expect a hearty meal?"

Luana placed both hands on his shoulders. "It's not a problem. We've been through this before. I have plenty of fresh fruit to offer, as well as cold cereal and bread."

"Who wants bread when you can't toast it?" He glanced at Mandy and Ellen. "We won't be going to church today, because if the power's out here, it's most likely out there, too. Besides, it's dangerous to go out in weather like this."

"My husband's right. A person could get hit by a falling branch or, worse yet, by a coconut falling from a tree. You certainly don't want to get clunked in the head by one of those." Luana moved to the refrigerator and took out a bowl of mixed berries. "We should be thinking positive and hope the electricity will be back on soon."

"In the meantime, what can we do to help?" Ellen asked.

Luana gestured to the pineapple sitting on the counter. "One of you can slice the *hala kahiki* and arrange it on a platter. The other can get the cereal out, along with a container of milk."

As Ellen went to get a knife out of the drawer, Mandy repeated the word for pineapple over and over in her mind. She was happy her vocabulary had grown with the Hawaiian words she'd learned so far.

"If we're stuck having cold cereal this morning, let's have it with coconut milk instead of regular milk," Makaio suggested.

"I'll get it out in case someone wants to try it, but I'm guessing most of our guests will want to stick with cow's milk."

"Coconut milk's healthier, but I guess not everyone realizes it." He pushed his chair aside and headed for the refrigerator. "Think I'll have a glass of it now, in fact."

Mandy couldn't help noticing how Makaio still limped as he walked. His therapy sessions were going well, but sometimes he tried to do too much and it set him back — like yesterday, when he'd tried to move something too heavy. Before she could ask if he would like her to get the coconut milk, he'd already taken it from the refrigerator.

"Do storms this bad hit Kauai often?" Ellen asked as she began cutting the pineapple.

"We get a fair amount of wind and rain, but severe storms, strong enough to knock out the power, don't happen often." Luana added several slices of papaya to the berries she'd placed on a large platter. "When they do, we're sometimes left without power for several hours."

"Right." Makaio poured some coconut milk into a glass and took a drink. "Last year, around this time, we lost power during a storm, and it didn't come back on for two whole days."

Luana fanned her face. "The temperatures were in the eighties, and it was impossible to cool the house down without air-conditioning."

"We're used to the heat and humidity during the summer," Ellen put in. "Since we Amish don't have electricity in our homes, we've never had air-conditioning to cool things down."

"Many Hawaiian natives and others who live here don't have it, either. They rely on the trade winds," Makaio explained. "The main reason we have AC is for the comfort of our guests, who aren't used to warmer weather. It would be nice if we could afford a generator for our establishment. Then we'd have some power to run lights and the refrigerator." He took another sip of coconut milk and set the glass back on the table.

Mandy stared out the window, watching the rain still falling quite heavily. Puddles quickly formed in the lawn, and pelted flower blossoms were scattered about. "What do you do for lights when the power goes out?" she asked, going to the cupboard to get the boxes of cereal for breakfast.

Luana pointed to the battery-operated candles sitting on a shelf across the room. "Makaio has a large lantern, also powered by batteries. It's good for many hours and puts out quite a bit of light. Our biggest challenge is cooking, but with the use of the barbecue grill, we manage to get by."

Mandy realized Ellen was right about things not being perfect on Hawaii, but like the Amish, the Hawaiian people knew how to survive without electricity.

■ ■ ■ ■

By eight o'clock that evening, the winds had died down, but the power at the B&B had not been restored. They all sat around in the living room with battery-operated candles for light while Makaio gave Mandy another ukulele lesson. After only a month's worth of practice, she'd gotten quite good at playing the instrument.

Ellen sat close to one of the larger candles and wrote a few letters to send home. She continued to write until the soothing music caused her eyes to grow heavy. In an effort to keep awake, she sat up straight and arched her back before picking up her pen. By nine o'clock, everyone but Mandy and Ellen had gone to bed.

"Sure wish we could have gone to church today." Mandy relaxed against the back of the couch. "I missed the music and looked forward to seeing Ken."

Ellen looked up from her letter writing. "Nothing else? What about the pastor's message?"

"Of course I missed his sermon. I only meant —"

"You don't have to explain, Mandy. If you ask me, you're getting a little too attached to Ken."

"I am not. We're good friends, and nothing more." Mandy abruptly stood. "I'm tired and going to bed. Are you coming?"

"I'll be there as soon as I finish this letter to Sadie. I'm bringing her up to date on how we're both doing."

"Say hi for me, too, please." Mandy picked up the flashlight Makaio had given her earlier and hurried from the room.

Ellen liked how quiet the B&B was right now. Their only two guests were pleasant and had retired to their room a short time ago. Awhile later, a knock sounded on the door. Since Ellen was the only one up, she went to see who it was. Seeing Ken through the peephole, she opened the door.

"Sorry for coming by so late. I meant to drop by earlier to see how you all were doing after the crazy storm, but I ended up helping my dad and brother pick up tree branches and other debris once the winds died down."

"We're all okay." She opened the door wider and offered him a seat.

Ken glanced around the dimly lit room. "Where is everyone?"

"They went to bed awhile ago." Ellen kept her voice down so as not to wake anyone.

"Even Mandy?" His tone revealed disappointment.

"Yes." Ellen figured Mandy hadn't had time to get undressed yet, but she wasn't about to tell her Ken was here. She'd no doubt come rushing out of their room, and they would sit and visit while Ellen played chaperone.

Ken stepped back toward the front door. "Well, I guess if everyone's okay, I'll head back home. Tell Mandy hi for me, and I'll talk to her soon."

Ellen cleared her throat, gathering up the courage to tell Ken what he needed to know. "Has Mandy told you she has a boyfriend back home?" She looked at him squarely, resting her hand on her hip.

"No, she's never mentioned it." He tipped his head.

"His name is Gideon, and once Mandy joins the church, they will no doubt get married."

"Oh." Ken shuffled his bare feet across the tile floor a few times. "It makes sense that someone as nice as Mandy would have a boyfriend waiting for her back home. I'm sure she will make Gideon a wonderful wife."

Before Ellen could form a response, Ken turned and rushed out the door.

Ellen stared at the candle flame flickering

close to her. She felt bad telling Ken about Mandy's boyfriend, but something needed to be done to discourage him from pursuing a relationship with her. She didn't want to hurt his feelings and had come close to calling him back. Her resolve won out, though. *I did it for Mandy's sake, as well as Ken's.* Ellen bit her bottom lip. *I had to make sure he didn't have any ideas of trying to sway Mandy to stay in Hawaii. It was time to break them apart, before one or both becomes too serious about the other. When Mandy is happily married to Gideon, she'll be glad she returned to Indiana and left her Hawaiian fantasy life with Ken behind.*

Middlebury

"I hate to do this to you," Sadie whispered to Barbara in the middle of their young people's singing, "but I've developed a *koppweh* and need to get going. You'll either have to leave with me or find another way home."

"I'm sorry you have a headache." Barbara patted her friend's arm. "If you don't mind, I'd like to stay for the rest of the singing. I'm sure someone here will be willing to give me a ride home."

"Danki for understanding." Sadie gathered up her things and headed outside to her horse and buggy.

Barbara felt a bit selfish for staying instead of accompanying Sadie, but Gideon was here tonight, and she hoped for the chance to speak with him. She enjoyed the opportunity to socialize and sing with Amish friends, too.

After the singing wound down, most of those who'd attended lingered for a while, visiting and snacking on leftover cake and cookies.

Gideon surprised Barbara when he sought her out. "Where's Sadie? I noticed the two of you sitting together earlier." He flashed her a smile.

"She came down with a koppweh and went home. Of course, I have no ride now, but I'm sure I'll find someone heading my way who'll be willing to give me a lift."

"Your house is on my way, so I'd be happy to offer you a ride."

Barbara smiled. "Danki, Gideon. I appreciate it so much." Her cheeks warmed.

As they headed for home a short time later, Barbara struggled with her feelings. She'd begun to care for Gideon as more than a friend, but she was sure he didn't feel the same way about her. *There's no hope of us being together, because Mandy will be coming back soon, and he's in love with her.*

Barbara would never intentionally do anything to come between Mandy and Gideon, but if by some chance, things didn't work out for them, she might find a way to reveal her feelings to him.

CHAPTER 28

Kapaa
Friday, March 25

Ailani had a baby girl two days ago. They named her Primrose, after Luana's favorite flower. The birth was not easy, but it was quickly forgotten once the precious baby was born. Because Ailani was still weak from the long labor she endured, she and Oke will be staying at the B&B until she's strong enough to take care of the infant on her own.

It was nice to make cookies yesterday for all of us to enjoy. Makaio and Luana left earlier today to run some errands. They also had a doctor's appointment to see how Makaio's leg is doing.

Mandy hoped things would go well for Makaio today. Luana had been so patient throughout his recovery.

She set her journal aside and smiled at Ellen, who sat beside her at the kitchen table, drinking a cup of lavender tea. "You know what, Ellen?"

Blowing at the steam swirling up from her cup, Ellen raised her eyebrows. "What, Mandy?"

"Seeing Ailani's baby makes me long for a child of my own." Mandy got out the soft cinnamon cookies and bit into one.

"I'm sure you'll have a baby someday — after you and Gideon are married." Ellen sipped the fragrant tea. "This lavender honey I added is quite good."

"I have to agree." She reverted back to Ellen's comment about her and Gideon. "What if we don't end up getting married?"

Ellen tapped Mandy's shoulder. "Of course you'll get married. Why do you think he's waiting for you to join the church? You have nothing to worry about. Once you get home, things will work out."

"But what if I decide not to join the church?"

"Not join? And do what, Mandy — stay here in Hawaii and marry Ken? Is that what you're hoping for?"

Mandy bit her lip so hard she tasted blood. "No, I . . ." Unbidden tears sprang to her eyes. She'd suppressed her emotions so long she felt as if she could burst. "It's

324

not like that."

"What do you mean?"

"Except for church, I don't see much of Ken anymore." Her throat felt sore when she spoke. "Something's changed. I can't imagine what I did, but it seems I may have said or done something to offend him. We were getting along so well before, but now I don't know."

"He's probably busy helping out at his parents' chicken farm."

Mandy drew in a few slow, steady breaths. "How busy could he be? He always had time to come by before. Ken hasn't even brought any eggs in a while. His brother's been making the deliveries." She clenched her fingers. "I feel like he's avoiding me for some reason."

"Maybe you're overthinking things, Mandy."

She tapped Ellen's arm. "Have you seen Ken recently? And if so, did he say anything to you about me?"

"Umm . . . no." Ellen pushed away from the table and rose. "Think I hear the baby crying. I'm going to see if Ailani needs any help."

Before Mandy could comment, her friend made a hasty exit. *Strange. Is Ellen trying to avoid talking to me about Ken?*

■ ■ ■ ■

As Ellen stepped into the living room, where Ailani sat rocking her baby, a feeling of guilt weighed heavily on her.

"Is everything okay?" Ailani asked. "It sounded like you two were having a disagreement."

"Oh, that. Mandy's a little worried about why Ken hasn't been around much lately."

"He's probably busy helping at his parents' farm right now."

"Yes. I told her the same thing." Ellen took a seat. She wasn't about to reveal to anyone, especially Mandy, what she'd told Ken the other evening.

She wondered how her best friend could be thrown off her normal path. Mandy had a nice boyfriend back home, waiting for her return. Ellen figured it was up to her to help Mandy see the light, but maybe she'd been wrong. Perhaps she should have kept her nose out of things.

Mandy is hurt because Ken hasn't been in touch with her lately, and it's my fault. If I hadn't told him about Gideon, he'd still be coming around. Her jaw clenched. *But Ken needed to know he has no future with Mandy, so I did it for both their sakes.*

Ellen felt sure things would be as they once were after they returned home. Her friend might miss Ken and everything she liked about Hawaii, but in time it would seem like a distant memory. In some ways, it was good Mandy had dropped her digital camera in the ocean during their whale-watching cruise. Having the pictures she'd taken would only have served as a reminder of what she'd left behind on Kauai. *I don't like admitting this, but I'm glad her camera is at the bottom of the ocean, never to be seen again. Those pictures would only keep her memory of Ken alive.*

Pushing these thoughts to the back of her mind, Ellen moved across the room to offer her assistance to Luana's daughter. "You look tired. Would you like me to hold Primrose for a bit?"

Ailani nodded. "I'd appreciate it. Since Mama took Dad to physical therapy, and Oke's at work, I've had full responsibility for the baby, and no matter what I do, she won't stop fussing." She appeared to be overwhelmed as she looked at Ellen with quivering lips.

Ellen's heart went out to the young woman. "Why don't you go lie down awhile? I'll take care of Primrose till your folks get back."

"Mahalo." Ailani rose from her chair and handed the precious bundle to Ellen.

After Ailani left the room, Ellen walked out to the lanai, while gently patting the baby's back. She heard water running in the sink and knew Mandy must be washing dishes in the kitchen.

It was a breezy afternoon, with comfortable temperatures — the kind of day one enjoyed being outside. After several minutes, Primrose stopped crying, so Ellen took a seat on the glider, softly humming as she rocked. The warmth of the baby and the infant's gentle breathing as she was lulled to sleep stirred something in Ellen's heart.

I understand why Mandy would want a baby of her own. I'd like one, too, but if it's meant to be, it'll happen in God's time. Mandy has a better chance at having a boppli *than I do.* She swallowed against the lump in her throat. *At least she has a boyfriend back home, eager to marry her. I don't even have a suitor. Maybe someday God will send the right man into my life.*

Middlebury

Sadie's stomach churned as she stepped into the phone shack to call Mandy. She hoped to unburden her worries, and the sooner the better. In the last few weeks she'd seen Gideon with Barbara a couple of times, not to mention hearing he'd taken her home from the singing a few Sundays ago. If Mandy didn't get home soon, Gideon might start courting Barbara or someone else.

Sadie wanted to speak with Barbara about this, too, but every time she started to bring up the subject, she lost her nerve. One time, she'd casually mentioned to Barbara about seeing Gideon a lot, but her friend made light of it, saying they were only good friends and he needed a sympathetic ear. Barbara said she was concerned, because with Mandy having been gone so long, Gideon was beginning to lose hope.

To make matters worse, the last time Sadie had spoken to Ellen on the phone, she'd learned Mandy had been seeing a lot of a young man named Ken. Ellen didn't say whether Mandy had fallen in love with this fellow, but she sounded concerned because Mandy was gone from the B&B so much.

"None of this would be a problem if they'd stuck with me and Barbara instead of heading out on their own when the ship docked at Kauai. We should have insisted they join our tour group that day," Sadie mumbled as she punched in the number for the bed-and-breakfast.

The phone rang a few times before someone picked up. "The Palms Bed-and-Breakfast."

"Mandy?"

"Yes. Is this Sadie?"

"Jah."

"It's nice hearing from you. How are things in Middlebury?"

Sadie shifted on the wooden bench, trying to find a comfortable position. "Everyone's fine, but —"

"Good to hear. Ellen and I are doing well here. We're busier than ever." Sadie couldn't get a word in edgewise, so she let Mandy continue.

"Luana and Makaio's daughter had a baby girl two days ago. She and her husband are staying at the B&B so she has more help until she gets her strength back." Mandy paused briefly, but before Sadie could respond, she rushed on. "The baby's so little, and you should see all her dark hair. Oh, and they call her Primrose. Isn't that a sweet name?" Her voice sounded so enthusiastic.

"I guess so; it's kind of tropical sounding, but certainly nothing like our traditional Amish names."

"Amish parents don't always give their

babies traditional names anymore, Sadie. I know an Amish couple who named their little girl Doretta, and I think it's a lovely name."

"You're right, and so is Primrose. I only meant . . ." Sadie cleared her throat. "Have you heard from Gideon lately?"

"Not for a week or so. I'm sure he's quite busy. He sent me a birthday card and gift, but I never got it."

"Maybe it got lost in the mail."

"Jah. That's most likely what happened."

"Have you talked to Barbara lately?" Sadie questioned.

"No, but then if she had called, I would have been too busy to talk very long."

"I see." Sadie licked her lips. She was quickly losing her nerve. "I saw Gideon and Barbara the other day, and I think —"

"What did you say, Sadie? I can hardly hear you anymore. The connection must be bad."

Maybe it's a sign I'm not supposed to say anything. Sadie tapped her fingers on the wooden shelf where the phone sat. *I probably shouldn't say anything about Barbara and Gideon right now. It may be best to keep my concerns to myself and wait to see how things go when Mandy gets home.*

"Sorry, Sadie, but I have to hang up now.

I heard a car pull in and need to see who it is."

"Okay. Take care, and I hope to see you soon."

When Sadie hung up, she leaned her head against the wall and sat several seconds, wondering if she should have called Mandy at all, for nothing had been accomplished as far as Gideon and Barbara was concerned. It was nice to hear Mandy's voice, though. It seemed like she and Ellen had been gone forever.

Kapaa

Mandy peeked out the window and saw Luana and Makaio getting out of their car. Makaio had a big grin on his face as they walked up to the house. She went to the back door and opened it for them. "How'd the physical therapy session go?"

"It went well." Luana, all smiles, too, pointed to Makaio. "Tell her the happy news."

"I had a good report today." His smile widened. "I can finally return to most of my duties here, which I kind of knew already. I've been feeling fine and did some gardening yesterday while you girls baked cookies." Makaio paused. "We hate to see you go, but when you're ready, I'll go on the

Internet and help you book your tickets."

Although eager to see her family and friends again, Mandy felt a sense of disappointment. This place and these people had become home to her. It wouldn't be easy leaving her special Kauai friends, whom she'd come to know and love.

CHAPTER 29

Friday, April 15, was Mandy and Ellen's last night on Kauai. Luana and Makaio had planned a going-away party for them, and Ken had been invited. Mandy's emotions ran high, feeling both happy and sad. Seeing him tonight, knowing it was the last time they would be together, nearly broke her heart. She wished she was free to share her feelings with him, but she would never be so bold. Besides, Ken had not given her any reason to believe he had feelings for her other than friendship — although after he'd looked at her a certain way or done something thoughtful, she'd wondered if he saw her as more than a friend. But that was before he'd stopped coming around so much.

It's better this way, Mandy thought as she sat between Ellen and Ailani on the couch. *I'll be returning to my Amish life, and he'll stay here with his family, like before I came to Kauai.*

She glanced across the room, where Ken sat in a chair, talking with Makaio and Oke. Ailani took pictures of everyone in the room, while Oke held the baby. Mandy noticed every once in a while, Ken looked in her direction, then glanced quickly away. Would he miss the friendship they'd established or forget about her soon after she was gone? He'd kept his distance these past several weeks and hadn't said much to her tonight. *If I only understood why he's stayed away, at least nothing would be left unsaid.*

Tears welled in her eyes, and she fought to keep them from falling onto her cheeks. In some ways, she wished he hadn't come. It may have made it easier. On the other hand, she was glad for the opportunity to see him one last time. If Mandy still had her camera, she would have taken a picture of him.

"We're certainly going to miss you both." Luana's statement pushed Mandy's thoughts aside. "I hope you'll call or write so we can keep in touch." Her eyes misted. "Maybe someday you can visit Kauai again, or we might go to Indiana to see you."

"It would be nice, but another trip for me would be expensive." Mandy was barely able to speak around the lump stuck in her throat. She'd known almost from the minute she and Ellen first arrived at the bed-and-breakfast that it would be hard to leave, but she'd never expected it would be this difficult to say goodbye. Of course, back then, neither of them had an inkling they'd be staying for several months. If not for Makaio's accident and Luana needing help at the B&B, they would have gone home long ago.

"I have something for both of you." Luana rose from her seat and left the room. When she returned, she handed Mandy and Ellen two quilted potholders and pillow shams, all sewn with colorful Hawaiian print material.

"They're beautiful. Mahalo," Mandy whispered tearfully.

Ellen, also with tears in her eyes, nodded. "Yes, we appreciate your thoughtfulness."

"Now don't forget to take home the ukulele I gave you." Makaio spoke up. "You've learned the basics, so now all you need to do is practice. It won't be long and you'll be playing as good as me." He looked over at his wife and smiled.

Mandy could only manage a nod. Every time she played the Hawaiian instrument, she would think of Makaio, as well as Ken because he, too, played the ukulele. Of course, she would also have the sunrise picture Ken had given her.

"Hold up your gifts so I can get your picture. These will be nice to put in my scrapbook." Ailani smiled. "I've enjoyed getting to know you. Mahalo for helping my ohana while Papa's leg was healing and for taking care of me and Primrose when we came home from the hospital." She bent to kiss the top of her baby's head.

"You're welcome." Mandy smiled. "It was our privilege to help your family."

Ellen nodded. "We appreciate all that's been done for us, too."

"I have something for both of you." Ken stood and made his way over to the couch. Then he handed Mandy and Ellen each a paper sack.

"How about you young people sitting on the sofa together so Ailani can take your picture after you've opened Ken's gifts?" Luana suggested.

The two friends scooted over and Ken took a seat beside Mandy. Even though they weren't talking much, she was grateful to be in his company this evening.

Mandy opened her gift and fought for control when she pulled out a lei made with kukui nuts. "Mahalo, Ken," she murmured. "This looks like the one you've worn a few times when we did some things together."

"It's the same one. I wanted you to have it as a symbol of our friendship, and so you would remember your time here on Kauai."

How could I ever forget it — or you? Mandy kept her thoughts to herself but nodded to Ken. She wished she could freeze this moment. Having him here, receiving his heartfelt gift made it even harder to leave tomorrow. Ellen, on the other hand, had made it clear she was ready to leave Hawaii and get home to her family.

Ellen opened her gift and revealed a pretty shell lei. "Thanks, Ken. It was nice of you to think of us."

"Okay, ladies, hold up those gifts, and everyone smile." Ailani snapped a few pictures before returning to her seat.

"What's for dessert?" Makaio asked.

"I made an angel food cake with strawberries and whipping cream, in honor of our most special guests," Luana replied. "I'll get it ready to serve right now."

"I'll give you a hand." Ellen rose from the couch.

Oke came over with Primrose, who'd begun to fuss, and handed her to Ailani. "I think she needs her *makuahine.*"

Makaio wandered out to the kitchen, and soon Luana announced it was time for dessert. Ken got up with Oke and Ailani, and they headed for the dining room.

Mandy remained seated a few minutes, closing her eyes to hold back the tears threatening to spill over. She wished she and Ken could spend a few minutes alone, but it was probably better they didn't. She couldn't be so bold as to ask if they could take a walk outside, and he had certainly not suggested it. Once more, she consoled herself with the fact that this was how it was supposed to be. The Hawaiian words *a hui hou,* which meant "until meeting again," floated through her mind, but she didn't voice them because deep down she knew she would probably never see Ken again.

Saturday, April 16
Ellen and I boarded the ship a few hours ago. After our evening meal, we'll be heading for the Big Island. Ellen's excited, but I have mixed feelings. We missed the opportunity to see the volcano and other things Barbara and Sadie got to view before their voyage home, but leaving Kauai is so difficult for me. I will miss Luana and Makaio, but Ken most of all. Even though we have no future together, it didn't make it any easier for me to part ways with him.

Mandy wondered if Ken would miss her. She knew Makaio and Luana would — especially with all the hugs Luana had given Ellen and Mandy when she drove them to the docks. The tears Makaio's wife spilled with their goodbyes were proof enough. The Palus were such a special couple.

Mandy thought about tomorrow and how she'd miss going to church in Kapaa. She would not be able to see Ken up front with the rest of the worship team. She'd miss the inspirational songs of praise, the pastor's encouraging message, and even the brightly colored Hawaiian clothes many people wore.

She looked down at her Amish dress. Her muumuu was packed away now, and it saddened her a bit, knowing she wouldn't have any reason to wear it again. She'd probably show it to her family, and then it would be put in a drawer to be looked at from time to time as a reminder of her days on Kauai.

Ellen had been eager to board the ship and talked about the delicious meals they would have on the cruise liner. She was also looking forward to seeing the volcano that Sadie and Barbara had seen before heading for the mainland.

After Ellen finished freshening up before dinner, Mandy quickly closed her journal.

She didn't want her friend to see what she'd written. She was fairly certain Ellen had suspicions about her feelings for Ken and didn't want to discuss the matter. Talking about it and thinking about it were two different things. Mandy's feelings for Ken were all she could think of right now, even though she tried to squelch them. The image of his face was constantly on her mind, not to mention how he'd looked at her when they finally parted last evening. If Ken had taken her into his arms, even for a casual hug, she didn't know what she would have done. Truthfully, she wished he had. Would she have been able to let him go?

Mandy closed her eyes, finding it hard to forget their final, silent goodbye. She'd walked with Ken to his vehicle, while the rest of them stayed inside. The short walk felt like miles, instead of a few feet. The silence between them was deafening. She'd studied every feature of his face. As he gazed into her eyes, she silently screamed, *Please, Ken, ask me to stay.* When he reached out to take her hand, it may as well have been a kiss. Coming from Ken, even this simple act of friendship had sent her heart soaring. The look on his face before he turned and got in his SUV nearly tore Mandy's heart apart. As difficult as it was, she kept silent and let Ken walk out of her life. He was English. She was Amish. What more could either of them say?

My fantasy is over now, she reminded herself. *It's time to face reality and focus on my life back home. Mom, Dad, and the rest of my family are waiting for me, and so is Gideon.* She massaged her forehead, continuing to mull things over. *Do I care for Gideon as much as I did before? Will Ken become a distant memory when I see Gideon again? Guess I won't know for sure until I see him again.*

Middlebury

"I'm glad spring is here," Peggy said Monday afternoon as she opened her store's front window and drew in a deep breath. "Can you smell the fresh air?"

Barbara nodded from where she sat behind the counter on a wooden stool. "It smells like clean towels when they've been hung outside to dry."

"On afternoons like this, I wish I could be home working in my garden, instead of cooped up in this stuffy store. When I sell the store someday, I'll be able to spend more time in my garden and do other things I enjoy." Peggy remained at the window a few minutes, then moved toward the door.

"Since there are no customers at the moment, I think I'll go outside and take a short walk. I'll keep an eye on the door, and if any customers show up, I'll hurry back inside."

"Go ahead. Take your time." Barbara motioned to the bolts of material lying before her. "While you're gone, I'll put these away."

"Danki, Barbara. Don't know how I'd get along without you." Peggy smiled. "You're a hard worker. It's a comfort to have someone I can depend on."

Barbara's face warmed. "I love working here and want to do a good job for you."

"Well, keep doing what you're doing, and you'll have a job here for as long as I own the store." With a parting wave, Peggy went out the door.

I hope she doesn't sell this business anytime soon. Barbara fingered a quilted potholder lying on the counter. *Wish I could buy the store when she decides to sell, but there's no way I can afford it.*

Sniffing the warm breeze coming through the open window, Barbara's thoughts wandered back to Peggy's other comments. She felt the same way as Peggy did about spring. It affected her soul, making her feel more alive. Springtime seemed to put the spirit of youth in people, young and old alike. The drudgery of cold winter months, long and gray, faded as each vivid new bloom brightened the landscape. Even from inside the store, Barbara could hear the birds singing and the leaves rustling in the gentle breeze. There'd even been a bee in the store earlier, which she'd quickly shooed out the window. Saying goodbye to the winter blues was something Barbara didn't mind at all. Spring was also a time when hearts seemed merrier, and the spirit of love seemed to be felt everywhere.

Will I ever be fortunate enough to find love? If I never get married, I'll continue working here as long as Peggy owns the store. Barbara picked up two bolts of material and carried them to the shelf where they belonged. She had started back to get the others when Gideon entered the store, smiling widely. "Did you hear the good news?"

"What good news?" She picked up another bolt of material, holding it under one arm.

"Mandy and Ellen are on their way home."

"Oh? I hadn't heard. When will they be here?" Barbara tried to sound nonchalant, but internally, she was shaking.

"It'll be a few more days. I talked to her daed yesterday. The man who owns the

B&B where they stayed is doing better now and can take over his job again. The cruise ship Mandy and Ellen are on was supposed to leave Kauai Saturday night." Gideon leaned on the counter. "Of course, it won't go directly to Los Angeles. It'll stop at another Hawaiian island for a good part of a day, then move on to stop in Ensenada, Mexico, before docking at the port in L.A. From there, they'll catch a train to bring them the rest of the way home." Gideon's smile widened. "Isn't it exciting, Barbara? Just think, by this time next week I'll be reunited with Mandy. Then we can start making plans for our future. I can hardly wait."

Barbara hadn't realized she'd been holding her breath until she felt the need to breathe. "That's wunderbaar." She forced a smile. *Mandy is a good friend, and I look forward to seeing her again, but once she gets home, I won't be seeing Gideon as often. He won't need a sympathetic shoulder to cry on, and Mandy might not appreciate me spending time with her boyfriend. I need to set my feelings for him aside and try to be happy for them.*

CHAPTER 30

Saturday, April 23

Ellen and I are on the train, heading toward our final destination. It's been difficult sitting all day and then sleeping in seats, but we didn't have enough money to pay for a sleeper car this time. Poor Ellen is especially glad to be off the ship, as the waters were quite rough coming back to the mainland, and she got seasick again.

Mandy paused from writing in her journal to glance out the window. Several buffalo were silhouetted against the setting sun. It was amazing to view such big animals grazing on the plains.

Shortly after noon, they'd left Albuquerque, New Mexico, and entertained themselves playing a few games until it was time for supper. Now, while Mandy caught up on her journal writing, Ellen nodded off.

Mandy had written in a previous journal entry about the things they'd seen on the Big Island. The volcano was interesting, but after being on Kauai, she couldn't help comparing the two islands. The area near the volcano on the Big Island looked so barren and full of lava rock. Although curious about the volcano, Mandy kept thinking about the beauty of Kauai. Even now when she closed her eyes, she visualized swaying palms, lovely flowers, and sandy beaches.

She thought about her Hawaiian friends — especially Ken. He'd looked so handsome in his Hawaiian shirt the evening he'd taken them to a luau. And even more handsome when he'd come to say goodbye the night before they'd left Kauai. Memories of the times they'd been together would stay with her forever.

Ken was so patient and kind when he taught me to swim, Mandy mused. *I could trust him with my fear of water, and he helped me relax and keep trying.*

At times, Mandy wished she'd never met Ken. But she was grateful for the opportunity to get to know him. *If only I could have the best of both worlds — the Hawaii life with Ken, and my Amish life with . . .*

Her thoughts swept her back to when their ship departed Kauai's tropical paradise.

She'd stood on the deck, tearfully watching until the island became a tiny dot against the huge horizon and then faded away. The farther away they got, the sadder Mandy felt. The ocean's vastness seemed to swallow her up, leaving a huge hole in her heart.

Desperately needing to focus on something else, Mandy turned to the journal page she'd written the day the ship stopped at the harbor in Mexico. Since she didn't have her camera anymore, it was important to fill her journal with as many remembrances as possible. She jotted in a short note about something she'd forgotten to mention — seeing several sea lions on the rocks and platforms. The creatures looked silly, flapping their flippers as they carried on with loud barking.

Mandy remembered her amazement at seeing so many brightly colored buildings in Ensenada. Some were chartreuse. Others were painted in bright pink, green, and blue. They were certainly in sharp contrast to the plain white of most Amish homes where she came from. It was interesting how each culture varied in their architecture, style of living, and food choices. Many things had been different in Hawaii than what she was used to at home.

Different is good when you fall in love with

it, though. Mandy drew a deep breath and closed her eyes. *Maybe I ought to follow Ellen's example and sleep.*

Monday, April 25
    We're in northeast Indiana and almost home. The scenery alongside the tracks looks familiar. Mom and Dad will be waiting in Elkhart for me to get off the train. I wonder if Gideon will be there, too.

Hoping to quell her nervous stomach, Mandy reached for the tote bag at her feet, placing her pen and journal inside. She glanced at Ellen, whose nose was pressed against the window like an eager child. No doubt she was anxious to get home.

"You know something?" Mandy lightly tapped her friend's arm.

"What?" Ellen turned to look at her.

"Since we've been gone so long and both lost our jobs, we'll need to start looking for some other employment as soon as possible."

Ellen groaned. "I sure hope we can find something."

"I can still do volunteer work at the thrift store in Shipshewana, but since the restaurant in Middlebury replaced me with someone else, I won't be returning there unless one of the other waitresses ends up quitting for some reason."

"Maybe your daed will have an opening at the meat-and-cheese store."

"I've worked there before and didn't like it much. I'd rather be waitressing, where I can visit with people." Mandy sighed, maneuvering in her seat to get more comfortable. "But I guess if it's all I can find, I'll do it, because I want to pay Mom and Dad back the money they spent on my cruise ship and train tickets to bring me home from Hawaii."

"I plan to pay my folks back, too." Ellen clasped Mandy's hand. "I'm sure we'll both find something, even if it's not our first choice for a job."

Elkhart

When Mandy stepped off the train, she spotted her parents right away. Ellen's folks were there, too, but she saw no sign of Gideon. She'd expected him to be at the train station, waiting for her. Giving Mandy little time to think about it, Mom quickly enveloped her in a hug. "It's good to have you home, Daughter. We've missed you so much!"

"I missed you, too." Mandy hugged Dad next, blinking happy tears from her eyes.

Despite missing her friends on Kauai, it truly was good to see her family again.

"Do you have any luggage besides what you're carrying?" Dad asked.

"We each have a small suitcase Luana and Makaio gave us," Ellen spoke up.

"I'll walk over with your daed to get it." Dad hurried off.

Ellen leaned close to Mandy and whispered, "Where's Gideon? I'm surprised he's not here."

Feeling a bit guilty, Mandy replied, "Maybe he's upset because I didn't give him much of my time whenever he called while we were on Kauai. He may think I was trying to avoid him. Perhaps he doesn't want to court me anymore."

"I couldn't help overhearing, Mandy," Mom interjected. "I seriously doubt he would think such things. Every time Gideon has seen your daed, he's asked about you, and he said on many occasions he couldn't wait for your return. I am fairly certain he had to work this afternoon. I wouldn't be a bit surprised if he doesn't drop by our house this evening."

Mandy's emotions swirled as she thought about seeing him again. Would she still have feelings for Gideon, or had they faded when she met Ken?

■ ■ ■ ■

Middlebury

Since Gideon had been at work when Mandy's train arrived in Elkhart, he hadn't been able to greet her at the station. It had been disappointing, but at least now that work was over he could stop by the Freys' house to welcome her back.

Filled with a mixture of excitement and apprehension, he clutched his horse's reins so tightly the veins on his hands stuck out. Maybe it was good his horse, Dash, was taking his sweet time. What if Mandy wasn't excited to see him? What if during her absence she'd changed her mind about being his girlfriend? Gideon didn't think he could deal with her rejection — especially after waiting all those months for her return. It would be one thing if she'd been here and they'd drifted apart, but if the miles separating them caused Mandy to forget what they once had, Gideon would be distraught. After all, he hadn't wanted her to go in the first place but had no way of stopping her. Of course, he had foolishly given Mandy his blessing, which he saw now as a big mistake.

"Take a deep breath and calm yourself,"

he mumbled, guiding his horse up the Freys' driveway. "In a few moments you'll see Mandy face-to-face."

After Gideon tied Dash to the hitching rail, he reached inside the buggy and took out the gift he'd bought for Mandy. He was especially eager to give it to her, since the birthday present he'd sent in January had apparently gotten lost in the mail.

Racing for the house, he took the porch steps two at a time and lifted his hand. But before he could knock, Mandy's brother Melvin opened the door.

"I heard your horse whinny and knew we had company." The boy looked up at Gideon and grinned. "Figured you came to see Mandy."

Gideon gave a quick nod. "Is she here?"

"Jah. She's in the living room, teaching everyone some words she learned from her Hawaiian friends." Melvin stepped aside. "Go on in. Bet she'll be glad to see ya."

Gideon followed him into the living room, where he found Mandy sitting on the couch, with her mother on one side, and her brother Mark on the other.

He cleared his throat and took a step forward.

"Look who came to see you, Mandy." Melvin pointed to Gideon.

Mandy stood and a bit awkwardly reached out her hands. "It's nice to see you again."

"It's good to see you, too. Welcome back." He clasped one of her hands and put the paper sack he held in the other. "I brought you a little welcome-home gift."

"Danki, but you didn't have to." Mandy's gaze darted from Gideon to her little brother and back again. She seemed nervous, reminding him of a skittish colt.

"I wanted to give you something. Go ahead and open it."

Mandy opened the sack. When she withdrew a pair of binoculars, her eyebrows lifted.

"I remembered how much you've enjoyed watching the birds in your yard. With spring being the time so many birds are around, I thought . . ."

"It's a nice gift, Gideon. Danki for thinking of me." Mandy's expression relaxed as she motioned to the only free chair in the room. "Please, take a seat."

Course I would think of you. I thought about you every day you were gone. Gideon sank into the chair. *This isn't how I'd planned to welcome you home, Mandy. I'd hoped we could spend some time alone this evening, and I could express my feelings without others listening.* He shifted uneasily, grasping the arm of the chair. *Maybe I should offer to take her for a buggy ride. It would give us a chance to spend some time alone. But then, her folks might think I'm rude and that I want her all to myself. I'm sure they're eager to visit with her, too.*

Staring at a stain on the hardwood floor, Gideon continued to fret, unsure of what to say or do. He'd never felt awkward around Mandy before; but then they usually didn't have all of her family sitting in the living room, staring at them.

As if by divine intervention, Mandy's mother stood and gestured to the other room. "Mandy, why don't you go with me to the kitchen and bring out some refreshments? Oh, and Gideon, if you'd like to join us, you can fix the kaffi. As I recall from your previous visits, you know just the right amount of grounds to put in the pot."

"Jah, sure, I can take care of the coffee." Gideon followed Mandy and her mother into the kitchen. He still wasn't alone with his best girl, but at least he didn't have her dad and three younger brothers staring at him. Gideon had noticed that Mandy's older brother, Michael, wasn't here this evening. He figured Michael and his wife, Kathryn, must have other plans and couldn't be part of their family gathering.

Or maybe they'd be here later. Surely they would also want to greet Mandy.

While Gideon got the coffee going, Mandy cut up some apples and arranged the slices on a platter. She glanced at him a few times but didn't say a word. Her silence made him feel even more uncomfortable. She used to be so talkative when they were together.

"I'll take the cookies I made earlier into the other room." Miriam smiled, giving her daughter's arm a tap. "After the kaffi is ready, you and Gideon can bring the fruit and coffeepot in." She picked up the cookie tray and some napkins, then hurried from the room.

I wonder if Mandy's mamm left us alone on purpose, so we could talk. Sweat beaded on his forehead as he moved closer to the counter where Mandy stood. "I've missed you greatly, and I'm so glad you're back."

"I missed you and all my friends, too."

Friends? Is that all we are, Mandy?

He shuffled his feet a couple of times, searching for something else to say that might break the tension. "So, how was Hawaii? I heard you liked it there a lot."

Her eyes lit up for the first time since he'd arrived. "Oh, I did. I liked everything about Hawaii, except for the vog."

"What's a vog?"

356

"It's sort of like fog, only it comes from the volcano on the Big Island. It was worse than normal for a few days while Ellen and I were staying on Kauai, and it bothered my allergies. Fortunately, it didn't last long, and it never occurred again during my stay," she quickly added.

"I see." Gideon didn't know why, but he was at a loss for words. It may have been his imagination, but things seemed even more strained between them — almost like they were strangers. He couldn't put his finger on it, but he noticed a change in Mandy. She was dressed the same way as she had before, but her enthusiasm in seeing him just wasn't there. It seemed as if her mind was someplace else.

Should I give her a hug or kiss? It might help break the barrier between us. Heart pounding, Gideon stepped up to Mandy and boldly drew her into his arms. He lowered his head, and was about to kiss her, when she pulled away and reached for an orange. "Maybe I should cut some orange slices to go with the apples."

He couldn't help noticing her cheeks had turned red. The old Mandy would have hugged him back and would certainly not have pulled away from his kiss. The young woman standing before him was not the same person as she had been before her trip. Gideon had a sinking feeling the old Mandy had been changed by her experience on Hawaii. The question was, could he bring her back?

CHAPTER 31

Kapaa

Ken glanced at the calendar on his cell phone. It was hard to believe the first Saturday of May had come around so quickly, or that Mandy had been gone two weeks. Ever since Ellen told him Mandy had a boyfriend back home and they might be getting married, Ken had felt strange. He'd begun to have feelings for Mandy, although he had never let on to her. It was hard, but after learning about her boyfriend, he'd kept his distance from her. In all the time they'd been together, Mandy had never mentioned having a boyfriend back home. But then, was there any reason for her to, since Ken hadn't known her that long? Maybe in time she would have opened up more. Since she was Amish, Ken had felt from their first meeting he needed to tread lightly.

Strange how his feelings for her came on so quickly. He'd had girlfriends before, but none he cared about as much as Mandy, and in such a short time, too. Ken must have read Mandy wrong, though, because he'd begun to think she had feelings for him, too. *Maybe it was wishful thinking. Most likely, she only saw me as a friend. Truth is, we are worlds apart.*

When he'd run into Makaio at the grocery store the other day, Ken found out Mandy had been in touch with Luana. She'd called the B&B soon after she got home. This meant Luana had Mandy's phone number. Ken fought the desire to ask for it, so he could give Mandy a call. But talking to her, knowing he wouldn't see her again, would only add to his frustrations. It was better for both of them if he made no effort to contact her and cut the friendship off clean.

There's no point in me dwelling on all this, Ken berated himself. *Mandy's back home where she belongs, and I'm here, in a place I hope to always call home.*

Ken's cell phone rang. Seeing Taavi's name pop up, he answered right away. "Hey, buddy, what's up?"

"The surf — that's what." Taavi chuckled. "How 'bout grabbing your surfboard and meeting me on the beach?"

Ken didn't feel much like going, but maybe it would improve the mood he was in. "Yeah, okay. I'll see you there in half an hour."

"The waves are a bit strong," Taavi called as Ken carried his surfboard across the sand to where his friend sat. "Maybe it's not such a good idea to go in. Might have been a mistake to come here today. Sorry for wastin' your time."

Ken shook his head determinedly. "Those monster waves don't frighten me. A little struggle in the water might help release some of my tension."

Taavi's brows furrowed. "Don't be stupid, man. There's no point taking any chances — especially if your mind is on other things."

"Come on, Taavi, you've surfed in waves higher than these, and not so long ago, either."

"Yeah, but I'm not comfortable going out there right now."

"Suit yourself. I'll take my chances." Ken carried his board into the water and paddled out to where the waves were breaking. Plenty broke near him, but none he could ride. As he sat on his board, bobbing in the water's rhythm, Ken glanced in the direction of the beach. He noticed quite a few surfers milling around with their boards, but only a few were in the water with him. *Oh, well. At least I won't have to worry about plowing into someone.*

Suddenly, a gigantic wave formed behind him. *Okay, here we go!* He worked his arms to catch a swell. When he stood up, everything seemed to be going fine as his board glided smoothly on the water's surface. He glanced toward the beach and pictured Mandy sitting on the sand, watching and waving to him. Then, before Ken had time to react, a massive wall of water engulfed him. It felt like he'd been smacked by a huge hand as he tumbled off the board and went under. The force shoved him deeper and deeper, somersaulting him into the ocean's blue depths. Over and over he rolled, trying to comprehend which way was up.

When the sea finally lost its grip, Ken knew he didn't have much time. Holding his breath and kicking as hard as he could, he followed the bubbles rising toward the surface. Ken saw light as he got closer to air, which by now he desperately needed. *Only a little farther. Keep going. You're almost there.*

Ken felt a hand grip him under the arm and soon realized it was Taavi pulling him onto his board.

"Are you okay, man?" Taavi took a deep breath of air, and Ken did the same. "You had me scared for a minute when your board made it to shore without you on it."

"Guess you were right about not going out there with those angry waves." Ken choked and coughed water out of his lungs. "Should have stayed on the beach with you."

"Doesn't matter. You're here now, and you're okay."

Together, they paddled back to shore on Taavi's board.

"Should never have even tried surfing today. It was stupid of me." Ken groaned, falling onto the sand, exhausted from the ordeal. "I've been kind of depressed lately and thought it might help."

"Want to talk about it?"

Ken shook his head. "Not now, anyhow."

To Ken's relief, Taavi didn't question him any further. Talking about his feelings for Mandy seemed pointless and would only make him feel worse. He needed to forget about her and move on with his life. It was time to start fresh.

"It doesn't seem the same around here without Ellen and Mandy," Luana said as she and Makaio enjoyed chilled pineapple juice together on the lanai. "Ken isn't coming around as much anymore, either."

Makaio nodded slowly. "I've noticed it, too. The last couple of times the eggs were delivered, Ken's brother Dan brought them over. The last time I saw Ken was at the grocery store. He asked if we'd heard anything from Mandy."

Luana set her glass on the wicker table between them. "My guess is he misses her."

Makaio quirked an eyebrow. "You mean, Ken?"

She tapped his arm. "Of course I mean Ken. Isn't that who we were talking about?"

"I mentioned his brother, too."

She pushed a piece of hair behind her ear and secured it with a decorative comb. "Didn't you ever notice the way Ken looked at Mandy?"

"Well, now that you mention it, I did get the impression he thought she was nice."

"It was far more than that. They had eyes for each other. There's no mistaking it."

Makaio waved his hand in her direction. "Maybe you thought there was a spark between them because you're such a romantic."

"I am a romantic, which is why I can tell when two people have a special connection."

"But didn't Mandy mention having a

boyfriend back home?"

Luana nodded. "His name is Gideon. He called here to talk to her several times."

"Well, there you go. If Mandy has a boyfriend, then she wasn't interested in establishing a relationship with Ken. I bet she only saw him as a friend."

"No, it was more, but it doesn't matter now because she's gone, and Ken will no doubt find someone else." She picked up her glass and took a drink. "I'm still analyzing the situation, so please bear with me. I understand Mandy has a boyfriend back home, but she was always so excited when Ken showed up. I could see her eyes light up."

"Come to think of it, I remember that, too."

"And she hardly spoke of her Amish boyfriend, but she couldn't say enough about Ken. It's my guess they tried to squelch their feelings for one another, knowing Mandy would eventually leave the island."

"You could be right."

"I believe Ken has been staying away from here lately to help himself cope." Luana took another sip and set her glass on the table. "He'd probably think about Mandy every time he came through our door."

"Well, they're both young and may have stars in their eyes, but I bet it won't be long and they'll be over this puppy-love thing." Makaio leaned over and gave Luana a kiss. "I say, let's leave it in the Lord's hands. He knows what's best for Mandy and Ken."

A car pulled into the yard, and Luana stood. "Looks like our daughter is here, and she brought the baby. I'll go out to greet them and bring little Primrose inside so her grandpa can hold her."

"I need to walk, so I'll come with you." Makaio grinned. "Last one there's a rotten egg."

Middlebury

It was Saturday, and Gideon had the day off. He'd arrived at the meat-and-cheese store where Mandy was working in hopes she would be free for lunch.

When he stepped inside, he spotted her near the back of the store, stocking shelves. "Hey, how are you doin'?"

She looked up at him and blinked. "I'm okay. I didn't expect to see you here today."

"Came to see if you'd be free to join me for lunch."

She glanced at the clock on the far wall. "Guess it's noon, but I only get an hour for lunch, so I'm not sure I'd have enough time to go out anyplace. Besides, I brought a sack lunch from home today. It's a nice day, so I planned to eat out back at the picnic table."

"I could buy some beef sticks and cheese and sit out there with you." Gideon didn't want to pass up this chance to spend a few minutes with Mandy. Except for the evening he'd dropped by her house and at church last Sunday, he hadn't had the chance to see or talk with her.

She smiled up at him. "If you'd like to join me for lunch, I'll get my food and meet you out by the picnic table."

"Okay, see you there." Gideon hurried over to the cooler where the cheese was kept and selected a bag of yellow curds, as well as a carton of chocolate milk. Then he picked out a teriyaki beef stick and paid for them at the register. He took his sack full of goodies outside and sprinted around back, where he found Mandy sitting at the picnic table by herself. *Whew! At least I'll have her all to myself.*

He took a seat across from her, and after their silent prayer, they both took out their lunches. As they ate, they talked about the nice weather they'd been having, but it didn't take long before the conversation lagged.

Desperate for an answer to the question

nagging him for some time, Gideon blurted, "Who's Ken?"

Mandy's eyes opened wide. "How do you know about him?"

"I don't know anything about him, but one day while you were in Hawaii, I called the B&B to talk to you and the lady mentioned you were at the beach with Ken."

Mandy's cheeks colored. "It's . . . uh . . . nothing to worry about. Ken and I were only friends. He was Ellen's friend, too."

"Oh, okay." Not quite satisfied with her answer, he continued probing. "You don't seem the same since you came home. You're almost a different person."

"I felt different when I was in Hawaii. You can't believe how beautiful and serene it is there."

"You're right. I can't, 'cause I've never been and probably will never have the opportunity to go."

"I didn't think I'd have the chance to go, either, but I did, and I'm glad. It was the opportunity of a lifetime, and I'll never forget the friends I made on Kauai." Mandy had a faraway look in her eyes, and it bothered Gideon. Her thoughts should have been here, with him, not on some tropical island.

"Is everything all right between us,

Mandy?" Gideon dared to ask. "I mean, are you and I still . . ."

His words were cut off when Mandy's dad came around the corner of the building. "Sarah's been at the cash register all morning and needs a break. Would you please take over for her, Mandy?"

She was immediately on her feet. "I'll be right there, Dad." Looking at Gideon, Mandy offered him a brief smile. "I'm sorry for cutting our conversation short, but I've gotta go."

"It's okay, but before you do, would you be free to come over to my house for supper this evening? Mom plans to make her wunderbaar fried chicken, and she always fixes plenty."

"I appreciate the invitation, Gideon, but I promised Ellen, Sadie, and Barbara I'd go out to supper with them. We've been wanting to get together and talk about our trip to Hawaii and haven't had a chance before now, since we're all working different schedules." Mandy gathered up what was left of her lunch and put it inside her tote.

"It's all right; I understand. We'll talk again soon."

After Mandy returned to the store, Gideon remained at the picnic table for several minutes. The sun felt good shining directly on his back. He took his hat off and ran his fingers through his thick hair. Hearing a whinny, he glanced at his horse stomping the pavement where he was tied to the hitching rail. Gideon wasn't ready to leave yet and sat awhile longer. Any other time, Mandy would have lingered a few minutes before returning to the store, but things had changed between them. There was no doubt about it.

Watching a hornet on the table not far from where his arm rested, Gideon took his hat off and shooed it away. When the bee flew closer and hovered near his face, he whacked it again, relieved to see it fly off.

What can I do to make things right? He was at a loss as to what to do next. *One thing's for certain — I miss the old Mandy and want her back.*

CHAPTER 32

The moon, hanging low in the east, was barely visible when Barbara came out of the house. *Thank goodness the days are getting longer.* She glanced at the sun, still high in the western sky, before climbing into the buggy. Daylight was a few hours from fading, and depending on how long she and her friends lingered at the restaurant, she might even get home before dark.

Barbara had decided to take a back road, so she'd left a little early. Traffic this time of year, especially on a Saturday, could get rather heavy. She wasn't in the mood to put up with impatient drivers when they got behind the buggy. The last thing Barbara needed was her horse getting spooked, especially the way she was feeling right now. Barbara always enjoyed spending time with her friends, but this evening she felt a bit uneasy. It would be bad enough to try and hide the nervousness, let alone eat with the butterflies in her stomach.

As the buggy pulled out onto the road, she heard her dog barking in protest. "Not this time, Duke. Where I'm going, they don't allow pets." Barbara smiled, thinking how her German shepherd loved going for buggy rides.

Keeping her attention on the road, she asked herself, *Will I be able to hide my feelings for Gideon from Mandy tonight?* She and Gideon had become good friends while Mandy was in Hawaii. Barbara found it easy to talk to him — even if most of their conversations were about Mandy.

Barbara's friendship with Mandy was important, too. They'd been good friends a long time. The last thing she wanted to do was break Mandy's trust. But how could she deny her feelings for Gideon? *I must keep them to myself and guard my heart so neither I, nor anyone else, gets hurt.*

Barbara turned her attention to the scenery along this stretch of road. While her horse, Gaffney, trotted at a comfortable pace, she enjoyed looking at the fields that had been planted a few weeks ago and were now sprouting the first leaves of corn and soybeans. Apple and cherry blossoms added colors of pink and white among the red and deeper rosy hues of azaleas and rhododendrons.

Barbara smiled when she saw a hen turkey, followed by a dozen of her poults, scurrying into some underbrush. She sighed, wondering if she would become a mother someday.

Shipshewana, Indiana

"It's nice we can be together this evening." Sadie smiled across the table at Mandy. "We've all been so busy we haven't had time to visit since you and Ellen got back from the islands."

"It's good we were able to get a table for four at this restaurant," Ellen responded before Mandy could comment. "Saturdays are always busy, especially with so many tourists in town."

Looking around, Barbara smiled. Being here before five o'clock helped, because the supper crowd hadn't arrived yet.

Sadie looked at Mandy again. "I can't believe how tanned you got while you were gone. You must have enjoyed the sun quite a bit." She turned to Ellen. "Looks like you got some rays, as well, although Mandy's skin is even darker than yours. Guess I'm a little envious of you two getting to be in Hawaii enjoying warm weather the whole winter. But I'm glad you had a good time."

"Thanks." Ellen picked up her menu. "I'm glad the Lord watched over us throughout the extended trip."

"I believe God allows things to happen to us, and He kept you there long enough for a purpose," Barbara stated.

"I agree." Ellen smiled. "That purpose, of course, was helping out at the B&B, and we were both happy to do it. Right, Mandy?"

Mandy barely nodded as she stared at the menu. For some reason, nothing appealed. After working all day at her father's store, she should be hungry. She glanced at the waistline of her dress, noticing how baggy it looked. Mandy hadn't mentioned it to anyone, but since returning home, she'd lost five pounds. The reason for her loss of appetite had to do with missing the friends she'd made on Kauai. Her heart wasn't in much of anything she did lately. In the waking hours, her thoughts were filled with things she saw and did on the island. When she went to bed, she dreamed of being back there. If only she hadn't dropped her camera overboard, she would have gotten all those pictures printed by now and put in a scrapbook. Instead, she came home with only souvenirs and memories of their trip. Over time those memories would begin to fade, which bothered Mandy the most, as she didn't want to forget the faces of the special friends she'd made.

She thought of all the pictures, resting on the ocean floor: Ken and her at the falls; the exciting luau; all the times spent on the beach; and the photos she'd taken in Luana and Makaio's yard. Such a great loss. At least among the nice gifts she'd received from the Palus, she had three other mementos that meant a lot to her — these were from Ken. Mandy kept them in one of her dresser drawers underneath the muumuu dresses she'd worn during her stay on Kauai. Each night in the quiet of her room, she'd retrieve them to look at before going to bed. To some, they may only seem like trinkets from Hawaii, but because the coral, lei, and sunrise picture had been gifts from Ken, they held deep meaning for her. It was good she didn't have pockets in any of her plain dresses; otherwise she would have carried the kukui nut lei close to her each day.

"It's your turn now." Ellen gave Mandy's arm a gentle tap. "The waitress is waiting to take your order."

"Oh, sorry. I must have been spacing off." She glanced at the menu one more time, then ordered a spinach salad.

"Don't you want anything else?" Sadie's forehead wrinkled. "A salad's not going to fill you much."

"I'm not in the mood for anything else." Mandy grabbed her glass of water and took a sip. Maybe coming here for supper wasn't a good idea, especially if her friends scrutinized everything she did. Mandy's conscience pricked her. *No one's actually been scrutinizing me. I'm being too sensitive.*

After the waitress left the table, Sadie took a photo album from her oversized purse and placed it on the table. "These are the pictures Barbara and I took during our trip to the Hawaiian Islands. I thought you might enjoy seeing some of the things we saw along the way."

Mandy swallowed hard. It was difficult to look at the lovely photos without feeling envious. "It's nice you have them to keep your memory of Hawaii alive."

"Don't you have pictures?" Barbara asked. "You bought a digital camera before we left for our trip to Hawaii. I would imagine you took many photos while you were on Kauai."

"I did, but the camera fell overboard when Ellen and I were on a whale-watching cruise."

"It was my fault," Ellen interjected. "I got seasick, and when Mandy tried to comfort me, she lost her camera."

"Such a shame." Sadie pursed her lips. "If you want copies of any of my photos, I'd be happy to have some made."

Mandy gave a brief shake of her head. "The pictures I had were mostly taken on Kauai, and there's no getting them back." She released a heavy sigh. "I felt such peace when I was there." Being home was good, but it wasn't like Hawaii. Mandy still felt as though a part of her remained on the island.

"Don't you feel peace here at home?" Barbara tipped her head, looking strangely at Mandy.

Mandy felt trapped and wasn't sure how to respond. "Well, I only meant . . ."

"It's okay." Ellen came to her rescue. "Being in Hawaii was peaceful for me, as well. There were so many beautiful flowers, colorful birds, and swaying palm trees. Luana and Makaio's bed-and-breakfast was peaceful, too, and they made us feel so welcome."

"They're good Christians," Mandy said. "I don't know what we would have done if strangers we met hadn't taken us to the B&B the evening we became stranded."

"I can only imagine how frightened you both must have been." Sadie cast a sidelong glance at Barbara. "How do you think we would have handled it if we'd been in such a situation?"

Barbara shrugged. "I'm not sure. As it was, we were scared not knowing at first what happened to you both."

"May I take a closer look at your album?" Ellen asked.

"Certainly." Sadie handed it to her just as the waitress came with the drinks they'd ordered.

"You have some nice pictures." Ellen turned each of the pages, pausing often to comment.

Mandy glanced at them, too. Seeing photos from the Big Island, Maui, Oahu, and especially Kauai, caused her to tear up. Barbara must have noticed, for she reached across the table and placed her hand over Mandy's. "Are you all right?"

"Just missing Hawaii." She looked away from the album. "Let's talk about something else now, okay?"

Sadie's brows squished together. "But I thought our meeting was to compare notes about our trip."

"It's fine. We can talk about it if you like." Mandy twisted the napkin in her lap. Once their meals came, maybe the conversation would change.

Barbara looked over at Ellen. "Before we say any more about Hawaii, I've been wondering how your new job is going. Do you like being a housekeeper at the hotel in Middlebury?"

"It's all right," Ellen replied, "but I preferred working at the B&B before we left for Hawaii. Of course," she added, "I work additional hours at the hotel, which means earning more money."

"How about you, Mandy?" Sadie questioned. "Do you like working at the meat-and-cheese store?"

"It's okay, but I enjoyed my previous job of waitressing more." She reached for her glass of iced tea and took a sip. "At the restaurant, I could visit with customers as well as the other waitresses during my breaks. We don't have nearly as many employees at my daed's store, and there's not a lot of excitement."

"You won't have to work there forever," Ellen stated. "Once you and Gideon are married, you can quit working at your daed's store and become a fulltime homemaker."

"Have the two of you set a wedding date?" Barbara leaned slightly forward.

"No, and since I'm not taking classes to join the church this spring, Gideon hasn't asked me to marry him. For now, at least, I'll keep working while I live at home."

"Oh, I see." Barbara leaned back in her seat.

Is that a look of relief on Barbara's face? Mandy wondered. *Could she be interested in Gideon? Does he have feelings for her? I can't help but wonder what happened during my absence. Maybe I'm overlooking something. If Gideon became interested in Barbara, surely he would have told me.* She pursed her lips. *I still care about him, but my feelings aren't as strong as they were before I met Ken.*

When their meals came, they prayed silently, then talked about some things going on in their area. By the time they were ready to order dessert, the conversation returned to Hawaii.

"Have you heard from Luana since we've been home?" Ellen asked Mandy.

"Only once, when I called to let her know we'd made it okay."

"I've been meaning to write them and say thank you again for everything they did for us, but other things have taken up my time."

"I'd have to say you two did a lot for the Hawaiian couple, as well," Sadie interjected. "You sacrificed by not returning home right away so you could help out when Makaio broke his leg."

"I didn't see it as a sacrifice." Mandy shook her head vigorously. "I enjoyed helping out. And by staying longer, Ellen and I were able to see a lot more things on Kauai then we ever expected. Also, thanks to our friend Ken, I learned how to swim, which I thought I'd never be able to do."

"That's wunderbaar, Mandy." Barbara's tone was enthusiastic. "Now you can go swimming in the ponds and lakes around here with the rest of your friends."

I'd rather go swimming in Hawaii, Mandy mused. Then another thought came to mind. *Would it be wrong for me to move to Hawaii and begin a new life? What would my family say if I did? Could I be happy living so far away?*

Since she hadn't joined the church yet, Mandy was free to choose what she wanted to do with the rest of her life, but going back to Hawaii would be a major decision, affecting everyone in her family, as well as Gideon.

Mandy determined to give it more time. *I haven't been home long enough to know for certain if this is the life I'm meant to have.*

CHAPTER 33

Middlebury

Excitement welled in Mandy's soul when she went to the mailbox the first Saturday of August and found a letter from Luana. She hurried back to the house and went straight to her room to read it privately.

Taking a seat on the end of her bed, Mandy tore open the envelope. It had been awhile since she'd heard any news from Hawaii, and she was eager to hear how everyone was doing.

The first part of Luana's letter was about her granddaughter, Primrose. Mandy read every word as though it was meant to be savored. The baby had grown several inches and started to roll over on her own. Luana said it pleased her to have Ailani working part-time at the B&B again. She brought Primrose with her, of course, and Makaio and Luana took turns watching her while their daughter made up the guest rooms each day. Mandy tried to visualize what the baby looked like and wished Luana had enclosed a picture.

Luana also wrote about the nice weather they'd been having and how well things were doing in her garden.

Mandy smiled, remembering how she had enjoyed spending time in Luana's garden, even when the weather turned hot and humid. Watching the gentle sway of palm leaves, listening to the birds sing, and breathing in the delicate scent of the tropical flowers in the yard filled her senses. She giggled, remembering how a cardinal had left its calling card on her muumuu.

Mandy stopped reading for a minute, while her mind wandered further. *I wonder how Ken is doing. Oh my, I wish I could stop thinking of him.*

As she turned the letter over to continue reading, a sudden coldness hit the core of her being. Her voice trembled as she read the next line out loud: "I ran into Ken's mother the other day when I was at the farmer's market. Ken has been seeing someone and is planning to get married in November."

Mandy's vision blurred as she stared at the words. *Could Ken have been seeing someone the whole time Ellen and I were on*

Kauai and not mentioned it? Maybe it was one of those young women I saw him talking to on the beach the day he'd been surfing. She shifted uneasily on her bed. *Or it could be someone he met after we left — perhaps one of the young women on the worship team at his church.*

Mandy's shoulders sagged as she reached up to rub her throbbing temples. She couldn't help feeling disappointed by this news, but she consoled herself with the knowledge that it was better this way. Ken obviously didn't care for her the way she did him, or he would have contacted her after she'd come home. Her throat constricted. *And he wouldn't be marrying someone else in November if he'd felt any love for me.*

Mandy finished reading Luana's letter, then with a heavy heart, tucked it inside a box in her closet where she kept mementoes. Glancing down, she spotted the ukulele Makaio had given her, leaning against the closet wall. Holding the instrument the way she'd been taught, she took a seat on her bed again and began to play a song he'd taught her. The longer she played, the more her heart yearned for Ken and the things she'd discovered on the island.

A long-distance relationship with him

wouldn't have worked, and since neither of them was free to leave their homes and families, it was all for the better. He had a fiancée, and she had Gideon. The brief encounter she'd had with Ken while visiting Kauai was like the vog. It swept in one day and was gone the next. Mandy had recovered from her allergic reaction to the vog. She hoped she could set aside her feelings for Ken, as well, and reestablish the relationship she'd once had with Gideon.

Ellen carried the laundry basket outside and set it under the clothesline. It was a beautiful sunny day — not too hot and not too muggy, which made it perfect clothes-drying weather. She was about to pick up a pair of her dad's trousers when Sadie rode into the yard on her bike.

"This is a nice surprise." Ellen smiled. "Are you here for a visit or only out for a ride?"

Sadie parked her bike and joined Ellen by the clothesline. "I've been meaning to talk to you about something, so I'm glad you're here this morning."

"Okay. We can chat while I hang the clothes, or take a seat at the picnic table under the shade of the maple tree when I'm done."

"I'll help you hang the laundry. When we're finished, we can sit and talk." Sadie picked up a towel and clipped it to the line.

Once all the wash swayed gently in the breeze, they both took a seat at the picnic table.

"What did you want to talk to me about?" Ellen asked.

"Barbara and Gideon."

Ellen blinked rapidly. "You mean Mandy and Gideon?"

"No. I'm talking about Gideon and Barbara."

"What about them?"

"I've seen them together several times since Barbara and I got back from Hawaii." Sadie paused. "Gideon even gave Barbara a ride home from one of the young people's singings a few months ago."

"Was this before or after Mandy and I arrived home?"

"It was before, but I saw them together again last night."

"Where?"

"At the benefit auction in Shipshewana. They were sitting next to each other during most of the bidding."

Ellen sucked in her lower lip. "Was Mandy there, too?"

Sadie shook her head. "I figured she'd be

with Gideon, but when I asked him about her, he said she had a koppweh and didn't feel up to going."

"I didn't go, either. Mom had a dress she wanted to make, so I stayed home to help with it." Ellen fiddled with the ties on her head covering. "Do you think Gideon's interested in Barbara?"

Sadie shrugged her shoulders. "Whether he is or not, I believe she's interested in him. While you and Mandy were on Kauai, Barbara talked a lot about Gideon. She kept saying how sorry she felt for him and that if he was her boyfriend, she'd have come home right away."

Ellen mulled things over. "Well, as you know, Mandy hasn't taken classes with us to join the church."

"Jah, and I'm surprised. If she and Gideon are making plans to be married, she'll need to get baptized and join." Sadie rubbed the side of her neck, her tone uncertain. "Maybe things aren't going well with them because of Barbara."

Ellen shook her head. "I don't think it's Barbara's fault. Mandy lost interest in Gideon while we were in Hawaii."

"Are you sure?"

"Jah. She rarely talked about him, and whenever he called, she didn't talk long at

387

all." Ellen paused, wondering if she should say more.

"Wonder why? I've always heard absence is supposed to make the heart grow fonder."

Ellen took a deep breath and sighed. "Mandy became infatuated with a young man named Ken. He came over to the B&B to deliver eggs and chicken, and it didn't take long before he started taking Mandy — and sometimes me — out to see some of the sights on Kauai."

"Did Mandy tell you she had feelings for Ken?" Sadie questioned.

"Not in so many words, but I could see it in her eyes when they were together and whenever she talked about him."

"Was he interested in her?"

"I believe he was. That is, until I . . ." Ellen dropped her gaze as she clasped her hands together in her lap.

"Is there something else you were going to say?"

"Jah." It wasn't easy to admit what she'd done, but she needed to get it off her chest. "One evening after a bad storm, Ken came by the B&B to see if everyone was okay. Luana, Makaio, and Mandy had gone to bed, so Ken and I visited a few minutes." Ellen's voice cracked. "We talked about Mandy, and in order to discourage Ken from pursuing a relationship with her, I told him Mandy had a boyfriend waiting for her back home, and they were planning to be married."

"You did the right thing. If I'd been there, I would have told him that, too. It would be horrible for Mandy's folks and everyone else she's close to if she'd stayed on Kauai and married an outsider."

"The time Mandy and I had in Hawaii was good, and I'm glad we had the opportunity to experience it, but it wasn't our world — the one we were born into and have become a part of since we were *bopplin*." Ellen lifted her chin. "Mandy's future is here with Gideon. We need to make sure no one — not even our friend, Barbara — comes between them."

Sadie's forehead wrinkled. "We can pray about the situation and maybe interject our opinion if asked, but the future of our friends is in God's hands, not ours."

Gideon shook his horse's reins to get him moving faster. He was on his way to Mandy's to take her for a buggy ride and felt anxious to get there. In the months Mandy had been back from her trip, things had been strained between them. She'd often had some excuse not to see him when he suggested they do something together. Since she'd agreed to his invitation this evening, he hoped things would go well. Her distant attitude certainly wasn't from a lack of him trying. Gideon had invited her out several times, as well as to his folks' for supper. When Mandy first returned from Hawaii and seemed so distracted, he'd figured it would take a little time before she readjusted to life at home. But it seemed to be taking forever, causing him to have more doubts. He and some of Mandy's other friends hadn't joined the church yet, deciding to wait until fall, and hoping Mandy would be part of their group.

Think positively, Gideon told himself as he started up the Freys' driveway. *If things go well tonight, Mandy may agree to take classes in the fall. Then she could join the church and we can be married. It's something to hope for, at least.*

Gideon pulled up to the hitching rail and was pleased when Mandy came out of the house right away and climbed into his rig.

"It's a nice night for a buggy ride," she commented, seating herself beside him. "When the sun goes down, I'll bet we'll see lots of twinkling stars."

"I'll bet, too." Gideon grinned at her, and a warmth spread through him when she gave a pleasant smile. *So far, so good.*

As they traveled the back road between Middlebury and Shipshewana, Mandy grew silent, but Gideon kept trying to engage her in conversation. She wasn't the talkative person she used to be. Before her trip to Hawaii, Mandy always thought of things to say. At times, she could be a real chatterbox.

Barbara talks to me more than Mandy does. Gideon glanced her way and frowned when he realized her eyes were shut. *Is she thinking about me or someone else? Could Mandy have fallen asleep?*

Mandy had a hard time staying awake. The gentle sway of Gideon's buggy and the rhythm of the horse's hooves clip-clopping along the pavement were enough to put anyone to sleep.

"Would you like to stop by the Hitching Post for some frozen yogurt?" Gideon asked when they arrived in Shipshewana.

"No, thank you. I ate too much of my mamm's zesty meatloaf for supper and don't have room for anything else. But if you want to stop for some, I'll sit and watch you eat it."

"No, it's okay." Gideon snapped the reins. "Let's keep riding." He turned his rig around and headed back in the direction of

Middlebury.

Is he taking me home? Does he think I'm bored? Mandy sat up straight. "How are things going with your job at the upholstery shop? Do you still enjoy working there?"

He nodded. "I've been helping out at my mamm's quilt-and-fabric shop some, too."

"Bet she appreciates it, but I'm surprised you have the time."

"I go there after work some afternoons."

"I figured with Barbara working at the store, your mamm wouldn't need more help."

"She gets pretty busy sometimes. Seems there's always something I can do to help. How do you like working for your daed?"

"It's okay, but I'd rather work at one of the local restaurants."

"Why don't you then?"

"There haven't been any openings since I got back."

They rode a short ways in silence, then Gideon guided his buggy onto a dirt road and pulled back on the reins. "Whoa!"

"What are we stopping for?" she asked.

"I . . . I've missed you, Mandy, and I'm hoping we can get back what we once had." Before Mandy could form a response, Gideon pulled her into his arms and kissed her. Although firm and gentle, like his kisses had always been, it didn't feel right to her. The kiss lacked the emotion she remembered from Gideon's kisses. *Maybe it's me. I'm not the same person I was before Hawaii. No matter how hard I've tried to get them back, the feelings I once felt for Gideon aren't there anymore. How can I verbalize this without hurting him?*

Mandy was the first to pull away. Unable to look at Gideon, she murmured, "I'm not going to join the church this fall, Gideon, so you're free to pursue someone else if you like."

"What?" His mouth hung open.

"I'm not sure if the Amish life is right for me, and it's not fair to keep you waiting." She placed her hand on his arm and gave it a gentle tap. "You're a good friend, and I don't want to hurt you, but I can't make any promises at this time."

"I can wait till you're sure." His tone sounded sincere.

"Please don't. You deserve to be happy."

"You make me happy, Mandy. You always have." He clasped her hand. "Will you at least pray about things and give it more time before you make a final decision about not joining the church?"

"Okay, but I can't make any promises." Mandy closed her eyes. *So much for trying to express my feelings to Gideon. I should have made things more clear. I doubt we'll ever get back what we once had.*

CHAPTER 34

The first Sunday of October, Mandy sat on a backless wooden bench in her brother Michael's barn, watching as Gideon, Barbara, Sadie, and Ellen were baptized and received into fellowship in their Amish church. They had waited until fall, hoping she would join, too, but she'd let them all down.

It was a beautiful autumn morning, and the doors of the barn had been left open on both ends, allowing a comfortable breeze to waft through. A fall-like aroma hung in the air, and Mandy breathed deeply of its earthy scent. When a rustling sound caught her attention, her eyes were drawn toward the entrance. A scattering of early fallen leaves had been captured in the draft and made their way inside, swirling in circles across the barn floor. Mandy's gaze followed the dancing leaves until they disappeared and whooshed out the opposite door.

When someone sneezed, Mandy hunched

her shoulders and focused on her friends up front. She remained that way until her brother's new puppy barked from outside, seemingly disgruntled for not getting any attention. Michael had surprised his new bride with a little basset hound a few weeks after they were married and said he'd chosen that type of dog because they were good with children. The puppy was adorable, and it was comical to watch it tripping over its own floppy ears. Mandy suspected by next year sometime she'd probably be an aunt. At least one happy event might be happening in the year to come.

A feeling of guilt swept over her. It felt awful to disappoint Mom and Dad by not being one of the candidates for baptism this morning, which meant no open door for her to be married in the Amish church anytime soon. Her friends were disheartened, too. Part of Mandy wanted to be free to explore her feelings and decide what she wanted to do with the rest of her life, but she also was drawn to joining the Amish fellowship. It was like being on a teeter-totter: up and down, up and down, as she tried to decide what to do. Should she have taken classes and joined the church with her friends? She couldn't answer that question right now.

Mandy stared at her hands, clasped firmly in her lap. *But I wasn't ready.* Next spring was a long way off, and unless something happened to change her mind, she would follow through with her decision to join the church then — for her family's sake, if nothing else.

As Gideon took his seat after being baptized and welcomed into fellowship with the church, he glanced quickly in Mandy's direction, noticing how forlorn she appeared, looking down at her lap. He felt disappointed she hadn't been part of their group today — especially when they had all waited until fall, hoping she would join them. Even harder was trying to come to grips with her reason for not taking classes and joining. Was it because she wanted to do something different with her life, or had Mandy refused to take classes because she didn't want to marry him? Gideon had committed himself to the church and wondered if Mandy ever would. She seemed like an outsider looking in — living among them, but not one of them.

Back in August when he'd taken Mandy for a buggy ride, her mood at times seemed cheerful. He'd felt enthusiasm one minute and disappointment the next — especially after she'd told him he was free to find someone else. *Maybe I should have listened to her then, instead of holding out false hope.*

His gaze went to Barbara. *Would she be a better choice for me?* Gideon had enjoyed his conversations with her during the time Mandy was gone. Barbara was attractive, had a sweet spirit, and most important she wanted to be Amish. But Gideon saw some problems: He didn't know how Barbara felt about him, and he wasn't sure whether Mandy had any feelings for him anymore. Likewise, he felt unsure of his feelings for Barbara and Mandy. He'd never been so confused.

Gideon had noticed how well his mother and Barbara got along. While Barbara was in Hawaii, Mom had mentioned several times how much she missed her. Furthermore, both of his parents had expressed concern because Mandy would not join the church. Mom even went so far as to say no son of hers should be made to wait around indefinitely for a young lady who didn't want to commit to the Amish way of life. He felt the pressure building but fought it off, needing to be cautious. Gideon didn't want any regrets where Mandy was concerned. Everything needed to be prayed about, allowing God to work things out.

Before directing his attention back to what the bishop was saying, Gideon made a decision. If Mandy didn't join the church next year, he would give up on their relationship and stop seeing her. In the meantime, regardless of what Mandy told him, he would try a little harder to get back what they once had.

At lunch following the church service, Ellen took a seat beside Mandy. "Is the dress you're wearing the one I made you in Hawaii for your birthday?" she asked.

"Jah, it's the green one." Mandy's expression was somber.

"Something doesn't look right with it." Ellen pulled at the material. "The dress looks as if it's hanging on you and doesn't fit like it should. I was certain it fit you properly when you wore it home from Hawaii."

"I may have lost a little weight since then," Mandy admitted. "But don't worry, I'm sure I'll gain it back and the dress will fit perfectly again."

"That makes me feel better, and I'm glad it wasn't because I measured wrong." Ellen looked at her friend long and hard. "I wish you could have been with us today when we went forward to be baptized. It was a meaningful occasion."

Mandy nodded. "I'm sure, and I'm happy for all of you."

"Why didn't you take classes with us? You've never truly explained."

"Jah, I did. I told you before. I don't feel ready." She drank some of her lemonade.

"When will you be ready?"

"How do we know when we're ready for anything? Maybe I'll take classes next spring, but I'm focusing on the now. I want to keep working and saving money, because I still haven't paid my parents all they spent for the ticket that brought me home from Kauai." Mandy squinted against the sun streaming into the window and scooted over a little to avoid it.

"What about Gideon? Do you think he will wait for you that long? He most likely wanted to be married this fall."

"Please, Ellen." Mandy's brows furrowed. "Don't make me feel any guiltier than I already do."

"Guilty for not joining the church or making Gideon wait?"

"I'm not sure." Mandy's voice lowered. "To tell you the truth, I'm not sure of anything anymore."

"I can tell." Ellen pushed the pickle on her plate around with her fork. "You're not the same person you were before we went to Hawaii. We've been home over five months, and by now you should have gotten over . . ." Ellen stopped talking when she noticed several women at the table looking their way. Now was not the time or place to express her feelings to Mandy. She would do it another day, when they could talk privately.

Barbara glanced at Mandy and Ellen, wondering what they were talking about. The two had their heads together, speaking in low tones. Then they stopped talking altogether, barely looking at one another.

During the church service this morning, it had been difficult for Barbara to concentrate on the preacher's message. She kept thinking about Mandy and how she'd disappointed all of them by not joining the church. *Gideon, most of all,* she thought. *I wonder if she'll ever decide to join, and if so, will Gideon wait for her or find someone else to court? I wish it could be me, but I doubt he sees me as anything more than a friend. If Mandy would break things off with him, I might have a chance.*

"Are you going to the young people's singing tonight?" Sadie nudged Barbara's arm, scattering her thoughts.

"Umm . . . I guess so. Are you planning to go?"

"I wouldn't miss it." Sadie smiled. "This will be our first singing as church members."

"Did you ever have second thoughts about joining the church?" Barbara whispered, leaning closer to her friend.

"Absolutely not. I've always looked forward to joining. Even as a little girl I knew what I wanted." Sadie chuckled. "I used to pretend I was the bishop, and I'd baptize my dolls."

Barbara laughed. "You were that eager?"

"Jah." Sadie nodded in Mandy's direction. "It saddens me to think you, Ellen, Mandy, and I made the trip to Hawaii together, but only three of us became members of the church today. From the time we were girls in school, I thought we'd all join together."

"I thought so, too." Barbara sighed. "A link was truly missing in what should have been a happy occasion for all of us this morning."

"Before we went to Hawaii, did Mandy give any indication she might not join?"

Barbara shook her head. "At least not to me. She may have mentioned something to Ellen, though. They're pretty close."

"I bet Mandy's folks are deeply hurt their only daughter hasn't committed to becoming a baptized church member. My parents would certainly be upset if I never joined."

"Do you think Mandy will end up leaving her Amish roots altogether?"

Sadie shrugged. "Could be. After talking to Ellen about the way Mandy acted when they were staying with the Hawaiian couple on Kauai, nothing would surprise me."

"She's told me a few things, too." Barbara pursed her lips. "The one I feel the most sorry for is Gideon. Mandy's been unfair, making him believe she would return from Hawaii and join the church, then staying longer than planned and not joining after she got home." She lowered her voice even more. "He deserves to be happy."

"Maybe he'll find happiness with someone else."

"You think so?" Hope welled in Barbara's chest.

"Anything's possible. Especially since things don't seem to be going well between him and Mandy these days."

A feeling of guilt settled over Barbara, for hoping Mandy and Gideon broke up, but she couldn't help wishing if things didn't work out between them, Gideon might turn to her. *He'd have to be blind not to see I have feelings for him. Every time he's around, I break out in a cold sweat. And sometimes when he talks to me, I feel like I can't speak without stuttering or saying something foolish.* She squeezed her eyes shut, thinking how nice Gideon looked in his Sunday best today. It was all she could do not to stare at him. *If I were in Mandy's shoes, I'd hang on to Gideon and never let him go.*

CHAPTER 35

By early January, Gideon had finally accepted the fact that his relationship with Mandy was over. Even if she did join the church this year, there was no hope of them being together. It hadn't been easy at first, but if he wanted to move forward with his life, he had to make this choice. He'd tried to continue courting Mandy for a while after he'd joined the church, but the feelings they'd once had for each other weren't there anymore. Fortunately, their parting wasn't bitter, and they'd agreed to remain friends. That wasn't to say he'd erased the last couple of months from his mind. The feelings deep in his heart would take effort and time to overcome, especially with the holidays still fresh on his mind.

Thanksgiving and Christmas had been difficult, since Mandy hadn't spent either holiday with him. But with the help of his family, Gideon had made it through. After

Christmas dinner, he and his brother Orley had taken a walk outside, and Gideon had taken the opportunity to unburden his soul. He'd explained the changes in Mandy since she returned from Hawaii and mentioned how she kept drawing further from him. Orley helped Gideon admit to himself the relationship was ending and that he shouldn't pursue Mandy anymore. If he wanted to remain friends with her, the best thing was to set her free. At the same time, Gideon would also be free to pursue a new relationship when the time was right. He'd taken his brother's advice, and by New Year's had come to terms with things and felt ready to focus on the future.

Gideon had asked Barbara to attend a singing with him this evening and was on his way to her house right now. He and Barbara had always gotten along well. Since she worked in his mother's store and they saw each other often, he felt comfortable around her. The sparks weren't there like they had been with Mandy in the beginning of their courtship, but maybe in time deeper feelings would come. Meanwhile, he enjoyed the stronger friendship developing between them. Gideon and Barbara saw eye-to-eye on many things, and most importantly, she had no desire to be anything but Amish. If things progressed with them, he'd probably end up asking her to marry him. "Think Mom would be happy if Barbara became her daughter-in-law someday," Gideon murmured.

As if in response, his horse whinnied and his ears perked up. The gelding acted frisky, prancing along the snow-covered road, blowing out his breath in steady streams as Gideon urged him forward.

Gideon had dressed warmly this evening, with a heavy jacket and gloves. Mom had given him a quilt to place across their laps. She'd also provided a thermos of hot chocolate, saying to make sure they kept warm, because the temperature was supposed to dip down this evening.

Gideon's thoughts returned to courting Barbara. Next week a group of young people planned a get-together that would include ice skating and a bonfire. He and Barbara would join them. He looked forward to the winter sport and having quality time with his new girlfriend.

Barbara's heart pounded as she stood at the living-room window, watching for Gideon's horse and buggy. Hours earlier, she'd debated on what dress to wear. Mom had stepped into her bedroom while she was trying on dresses and suggested Barbara wear a blue dress because it brought out the color of her eyes.

Barbara turned from the window when her mother entered the living room. "I'm a little naerfich tonight," Barbara admitted.

"I remember during my courting days, I was so nervous my knees sometimes knocked." Mom gave Barbara a hug. "I worried someone would notice, but no one said a thing."

"My knees aren't knocking, but I feel like I've got butterflies in my stomach."

Mom smiled. "You'll be fine, Daughter."

Barbara kept it to herself, but every time she and Gideon were together she found herself falling harder for him. She was amazed they'd become a courting couple. She'd thought for sure he would end up marrying Mandy.

Of course, Gideon hasn't proposed to me, and maybe he never will. He might only see me as a good friend — someone to fill the void since he and Mandy broke up.

Barbara took a seat on the couch. She remembered how when Gideon first asked her out, she'd asked Mandy how she felt about it. To Barbara's surprise, Mandy had given her blessing, stating she didn't have romantic feelings for Gideon anymore.

She sighed. *I can't believe Mandy would give up what she and Gideon once had, but I guess she has her reasons.* Barbara was glad she could freely express, at least to Sadie, how she felt toward Gideon. Until he declared feelings of love for her, she would remain quiet. But if the day ever came he asked her to marry him, Barbara's answer would be yes.

Shipshewana

On Monday morning, Mandy's day off at the meat-and-cheese store, she headed to the thrift shop where she volunteered one day a week. She enjoyed working there. It broke up the week and gave her something to look forward to. She couldn't wait to see what had come in since the last time she'd volunteered her services. All kinds of housewares and clothing were normally donated. Mandy would sort through the boxes and bags and then clean or repair what was needed.

She snickered, thinking about the wigs that had come in a few weeks ago. It would be comical to wear one of them while dressing up for a skit of some kind. Another time she'd opened a box of dishes, but many of them were chipped so they couldn't be put out.

Mandy pulled her thoughts together when the vehicle she rode in slowed down and turned the last corner before the thrift store. It had begun to snow pretty hard, and she breathed a sigh of relief when her driver dropped her off in front of the store.

Mandy shivered as she stepped through the door. "Brr . . . It's sure cold out there." She stomped her feet and brushed crystal flakes from her shoulders. "The snow's coming down harder," she told Mary Jane Bontrager, the woman in charge of the store for the day.

Mary Jane crinkled her nose. "We probably won't get too many customers. Only the brave or someone desperately seeking a bargain would be likely to come out in weather like this."

"I did." Mandy snickered. "But then, I enjoy my work here. It's a nice change of pace."

"I like it, too." Mary Jane gestured toward the back of the store. "Someone brought in several boxes of used items last week, but I haven't had time to go through any of it. Would you mind sorting?"

"Sure, no problem. I'll begin as soon as I hang up my jacket and outer bonnet and put my lunch tote away."

Mandy moved swiftly for the back room.

Once she'd put her things away, she located the boxes and got right to work. The first box was filled with children's toys, so she put them in two piles and would take care of cleaning them as soon as she sorted the items in the other boxes.

The clock clicked close to noon, and Mandy was about to stop and eat lunch, when she discovered something in the third box that nearly took her breath away. She studied the beautiful blue-and-white quilt. It didn't look like a traditional Amish quilt when she opened it the whole way. This one reminded her of the photo she'd seen of Luana and Makaio's quilt while staying at their bed-and-breakfast. After inspecting the covering closely, she discovered the initials *L* and *M* sewn in one corner of the quilt. Although it seemed impossible, Mandy wondered if by some miracle this could actually be Luana and Makaio's missing quilt. *But how would it get all the way from Hawaii to Indiana?*

Mandy knelt on the floor beside the cardboard box, holding the quilt. Gazing at the beautiful Hawaiian design put a lump in her throat. She felt a strong need to purchase this quilt, even if it wasn't Luana's. She couldn't imagine leaving it here in the store for someone else to buy, and she felt sure they would. An item this lovely wouldn't last long.

Carrying the quilt up to the front counter, Mandy held up her find. "What price will you put on this?"

Mary Jane studied the covering a few seconds, pursing her lips. "I'm normally the one who prices things here, but . . . Oh, I don't know. The quilt's design is unusual, especially for around these parts. Why don't you decide on a price? You have an eye for finely made quilts, so you can probably price it as well as I could."

Mandy shook her head. "You don't understand. I want to purchase this quilt. It reminds me of Hawaii, and it looks like the picture of a quilt that used to be owned by someone I met on Kauai."

"I'll tell you what. Since it means so much to you, why don't you give a donation to the store for whatever you can afford? Then the quilt will be yours."

Mandy didn't have a lot of money, but she'd been saving up since she began working at her dad's store. "Would a hundred dollars be fair?"

Mary Jane gave an affirmative nod. "Consider it yours."

Holding the covering close, Mandy's heart swelled. She'd replaced her digital camera a few months ago, so when she went home this evening, she would take a picture of this outstanding quilt and send it to Luana. If, by some miracle, it turned out to be her and Makaio's quilt, Mandy would make sure it was returned to them, even if it meant taking it there herself.

Mandy smiled. *Now wouldn't it be something if I got to go back to Kauai and could present something so special to Luana and Makaio? I hope and pray this is truly the lost quilt they received on their wedding day.*

CHAPTER 36

Bundled in a heavy jacket, thick brown scarf, and matching gloves, Mandy stepped outdoors, where a strong wind continued blowing from overnight. Hopefully it would ease up soon, like it was supposed to. Making her way down the slippery driveway, she pulled her scarf up to the bridge of her nose.

Shivering against the cold, she opened the mailbox and pulled out a stack of mail. Thanks to the gloves she wore, her grip wasn't so good. Before she could react, a gust of wind whipped it right out of her hands and sent the mail flying down the road. She raced after it, trying to hold her balance as she slipped and slid in the snow. She grabbed one letter, but ended up bending it. "Oh, great! Come on, Mr. Wind. You're supposed to be calming down by now."

Mandy removed her gloves and managed to pick up the rest of the mail as the wind subsided, almost instantly. She stopped and looked around. *Guess the wind must have heard me.* She giggled. After thumbing through the retrieved items, she saw only a few bills and some advertising catalogs. It had been almost two weeks since she'd sent Luana a letter with the picture of the quilt she'd found at the thrift store. So far, there'd been no response. She hoped her letter hadn't gotten lost in the mail. If Luana had received it, she should have responded by now. Even if she thought the quilt wasn't hers, surely she would have written back.

Meandering back and being careful not to fall, she inhaled a breath of frosty air. Looking out across the field and the tree line adjacent to their property, Mandy paused for a minute to watch a steady stream of smoke, almost fog-like, wafting slowly in the afternoon's breeze. No doubt someone up the road had stoked their woodstove. The whitish haze was a stark contrast against the bare dark trees at the far end of the field. At least the stronger winds had finally settled down.

Winter had its own fragrance. Even snow sometimes smelled like rain. One thing she could always count on this time of the year was the pleasant aroma of wood smoke in the air. As much as she missed Hawaii, if she lived there she'd probably miss some things about winter here.

As Mandy approached their phone shack, she stopped to check for messages. The chilly wind picked up again, as quickly as it had stopped, causing the falling snow to pelt Mandy's face. She found welcome relief inside the small wooden building, despite its lack of heat.

Taking a seat on the cold metal chair, Mandy pressed the answering machine button. The first two messages were for her father, and the third one was for Mom. Mandy waited for the fourth message to come up. Her heartbeat quickened when she heard Luana's voice.

"Mandy, this is Luana Palu. I received your letter, and I'm so excited. After comparing the picture you sent me with the one I showed you of our missing quilt, I've concluded that the one you found is almost certainly Makaio's and mine. I can't begin to imagine how it could have gotten all the way from Hawaii to Shipshewana, Indiana. You finding it has to be more than a coincidence. I see it as a God-sent miracle."

Tears welled in Mandy's eyes and spilled over onto her cheeks as Luana's message continued. "If you would be willing to send me the quilt, I'll gladly pay you for it, and also reimburse your postage. Please give me a call as soon as you can."

When the message ended, Mandy remained in the phone shack several more minutes, feeling elated with this awesome news and thinking things through. She could box up the quilt and mail it tomorrow, but it might take a few weeks to get there, or might never make it at all. Apparently it had taken nearly two weeks for her letter and picture to reach Hawaii, or she would have heard from Luana sooner.

I'd rather take it there myself. Mandy moistened her chapped lips with her tongue. *Mom and Dad won't approve of me flying, even though I haven't joined the church, but I'm going to talk to my cousin Ruth and see if she will help me book a flight to Kauai.*

South Bend, Indiana

Mandy's heartbeat quickened when, one week later, she sat in the airport, waiting to board her plane. Flying was a new experience for her, and traveling alone for such a distance made it even more frightening. Yet her excitement over making this trip to Kauai overrode the nervousness. She could hardly wait to see Luana and Makaio's expression when she took their quilt from her suitcase and presented it to them. She'd never dreamed she'd have an opportunity to visit Hawaii again, let alone hand-deliver their lovely wedding quilt.

Mandy reflected on her parents' reaction when she told them Ruth had not only booked her flight to Kauai but also loaned her part of the money for a round-trip ticket. Mom was stunned and begged Mandy not to go. Dad said it was Mandy's choice. He not only gave her time off from work, but he encouraged Mandy to do what she felt was right.

It's not like I'm going to stay there forever. She gripped the handle of her carry-on bag. *I'll only be staying at the B&B two weeks. Then I'll return home, and everything will go back to normal.*

Mandy's flight would go to Detroit, Michigan. From there she would change to a plane taking her to Los Angeles, and another plane would fly on to Lihue, Hawaii. The airport in Lihue wasn't far from where the cruise ship docked when she and Ellen got stranded on Kauai.

She smiled inwardly, thinking about Ellen's response when she'd told her about finding the quilt and the plans she'd made to take it to Kauai herself. Ellen had clasped Mandy's hand and cautioned, "Don't miss

418

your plane on the day of your return flight or I'll have to come and get you. Of course, since joining the church, I won't be allowed to fly unless it's an emergency."

Mandy had giggled and replied, "If I get stranded again, you'll be the first person I call, because it will be an emergency."

"Will you see Ken while you're there?" Ellen's furrowed brows revealed concern.

"No, he got married in November, so it wouldn't be right for me to seek him out. I'll be enjoying my time with Luana and Makaio, though, and it'll be fun to see how much little Primrose has grown."

"Please give them my best." Ellen's sincere hug told Mandy her friend had sent her off with a blessing. Even Sadie, Barbara, and Gideon wished her well, saying they would pray she had a safe trip.

It's nice to have good friends, Mandy thought. *Both here and in Hawaii.*

On the plane, Mandy sat with her nose pressed against the window, in awe of all she saw. Flying wasn't nearly as frightening as she'd imagined. In fact, she rather liked it.

When the airplane first took off, she'd seen what looked like miniature buildings and vehicles below, but as the pilot took them higher into the sky, the buildings were replaced with nothing but white, fluffy clouds, giving the appearance of cotton. In some places, the edges of the clouds were lit up by the sun's reflection. It was so different than watching clouds from the ground. Some were tall and billowy, like pillars against the bluest of skies, and others so distinct she could imagine touching them.

"Beautiful," Mandy whispered, briefly closing her eyes. Being up this high gave her an inkling of how it must be for God looking down on the world He created.

Mandy's eyes snapped open, and she clenched her fingers when a vibration went through the plane. Quickly, she looked out the window again but saw nothing amiss.

"Is this your first time flying?" the elderly lady beside her asked.

"Yes, it is." Mandy smiled. "Can you tell?"

The pleasant woman nodded slightly.

"This is all so new to me. Since the minute I took a seat, I've been intrigued with everything going on." She extended her hand. "Sorry, I should have introduced myself earlier. I'm Mandy Frey."

"Nice to meet you. I'm Charlotte Lowell." She shook Mandy's hand. "I felt the same way on my first flight many years ago. The bumps and vibrations we might be feeling are nothing to worry about. It's only a bit of turbulence."

Mandy felt herself relax. On this, her first opportunity to fly, she felt as if God had put this nice lady beside her on purpose.

Please keep us safe as we make this journey, she silently prayed. *And watch over my family and friends while I'm gone.*

Kapaa

"Your feet are gonna start to ache if you don't sit down and relax," Makaio told his wife. "Mandy's room is ready, and it won't be time to pick her up at the airport for two more hours. So you may as well join me for a glass of mango lemonade and some of those macadamia nut cookies you made this morning."

Luana shook her head. "Those cookies are meant to be a treat for Mandy when she gets here. They're one of her favorites."

"Doesn't mean we can't eat a few of them now." Makaio stepped up to Luana and kissed her cheek. "*E hele mai* — come and take a seat."

Luana sighed. "Oh, all right, but we're only drinking the lemonade. If I set out any of the cookies, you won't be able to stop at one. Pretty soon, the whole jar will be gone." She went to the refrigerator and took out the pitcher of lemonade, placing it on the table, along with two glasses. After taking a seat, she poured for both of them.

"Ah, this hits the spot." Makaio drank half his drink then paused and smacked his lips. "Yep, that's real good stuff."

Luana glanced at the clock again. "Where do you think she is now?"

"Who?"

She swatted his arm playfully. "Mandy. Who else?"

He shrugged. "Somewhere over the Pacific Ocean headed toward here. Probably two hours out if the plane's on time."

"Maybe we should head for the airport now. She's supposed to arrive at 8:21 p.m., and I want to make sure we're there on time to pick her up."

Makaio rolled his eyes. "It takes less than thirty minutes to get to the airport from here."

"But traffic could be bad. You know how it gets sometimes coming out of town."

"You're right, but it's usually worse when people are getting off work or heading out to a luau or some other function." He gestured to his watch. "Let's wait another half hour."

"Okay." Luana leaned back in her chair

and tried to relax. The last time she'd been this excited was when she became a grandma. She'd missed Mandy and looked forward to seeing her again. To add to her excitement, she could hardly wait to see the quilt Mandy had found. It still didn't seem possible it could be her and Makaio's wedding quilt.

No matter how hard Luana tried to keep her emotions in check, the thought lingered: *What if it isn't our quilt after all? If not, it'll feel like we've lost it all over again. But then, how many quilts would have the initials L. M. sewn in the corner, as the picture of the one Mandy found showed? Well, in a short time, my questions will be answered and we'll know for sure.*

CHAPTER 37

Lihue, Hawaii

The minute Mandy entered the baggage claim area, she spotted Luana and Makaio, both wearing eager expressions. She ran toward them, excitedly. Before any words were spoken, Luana's warm hug encompassed Mandy.

"It's so good to see you," they said in unison.

Then Makaio stepped forward and pulled Mandy close. Tears flooded her eyes, and she gulped on a sob. In some ways it felt like she'd been gone longer than nine months. In another way it seemed as if she'd never left at all — most likely because there hadn't been a day when her thoughts hadn't returned to the islands and the people she'd come to know and love. Oh, how she had missed the warmth and beauty of Kauai. Even more, she'd missed spending time with her Hawaiian friends. It would probably be harder to leave this time, but at least she'd have fourteen full days to spend with Luana and Makaio before returning home.

"Let's get your suitcase." Makaio pointed to the revolving conveyor belt where her checked luggage would be coming.

As Mandy stood waiting for her suitcase to appear, she took in the sights around her. She saw the familiar landscape of the hills in the distance and felt a warm breeze coming through the open areas in front of the building.

"There it is!" she shouted, when her luggage appeared. "The one with the green ribbon tied to the handle."

Once Makaio retrieved her luggage, the Palus led the way to their car. Before getting in, Mandy paused and lifted a silent prayer: *Thank You, Lord, for bringing me here safely.*

"How were your flights?" Luana asked as Makaio directed the vehicle onto the main road.

"A little bumpy sometimes, but it didn't bother me much — especially when the nice lady sitting beside me helped calm my fears." Mandy rolled down the back window a crack and breathed in the fresh, balmy air, feeling her whole body relax. "I could get used to traveling by plane. It's so much quicker," she commented, resting deeply against her seat.

"Were you nervous making connections?" Makaio asked.

"A little at first, but my cousin Ruth has flown before, so she told me what to expect." Mandy put the window down farther and held on to her head covering.

"You didn't break any church rules by flying, I hope." Luana looked over her shoulder with concern.

"No, because I have not yet joined the Amish church — although, my mother wasn't too happy about me coming."

"She didn't want you to return our quilt?" Luana's tone was one of surprise.

"Mom wanted me to mail the quilt, but I felt better returning it to you in person."

"Speaking of the quilt," Luana said, "I can hardly wait to see it. I'm almost one hundred percent sure from the picture you sent that it's the same one we were given as a wedding present."

Mandy smiled. "One of the first things I'll do when we get to the B&B is open my suitcase."

Kapaa

When Mandy entered the bed-and-breakfast, she felt as though she was at home. With the exception of a few new plants in the living room, everything looked exactly as it had when she and Ellen left last April.

"We have the Primrose Room ready for you. Is that okay?" Luana asked.

"Yes, it'll be perfect. Speaking of Primrose, when will I get to see your sweet baby granddaughter?"

"Ailani will be coming to work tomorrow. She always brings the baby with her." Luana picked up a framed picture sitting on a side table. "Can you believe how much my granddaughter has grown?"

"She's adorable."

"Yes, we feel truly blessed."

It was tempting to ask how Ken was doing, but Mandy figured it wasn't a topic that should be discussed, since as far as she knew, he'd gotten married back in November. Even though she no longer dwelled on the feelings she'd once had for him, occasionally she thought about the friendship they'd established and hoped he was doing well.

Makaio set Mandy's suitcase on the floor. "Should I take this to your room now so you can unpack your things?"

"You can leave it there for the moment.

I'm going to open it now and take out the quilt."

Mandy went down on her knees and unzipped the suitcase. Then she lifted the covering out and handed it to Luana.

Makaio inhaled sharply, and Luana gasped, clasping her hands to her chest. "It . . . it's our beautiful wedding day quilt!" She lifted one corner and pointed to the initials. "See here — *L. M.*" Tears gathered in her dark eyes and dripped onto her cheeks. "I truly never thought I would see this again, much less that it would be found in such an unexpected place."

Makaio slipped his arm around his wife's waist, then gave Mandy a wide grin. "*Mahalo nui loa* — thank you very much."

Wiping away her own tears, Mandy barely managed to say, "You're welcome."

It did her heart good to see and actually feel how much they appreciated receiving this quilt. Luana and Makaio showed Christ's love to others as they entertained strangers almost on a daily basis. It was her utmost pleasure to see them get something in return. She thanked God for allowing her to be instrumental in getting their beloved Hawaiian quilt back where it belonged.

"We can talk more about the quilt after you're settled in," Luana suggested. "I'm sure after your long day of travel, you must be exhausted."

"I am a little weary," Mandy admitted. "It's hard to believe I started out this morning in Indiana and arrived here on Kauai before the day was out."

"While Makaio is putting your suitcase and carryall in your room, I'll put some water in the teakettle, and we can have a little snack out on the lanai before it's time for bed. It'll be good to catch up with each other's lives." Luana winked at Mandy. "Oh, and I made your favorite macadamia nut cookies."

Mandy moistened her lips. "Sounds wonderful."

The following morning when Mandy woke up, she took her purple muumuu out of the suitcase and slipped it over her head. While she was in Hawaii she would dress like she had during her previous stay. Once Mandy joined the church, which she felt obligated to do, there would be no opportunity to wear the dress again. It was like one last fling during her rumschpringe days. *At least I'm not doing anything totally crazy or wild like some young people do,* she thought, looking at herself in the mirror.

It was tempting to go outside, pick a

pretty flower, and put it behind her right ear. Instead, Mandy secured the black scarf she'd brought along to the back of her head in preparation of going to the kitchen to help Luana with breakfast. It would be like old times, except this morning she was the only guest in the house. Luana had mentioned last night that they didn't have any other B&B guests scheduled for the next two days. Mandy had already determined when those guests checked in, she would help out by making beds, cleaning rooms, and offering to do anything else that would help Luana. It was the least she could do in exchange for the free room they'd offered her. Makaio had tried to reimburse Mandy for the amount she'd paid for the quilt when she'd found it at the thrift store. But she'd been adamant, saying the money she'd paid should be considered a gift.

Mandy lifted the window to enjoy the Hawaiian breeze and listen to the birds' sweet melodies coming from the trees. A flash of gray and white appeared, landing on a branch. The red-headed bird looked like one she'd seen once before in the Palus' yard. *Weerit, churit, weerit, churit,* it chirped.

"Hey, I should be the one scolding you." Mandy giggled, remembering how a bird looking a lot like this one had left its calling card on her muumuu. Even the memory of Ken wiping the splotch from the shoulder of her dress held a special place in her heart.

When good smells from the kitchen began to waft upstairs, Mandy quickly closed the window. *I need to quit thinking about Ken and see if Luana needs help with anything.*

Mandy's nose twitched when she entered the kitchen and smelled a sweet aroma. "Something smells familiar." She peered over Luana's shoulder and studied the batter in a large bowl. "Is it my favorite mango-flavored pancakes with sweet coconut syrup?"

Nodding, Luana smiled. "It's one way I can thank you for bringing our quilt back to us."

"It was my pleasure, and I'm happy it all worked out. I will carry the memory of giving it to you for the rest of my life." Mandy slipped into a colorful apron. "Now what can I do to help?"

"Nothing really, unless you want to . . ." A knock at the door interrupted Luana. "Would you mind seeing who that is, Mandy? I'm about to start cooking the pancakes, and I don't want them to burn." She reached over and grabbed the spatula from the pan.

"No problem." Mandy hurried across the

room. Turning the knob, she opened the door. Heat flooded her face when she looked into Ken's blue eyes as he stood, holding a carton of eggs.

"Mandy!" His eyes widened. "I sure didn't expect to see you here this morning. What brings you back to Kauai, and how long will you be staying?"

Lightheaded, Mandy felt her heart beat so fast she could almost hear it echo in her head. Ken was as good-looking as she remembered, and his pleasant, deep voice still sounded the same. The only thing different about Ken was that he'd cut his hair, although it was still thick and curly. She had to catch herself to keep from giving him a hug. *But you mustn't even think such thoughts,* her conscience reminded. *He's a married man.*

"I found Luana and Makaio's lost quilt in a thrift store in Shipshewana, so I brought it back to them." She spoke quickly, trying not to stare at his handsome face and barely making eye contact with him.

"Wow! How about that!" He set the eggs on the counter and stared hard at Mandy. "I can hardly believe you're here. I've missed seeing you and —"

"How have you been? I'm looking forward to meeting your wife."

Ken tipped his head to one side. "My wife?"

"Yes. Luana wrote in a letter she sent me about you getting married last November."

Ken's eyebrows furrowed. "Me, married?" With his eyes fixed on Mandy, he brushed some hair off his forehead. "Oh, you must be talking about my brother, Dan. He got married in November."

"Oops! Guess I messed up and wrote the wrong name," Luana called from across the room. "I must have been preoccupied when I wrote that letter. Come to think of it, I was holding Primrose at the time."

Mandy's lips parted, but no words came out. So Ken was still single. It was difficult not to get her hopes up, but a longing welled in her soul like nothing before. *Could there be a chance Ken might . . . No. He only sees me as a friend. That's how it was before I left, and I'm sure nothing's changed.*

CHAPTER 38

Mandy's legs trembled like they had when she and Gideon first started courting. Only Ken wasn't courting her. He merely stood staring at her with a wide smile. She could hardly believe he hadn't gotten married.

What does it matter? she asked herself. *I'll be returning home in two weeks and will start classes to prepare for joining the church this spring.* She shifted uneasily. *I wonder what would happen if I didn't join and stayed here instead.*

Mandy's thoughts swirled until she felt as if her head might explode. She remembered when Luana had told her how she and Makaio left their family and friends on the Big Island to begin a new life as owners of the B&B here. *Would it be wrong to leave my family and stay in Kauai permanently? I would miss everyone, but I'd go home for visits. It would be hard on my folks, though, especially Mom. She wants all her children living close, which I totally understand. If I was married and had children, I'd wish for the same thing.*

"Why don't you two go out to the lanai and get reacquainted?" Luana suggested. "After you've visited awhile you can join Makaio and me in the dining room for breakfast."

"I should help you," Mandy offered.

"No, it's fine. You're our guest here this time, and guests don't help with the cooking."

Mandy was tempted to argue, but Ken had already started out the door, so she thanked Luana and followed him to the lanai.

"I still can't believe you're not married," Mandy murmured, taking a seat beside him on the porch swing. "I thought maybe it was one of the young women you were talking to on the beach when I was here last year."

He shook his head. "No serious girlfriends for me. But speaking of marriage . . . Since you have a boyfriend in Indiana, I figured you'd be married by now." He took a step back. "You're not, are you?"

Mandy's mouth opened slightly. "No, I'm not married, but who told you I had a boyfriend?"

"Ellen."

"When?"

"Remember the night of the bad storm?"
Mandy nodded.

"Well, I stopped by here after it had subsided, to see how you were all doing. Everyone but Ellen had gone to bed, so she and I visited a few minutes. During our conversation, she mentioned you had a boyfriend back home and said after you joined the Amish church you would most likely get married."

A shock wave rippled through Mandy, and she grabbed the edge of the swing, fearing she might fall off. *Why would my good friend tell Ken about Gideon? Did she do it on purpose to make sure he didn't develop strong feelings for me? Could this be why Ken pulled away and didn't come around much after that night?*

"So what about your boyfriend?" Ken's question broke into Mandy's thoughts. "Has he asked you to marry him?"

Slowly, she shook her head. "I haven't joined the church. Gideon and I broke up awhile back." Mandy paused to draw a quick breath. "He's seeing someone else now."

Ken blinked. "Really? You're unattached?"
"Yes."

A wide smile stretched across his face as he moved closer and reached for Mandy's hand. "Would you be willing to let me court you? That's how the Amish refer to dating, right?" He looked deeply into her eyes.

"It is, and I would." Mandy swallowed hard. "There's just one problem; I will only be here two weeks, then I'll have to return to Indiana, because I bought a round-trip plane ticket."

"Is it refundable?"

"I don't think so. My cousin booked the ticket for me, and Ruth got the cheapest one she could find."

His fingers tightened around hers. "You can't leave in two weeks, Mandy. We need more time to court." Ken's tone sounded desperate and sad at the same time.

His look of sincerity brought a smile to her lips. *Ken cares about me. He always did. He only kept his distance because of what Ellen told him about me and Gideon.* Mandy felt torn. She wanted desperately to stay and develop a relationship with Ken, but staying longer would mean losing part of the money Ruth had loaned her for the plane ticket. It would also disappoint her parents. They were expecting her to return and take classes in the spring. Mandy didn't want to hurt them, but if she said goodbye to Ken again, her heart would break, even more than it had the last time she'd left Kauai.

"I need to pray about this." She gazed at his handsome face. "Can we talk about it again in a few days?"

"Of course, but I want to see you every single day you're here." He lifted his hand and gently caressed her face. "I've missed you so much."

Ken leaned closer, and Mandy felt in her heart he was about to kiss her, but Luana called them to breakfast. "Guess we'd better go eat." She rose from the swing. "I'm glad you came over this morning."

"Same here." Still holding Mandy's hand, Ken brought it slowly to his lips and feathered a kiss across her knuckles. She had a sense of what it was like to float, when together, they headed for the dining room. Mandy didn't know how things would turn out for her and Ken, but she was sure of one thing: she'd never been happier.

After Ken left, Luana noticed Mandy seemed quieter than usual. The bubbly spirit she'd exhibited earlier this morning had suddenly vanished. "Are you tired, Mandy? Would you like to go to your room and take a nap?"

"I'm not sleepy, but I would like to talk to you about something."

"Certainly. Why don't we take a seat in

the living room where it's nice and cool? Ailani's car broke down, and since Makaio went to pick her and Primrose up, we should take advantage of our quiet time together." Luana chuckled. "If my precious granddaughter decides to start hollering, we won't be able to hear ourselves think."

"I'm looking forward to seeing her, though. I can't wait to take a few pictures of your grandbaby." Mandy followed Luana into the other room and took a seat in the rocking chair.

Luana sat on the couch across from her. "Now what was it you wanted to talk to me about?"

"I'm confused about Ken."

"What do you mean?"

Holding the armrests, Mandy got the rocking chair moving. "He wants to court me."

Luana tipped her head. "Court?"

"Yes. It's what the Amish call dating."

"Ah, I see. I'm beginning to understand why Ken didn't come around much after you left."

"Why is that?"

"He missed you. Coming here probably made him think about you even more." Luana smiled. "I suspected he'd fallen head over heels for you, but it wasn't my place to say anything. I figured once you went home, Ken would move on with his life and find someone else."

Mandy nodded. "I thought so, too, and when you wrote and said he was getting married, I tried to accept the fact that a relationship between him and me was not meant to be."

"And now how do you feel?"

"Confused."

"About your feelings for Ken?"

"No, I'm clear about that. Seeing him again this morning and learning he isn't married made me aware my feelings for him hadn't changed." Mandy paused and lowered her head. "I'm in love with him, but I don't see how things could work out between us when I live so far away."

"Have you considered staying in Kauai?" Luana questioned.

Mandy nodded. "I love it here, but all of my family live in Indiana, and I need to consider them. I don't know if I could move here permanently without their blessing. I'm not sure I'd be truly happy living so far from them, either."

"The first thing you should do is pray about it." Luana reached for the Bible on the coffee table and opened it to a passage she had underlined some time ago. "Listen to what it says in Proverbs 3:5–6: 'Trust in the Lord with all thine heart; and lean not unto thine own understanding. In all thy ways acknowledge him, and he shall direct thy paths.' "

Mandy's chin quivered as she rose from her chair. "Mahalo, Luana. I needed the reminder."

When Ken returned home later that morning, he had a hard time concentrating on his work. Beautiful Mandy, whom he'd fallen in love with during her stay on Kauai last year, would be returning to the mainland again unless he could convince her to remain here with him.

What should I do, Lord? he silently prayed. *I want to be with Mandy, but I can't force her to stay. Her family is in Indiana — so far away.*

Fate could be a strange thing sometimes, if this was actually fate. Ken never thought he'd see Mandy again, especially when Ellen had told him about Mandy having a boyfriend and given the impression they'd be getting married. He'd tried so hard to forget her, but nearly every day Mandy's sweet face was vivid in his mind. Ken had even gone out on a couple of dates, but he couldn't get Mandy out of his thoughts. The few times he'd taken a girl out for dinner, his mind had been elsewhere. He'd finally given up, deciding it might be too soon to think about dating anyone. Maybe a few years down the road it would get easier.

Ken gripped the handle of the shovel he'd been using to clean the chicken barn. *Is it possible God used Luana and Makaio's missing quilt to bring Mandy back to Kauai? Maybe this is where she belongs.*

He took a seat on a bundle of straw, watching the chickens move about and hoping they might divert his spiraling thoughts. *What should I do? Mandy's met my parents and brother, and they got along well. I'd like the chance to meet her parents and siblings, too. It'd be great to see the area she grew up in.*

As Ken sat pondering, one of the barn cats rubbed against his leg, jarring his thoughts. The cat purred then leaped into Ken's lap. "You're supposed to be keeping the mice down, not lounging around." He snickered and stroked the feline's ear. "Guess I shouldn't be sitting here, either."

Ken sat a few more minutes then placed the cat on the floor and stood. He picked up his shovel and opened the door to the large pen. He was about to start cleaning, when Taavi walked in.

"Hey, Ken! Thought I'd stop by to see if

you wanna go surfing with me. The waves are looking real good today."

"Wish you would have called me instead of coming all the way out here." Ken set the shovel aside and reached into his pocket for his cell phone. "Oh, yeah, it's in the house on the charger." He slapped his forehead.

Taavi snorted. "Well, you answered your own question, buddy." He pointed to Ken's feet. "You sure look funny wearin' those clod-hopper boots."

"What? Do you think I'd wear a pair of flip-flops out here? No way!" Ken lifted his gaze to the ceiling.

"So what do you think about heading to the beach. You wanna go?"

"Any other time I'd jump at the chance, but I have work to do." Ken picked up Fluffy, his favorite chicken, and stroked the hen's feathers. "Not only that, but Mandy is back for a couple of weeks, and when I'm done working for the day, I'll be with her."

Taavi leaned against the wall. "You weren't the same after Mandy left last year. Fact is, you acted like a love-sick seal. So guess I won't be seein' much of you till she goes home again — unless, of course, you beg her to stay."

"I'll stop by soon or give you a call." Ken set the chicken on the floor. "You might want to know how things turned out."

"Sounds good." Taavi thumped Ken's back. "Say hi to Mandy for me."

After his friend left, Ken contemplated the situation with Mandy. *Is her place really here on the island because she brought back Luana and Makaio's quilt? Or maybe,* he thought, grabbing the shovel again, *my place is in Indiana with her.*

CHAPTER 39

For the next ten days, Mandy and Ken spent every free minute together. In addition to him visiting Mandy at the B&B, he took her to see several sights she hadn't seen before. Today, Ken had some time off, so he'd booked a one-hour trip with the Wings of Kauai. He wanted Mandy to see the entire island from the air. This would be his special treat before she went home. Ken couldn't wait to see her surprised look when he told her about the island air tour. Hopefully, it would be something she'd remember for a long time to come.

Since Mandy's return to the island, Ken had removed his surfboard from the roof of his SUV. He figured there'd be no time for hanging out on the beach, nor did he want to waste a minute without Mandy at his side. He'd taken his vehicle to the gas station and through the car wash so that everything could be perfect for her.

Ken glanced at the passenger seat, where Mandy sat in his SUV, holding a camera. He was glad she'd gotten a new one and was enjoying taking photos. *But no photo can ever replace the real thing.* Ken reflected on how he had longed to see Mandy's sweet face during the months she'd been gone. She'd been in his thoughts daily, and his dreams at night. Having her sitting beside him now was an answer to prayer.

Ken had been praying about their situation and discussed it at length with his folks. As of last night, he'd finally come up with a way for him and Mandy to be together on a permanent basis, even though it meant giving up the dream he had of owning his own organic hydroponic nursery on the island he loved so much.

"Guess where we're going?" He waited for her response.

Tilting her head she looked at him. "I don't know. Where?"

"To the airport. I booked us an island tour with Wings over Kauai."

"Really? It sounds like fun. I'm looking forward to riding in a plane again. It should be fun to see the island from the air."

"It will be fun, but riding in a small plane will be a little different than the big jet you were on coming here."

"I figured it would be since it's so much smaller." She giggled. "No flight attendants to offer cold drinks and snacks."

"There will be water and soda pop on the plane, but the only passengers will be us, the pilot, and four others who signed up for the flight."

Smiling, she lifted her camera. "I'm anxious to get some pictures. I need something to take home to remind me of this trip."

For the first several minutes, Mandy sat with her nose pressed against the window on her side of the airplane. Due to distribution of weight, Ken sat next to the pilot, and the other passengers were in the back, with one middle-aged woman sitting across from Mandy.

Mandy's stomach flew up as the small plane took off, but she didn't mind. What an adventure it was to look down and see the layout of the land, with all its peaks and valleys. Everyone on board wore headphones so they could communicate with the pilot, as well as with each other. The plane flew out over the ocean, and the pilot called their attention to some whales. It was different seeing them from this perspective.

Mandy wished she and Ken were the only ones in the plane so she could speak to him freely, without others hearing their conversation.

As they continued on, several waterfalls came into view. One of them was the same falls she and Ken had visited last year, when the nice lady offered to take their picture. Of course, seeing it from above put a different slant on things. All the while, Mandy snapped more pictures.

When the Na Pali Coast came into view, she couldn't help exclaiming, "How amazing! It looks different than when we saw it by boat, but beautiful, nonetheless. Only God could have created something this spectacular."

Ken looked over his shoulder and smiled at her. Then he gave a thumbs-up.

I love him, she thought. *How am I ever going to leave here when it's time to go? I wish it were possible for me to stay. I'll miss Ken terribly when I return to my home on the mainland.*

Ken's heart pounded as he drove Mandy back to the B&B later that afternoon. He needed to tell her how he felt, but was unsure of her reaction.

"Mahalo, Ken, for giving me such a nice day." Mandy held up her camera. "I took enough pictures to help me remember my time on Kauai this time." She sighed deeply and leaned back in her seat. "I'm going to miss being in Hawaii, but I'll miss you most of all."

Pleased with her declaration, Ken couldn't wait any longer. He pulled off at a wide spot on the shoulder of the road. "There's something I need to tell you."

Mandy tipped her head. "What is it?"

He reached for her hand. "It may seem like it's too short for the declaration I'm about to make, but we spent a lot of time together when you were here before." He paused, searching for just the right words. "Every minute you were with me was special. Truth is, these last couple of days, we'd no sooner part than I'd began counting the hours till the next time we could be together."

"I felt the same."

Gently, he held her fingers. "I'm in love with you, Mandy."

Her eyes glistened with tears. "Oh, Ken, I love you, too. I began to feel it soon after we were formally introduced, but I feared so many things. With the distance between our homes, I didn't see how anything could work out."

"I didn't believe so for a while, either, but after praying and thinking everything through, I've come up with a plan."

"You have? What is it?"

"I'm going back to Indiana with you."

"To meet my family?"

"Yes, and also to look for a job so I can be close to you, because if you'll have me, I want you to become my wife."

"I would be honored to marry you." Mandy spoke in a soft, shaky voice. "But you can't move to Indiana. You have a job right here, helping your parents raise chickens. Life in Middlebury is a lot different than Kauai. There are no sandy beaches, palm trees, tropical flowers, or places to go surfing."

Mandy's somber expression concerned him. Was she having second thoughts about being with him?

"If you leave Kauai, you'll miss the island, as well as your family and friends."

"I'll have you, and I'll make new friends." Ken shifted in his seat, never taking his eyes off Mandy. "I've already talked to Mom and Dad about this, as well as my brother, Dan. He said he'd take over my responsibilities with the business, and Mom and Dad are fine with it, too. They'll come visit whenever they can. My family wants me to be happy, and my happiness is with you."

"What about your dream of owning your

own organic hydroponic nursery?"

"I'm willing to give it up to be with you. Staying in Hawaii and owning my own business may not be God's will for me. Truthfully, sometimes the things we think we want are not what is best for us."

"I believe you're right. I've been rather selfish thinking only of my own needs and longing for Hawaii, when I should have been asking God what is best for me."

Ken leaned forward and drew Mandy into his arms. Then he kissed her gently on the lips.

When they pulled apart, Mandy stared at him with a dazed expression.

Did I kiss her right? Should I have asked her first? Does she want me to go to Indiana with her? Many doubts filled Ken's mind, but one thing he believed without question: the kiss felt right. In fact, it was perfect. And if Mandy's sigh was any indication, maybe she felt it, too.

For a while they sat together, holding hands but saying nothing. Words weren't necessary as Ken looked into her beautiful brown eyes. The tiny flecks of green in Mandy's eyes looked even more vivid as traces of tears remained.

Ken traced her jawline with his fingers, then moved his hand to the back of her

451

head. He didn't have to pull her close, for she willingly went toward him, and they kissed again. It was so sweet, Ken felt as though he were floating.

Mandy swallowed hard, then cleared her throat. Her cheeks were still flushed, no doubt from what they'd shared seconds ago.

"You're not thinking of joining the Amish faith, are you?" she asked.

Sorry to see the moment end, Ken breathed deeply. "I will if it's the only way we can be together."

"No, Ken. I cannot ask you to make such a sacrifice." Mandy paused. "It's a difficult transition that not many English people have been able to make." She smiled tearfully, gently touching his face. "I'd thought I would join the Amish church this spring, but it would only be to please my parents. I can be happy attending any church as long as it teaches God's Holy Word."

"What exactly are you saying?"

"From the time I was a young girl, I was taught it would be my choice to join the Amish church. Mom and Dad often said it wasn't a matter of what church you belonged to. What counts is what's in a person's heart and whether you choose to follow God." Mandy paused before she continued. "So, even though they may be

452

disappointed because I'm not becoming part of the Amish church, they will be pleased I have found a Christian man. I only wish we could both live near our families. Hawaii's a long way from Indiana, and you had no plans to leave here until now."

"True." Ken took her hand. "But we can live in Indiana to be near your family and take our vacations on Kauai, where my folks live. It only takes a portion of a day to get here by plane, so we can go once or twice a year — maybe more if I should end up opening my own business in Indiana."

"When I first went to Kauai, I thought it was the island I loved, but I've come to realize it wasn't the island, but rather the people I'd met while living there. I've also learned it doesn't matter what church we attend, as long as we are serving the Lord." She leaned her head on his shoulder. "I want to serve Him with you."

EPILOGUE

Middlebury, one year later

Mandy's heart swelled to overflowing as she stood at the altar beside her groom, preparing to recite her wedding vows. A meaningful life's journey was about to begin for her: not pure Amish, but still living a Christian life, ready to serve God.

She took a deep breath to steady her nerves, and then the vows flowed from her heart: "I Mandy, take you, Ken, to be my husband, secure in the knowledge you will be my constant friend, my faithful partner in life, and my one true love. On this special day, I affirm to you in the presence of God and these witnesses my sacred promise to stay by your side as your faithful wife, in sickness and in health, in joy and in sorrow, through good times and bad. I further promise to love you without reservation, comfort you in times of distress, encourage you to achieve your goals, laugh with you and cry with you, grow with you in mind and spirit, always to be open and honest with you, and cherish you for as long as we both shall live."

Tenderly holding her hand, Ken repeated his vows. As he spoke the words, Mandy listened intently while gazing into his vibrant blue eyes, filled with happy tears.

Thank You, Lord, for bringing this special man into my life.

When their vows concluded, Mandy stood beside her groom, listening to the song "Each for the Other" sung a cappella by three members of the church worship team.

As the trio sang "Each for the other, and both for the Lord," Mandy stole a look at the people who had come to witness their union this sunny but cold Saturday afternoon.

Mandy's folks sat on one side of the church, along with her brothers, Milo, Mark, Melvin, and Michael, as well as Michael's wife, Sarah.

Ken's parents; his brother, Dan; and Dan's wife, Sandy, sat on the other side of the church. It pleased Mandy that Ken's cousin Brock had been able to take over the responsibilities of the Freys' chicken farm so they could all be here for the wedding.

Mandy's best friends, Ellen, Sadie, and

Barbara, were seated in the pew behind Mandy's family. Gideon sat beside Barbara, whom he planned to marry in the spring. Mandy was glad they could still be friends. Barbara was the better choice for him, since she shared his dedication to the Amish church.

They were meant to be together, Mandy thought, *just as Ken is the man God intended for me.*

She looked forward to spending their honeymoon in Kauai, where Luana and Makaio had promised to give them a wedding reception. When Mandy and Ken returned from Hawaii, they would begin making plans for the bed-and-breakfast they wanted to open. It would be an exciting adventure, although a bit frightening. But with God's help, she felt confident it would succeed. Like Luana and Makaio, she and Ken would minister to many people in the days ahead. . . . and perhaps entertain a few angels unaware.

Luana's Hawaiian Teriyaki Burgers

1 1/2 pounds ground beef
1 small onion, chopped
1 egg
1/4 cup soy sauce
2 cloves garlic, minced
1/2 teaspoon fresh ginger, minced
2 stalks green onion, chopped
1 tablespoon sesame oil

Combine all ingredients in large bowl; mix well. Form into patties. Fry, grill, or broil. For additional taste, serve with a slice of pineapple on top of each burger.

Mandy's Organic Chicken Chowder

2 tablespoons butter
1/4 cup onion, chopped
1 1/2 cups cooked chicken, cubed
1 1/2 cups carrots, diced
1 1/2 cups raw potatoes, diced
2 chicken bouillon cubes
1 teaspoon salt
1/8 teaspoon pepper
2 cups water
3 tablespoons flour
1 1/2 cups milk

Melt butter in a 3-quart saucepan. Add onions and sauté until tender. Add chicken, carrots, potatoes, bouillon cubes, salt, pepper, and water. Cover and simmer until vegetables are tender. Combine flour and 1/2 cup milk in a jar. Shake until blended. Add to vegetables along with remaining milk. Cook on medium heat, stirring constantly, until mixture thickens. Yields 1 3/4 quarts.

HISTORY OF HAWAIIAN QUILTS

The introduction to sewing and quilt making came to Hawaiians from the wives of American missionaries in 1820. Patchwork quilts were made in the missionary boarding schools, where girls were taught to sew. Even though the missionaries are credited with teaching new concepts and techniques in quilt making, the development of the Hawaiian appliquéd quilts lies with the Hawaiian women. Many of the designs and methods they used are found only in Hawaii. Hawaiian quilt making became a form of self-expression during nineteenth-century westernization. Every stitch had a meaning and every part of the design a purpose.

Quilting frames in Hawaii were set close to the ground so quilters could sit on their handwoven *lauhala* mats. A wide variety of fill material for the quilts was used in Hawaii, including soft fibers from tree fern, cotton, wool, and animal hair. As three layers were stitched together. The quilters started at the quilt's center and worked toward the edges.

Quilts found on the mainland that are the most similar to Hawaiian quilts are appliquéd in the Pennsylvania Dutch tradition. Their quilts often consist of a central medallion appliqué that resembles the Hawaiian technique and repeats the same floral design in four large blocks. The Hawaiian women designed their quilts based on floral surroundings, legends, and innermost feelings of love. Every quilt had a purpose, and no two quilts were alike.

DISCUSSION QUESTIONS

1. For some time, Mandy had a desire to visit Hawaii. Her boyfriend, Gideon, wanted her to stay but gave his blessing so she could pursue her dream. Have you ever wanted to do something so badly you didn't consider another person's feelings? Like Gideon, have you ever given someone your blessing, even though you felt what they were doing was wrong?

2. On the cruise ship, someone mistook Mandy and her Amish friends for nuns. Have you ever assumed something about a person based on their outer appearance?

3. Mandy was afraid of water and was unable to swim, yet she set her fears aside to go on the cruise to Hawaii. Have you ever wanted to do something so much you were able to set your fears aside in order to pursue your goal? Or have you ever held

someone back from doing what they wanted, because of your own fears?

4. When Mandy and Ellen became stranded on Kauai, a caring Hawaiian couple took them in. Would you be willing to take in strangers at a moment's notice and make them feel welcome? If you have entertained strangers, how did it all work out?

5. Since Mandy's and Ellen's luggage was left on the ship, they only had the dresses they were wearing when they became stranded. Luana suggested they go shopping for a modest-looking Hawaiian dress. Mandy was content to accept the style of clothing on Kauai, but dressing that way made Ellen feel uncomfortable. How do you feel when you're subjected to uncomfortable situations? Do you conform or stay with what you believe is appropriate for you? Why?

6. When Makaio was injured, should Mandy and Ellen have agreed to stay on Kauai longer to help at the B&B, or would it have been better if they'd returned home right away?

7. After Barbara and Sadie returned to

Indiana without their two Amish friends, Barbara found herself drawn to Mandy's boyfriend, Gideon. She did not act upon her feelings and kept them to herself. What would have happened if she had let him know how she felt? Have you ever been in a similar situation? If so, how did you respond?

8. Ellen realized Mandy was captivated by Hawaii and a certain young English man, so she intervened without Mandy's knowledge. Is there ever a time we should intervene if we feel someone we know is about to make a wrong decision that could change the course of their life? Should Ellen have gone to Mandy and discussed her feelings instead of going behind her back and attempting to manipulate the situation?

9. Even though Luana had lost a sentimental quilt, she didn't let it consume her. She moved on with a positive attitude. Have you ever lost something that had either monetary or sentimental value? What was the item, and how did you cope with the loss?

10. When Mandy returned home from

Hawaii, Gideon saw a change in her. It was almost as though they were strangers, and he didn't know how to get back what they'd once had. Life is full of changes, some good and some bad. How do you deal with a friend or loved one who has changed?

11. Gideon's mother, Peggy, was unsure of him choosing Mandy for a wife. However, instead of meddling, she prayed about it, allowing God to work things out for her son. What happens when we allow God to work in our lives, rather than taking matters into our own hands?

12. Mandy's desire to live a different life from the one she'd always known was hard for her family and friends to accept. If you had a child who wanted to serve God in a different church than the one in which they were raised, how would you respond?

13. Did you learn anything new about the Amish by reading this story? If so, what was it?

14. Were there any Bible verses mentioned in this story that spoke to your heart? If

so, what were they, and how did they bolster your faith?

ABOUT THE AUTHORS

New York Times bestselling, award-winning author **Wanda E. Brunstetter** is one of the founders of the Amish fiction genre. Wanda's ancestors were part of the Anabaptist faith, and her novels are based on personal research intended to accurately portray the Amish way of life. Her books are well-read and trusted by many Amish, who credit her for giving readers a deeper understanding of the people and their customs. When Wanda visits her Amish friends, she finds herself drawn to their peaceful lifestyle, sincerity, and close family ties.

Wanda enjoys photography, ventriloquism, gardening, bird-watching, beach-combing, and spending time with her family. She and her husband, Richard, have been blessed with two grown children, six grandchildren, and two great-grandchildren.

To learn more about Wanda, visit her

website at www.wandabrunstetter.com.

Jean Brunstetter became fascinated with the Amish when she first went to Pennsylvania to visit her father-in-law's family. Since that time, Jean has become friends with several Amish families and enjoys writing about their way of life. She also likes to put some of the simple practices followed by the Amish into her daily routine. Jean lives in Washington State with her husband, Richard Jr., and their three children, but takes every opportunity to visit Amish communities in several states. In addition to writing, Jean enjoys boating, gardening, and spending time on the beach.

The employees of Thorndike Press hope you have enjoyed this Large Print book. All our Thorndike, Wheeler, and Kennebec Large Print titles are designed for easy reading, and all our books are made to last. Other Thorndike Press Large Print books are available at your library, through selected bookstores, or directly from us.

For information about titles, please call:
(800) 223-1244

or visit our Web site at:
http://gale.cengage.com/thorndike

To share your comments, please write:
Publisher
Thorndike Press
10 Water St., Suite 310
Waterville, ME 04901